Tremendous acclaim for Patricia Anthony's superbly inventive novel of the alien occupation of earth.

'Incisive . . . rewarding.' *Publishers Weekly*

'Brilliant.' *Library Journal*

'Engrossing entertainment.' *Booklist*

'*Brother Termite* is superior science fiction – a wild, weird story in its own right that is also very thought-provoking when looked at as a reflection of contemporary human society.'
The New York Review of Science Fiction

Also by Patricia Anthony in New English Library paperback

Cold Allies

About the author

Patricia Anthony's short stories have appeared in major science fiction magazines and anthologies. Her first novel was *Cold Allies*. *Brother Termite* is her second and *Happy Policeman* her third. Her fourth is imminent. She lives in Dallas, Texas.

Brother Termite

Patricia Anthony

NEW ENGLISH LIBRARY
Hodder and Stoughton

Copyright © 1993 by Patricia Anthony

First published in Great Britain in 1995 by
Hodder & Stoughton
A division of Hodder Headline PLC

A New English Library paperback

The right of Patricia Anthony to be identified as the Author of
the Work has been asserted by her in accordance with the
Copyright, Designs and Patents Act 1988.

10 9 8 7 6 5 4 3 2 1

A CIP catalogue record for this title is available from
the British Library

ISBN 0 340 61843 4

Printed and bound in Great Britain by
Cox & Wyman Ltd, Reading, Berkshire.

Hodder and Stoughton
A Division of Hodder Headline PLC
338 Euston Road
London NW1 3BH

For Pat LoBrutto.
He always believed.

1

THE BULLETPROOF GLASS IN THE Oval Office windows cast a gloom over the day, the sort of greenish pall associated with bad storms. Appropriate clouds rose from the Ellipse, pluming easterly in the late autumn breeze. On E Street a string-straight line of troops prepared to advance. The White House chief of staff knew that had the French doors been open he would be hearing the chuck-chuck of the tear-gas guns, the rattle of the Uzis' rubber bullets, and the screams.

Eisenhower had warned him this would happen.

Doggedly he swiveled away from the riot, his leather chair squeaking, to face the mantelpiece and the portrait of Millard Fillmore that hung above it.

The door behind him opened with a click. His secretary announced, "Sir. The NSC's finally arrived through the Treasury Building tunnel. They're waiting for you."

Wearily he rested his chin on his hand. The President, in one of his frequent tutorials on politics, had assured his chief of staff that governments existed only by the apathy of the governed. The people outside, with their placards and Molotov cocktails, seemed troublesomely unapathetic.

With a surge of will he pictured himself as a pool. The riot and the oil painting of Millard Fillmore were pebbles tossed into water. The ripples they made widened until the warm waves of their company gently rocked him.

The roundness of stones in the bottom of a stream; the circular pattern of fishes' scales. He sat in the silence of the huge office but pictured the triangular thrust of the Rockies with their beards of conical firs, shapes within shapes within shapes. Perhaps soon he would take a needed Colorado vacation. Perhaps one day he would do the unthinkable and retire.

"Sir? You hear me?"

"Yes." He refused to turn around.

Muffled footsteps on the thick wool carpet. Natalie came into view behind his left shoulder, just inside the range of his peripheral vision. Her blouse, sewn from a material of disorderly, multicolored shapes, sent chills of disquiet down his neck. To avoid the sight of that blouse, he moved his gaze toward the window and the riot again.

"Who are the demonstrators?" he asked.

"Germans, French, some Scandinavians," she replied, seating herself in the Louis XV chair next to his desk.

"What are they protesting?"

"The tariff bill. They think the Chinese and Koreans are about to undermine their economic freedom."

There was a new box of pencils on his desk. He picked up the container and slid off the top. Inside, pencil ends nested like flat, hexagonal atoms. He drank in the scent of wood and graphite, running his finger down the first queue. "This," he said fondly, "is freedom."

Holding the corner pencil down, he upended the box, letting the others spill onto the desk. Then he righted the case and lifted his opposable claw from the single survivor. The pencil toppled from its pleasant upright alignment and fell against the side of its container. "That is freedom to you," he said.

Natalie pondered the box, then picked up a pencil from the heap and dropped it, with a dull tap, in with the other. "It looked lonely," she explained.

In the box the two pencils lay at an antagonistic angle. Yes, he had missed the point. Two crossed pencils were more symbolic of what humans judged to be freedom.

"There are plots to kill me," he told her.

"I know."

"Who could be behind it?"

"Anyone," she said with a shrug. "Everyone."

He peered down the long velveteen spread of the south lawn to the single army tank at the barricade and the advancing troops behind it. The helmets of the UN peacekeeping forces were an inappropriately cheerful sky blue. "They expect me to do something, but I don't understand tariffs. And why should economics be so important?"

"Pocketbook issues always get people into a sweat."

The White House chief, like all Cousins, was used to concrete answers. Good data, he felt, should line up in neat rows like pencils in a new box. "What specific pocketbook issues?" he asked, hoping she would come to the point.

"Oh, cheaper cars."

In the window his own image was superimposed on the riot, as though he had given it a seal of approval. His eyes were huge onyx almonds on a pale hot-air balloon of a head that seemed tethered above his black uniform. On his shoulder his insignia and nameplate gleamed.

"Cheap cars are unimportant," he told her, "when compared to the peace of Communal thought."

Light as a leaf drifting onto the surface of a pond, his attention settled on her. The colors of her blouse were hectic blues and reds and greens, the shapes ill-formed triangles that pointed, higgledy-piggledy, in all directions. "This blouse," he said.

She touched her collar in evident surprise. "New. You like it?"

"Don't wear it again. Muted colors, as I told you. Grays and blacks and navies."

"Gray makes me look ten years older," she argued. "And I spent good money on this blouse. You know, I could make a lot more in the private sector. I have great front-office appearance. Not, of course, that *you* would ever notice, but the senators do. You don't pay me enough—"

He stood and lifted his hand as a signal that she had won the fight. Natalie, at five feet one-half inch tall, had been one of the few applicants his size. "Use the White House credit card to buy yourself another."

"And a new pair of shoes."

He cocked his head to the right in query.

"I bought shoes to match this blouse. So you owe me."

"All right."

"And a purse." Natalie's mouth was in a tight line. It was a dangerous expression, he knew. A sign of anger. Perhaps the blouse was a pocketbook issue.

"Buy whatever you like," he said. She bared her teeth in a smile, and he began to wonder if he was being overly generous.

"Sir? Better get down to the basement."

As he turned to go, the room assaulted him with its disorganized design, one that had no relationship at all to nature. Humans had a primitive idea of harmony. Only once had he seen the order of fractals in a piece of human art: a Renaissance oil that showed the subject standing next to a painting of the same subject and the same painting, copies of the large painting growing smaller and smaller until the final one was done in a suggestion of tiny brushstrokes.

Chaos, he thought as he strode across the presidential seal woven into the dark blue carpet. Chaos was going to kill him.

2

A BROODING WILLIAM HOPKINS AND
a nervous Speaker of the House were lurking at the West Wing stairs.
Dropcloths were spread nearby, and Secret Servicemen were gathered
in a somber knot watching a pair of painters apply eggshell latex over
three lines of graffiti on the wall. The red paint was stubbornly bleed-
ing through the beige.

The sharp, aggressive strokes of the letters were plain enough,
but the White House chief found the message bewildering:

BLACK UNIFORMS,

LIGHTNING BOLT INSIGNIA.

REMIND YOU OF ANYTHING?

Reen idly fingered the outline of the white lightning bolt on his
chest.

"Reen," Hopkins called. The FBI director was smiling as he
walked across the carpet. It looked as though his hand was fighting
an urge to pop out of his pocket and grasp Reen's own, but Hopkins
had worked with the Cousins long enough to have learned reticence.

"Director." The chief of staff nodded. Then his gaze fell on the
man behind Hopkins's broad back. Of late the two habitually traveled
together, the huge Bureau director and the diminutive congressman,
as though the latter were a dog on his leash.

Reen searched his mind for the congressman's name and then remembered the word association Marian had taught him: What was the sound a Chihuahua would make, dropped from a twelve-story window?

Oh, of course. "Speaker Platt," Reen said before the FBI director's form eclipsed that of the other man.

Hopkins's sloping shoulders ballooned out into a puffy midsection, and his feet seemed too small to balance his bulk. As the man leaned over, Reen had the unsettling notion that he was about to be engulfed by a sofa.

Hopkins breathed whiskey-and-mint-scented breath into what he incorrectly imagined to be Reen's ear. "Wanted to talk with you for a minute before we had to go down to the meeting."

"Yes?"

"You know, I appreciate how you've adapted to us, but there's some stuff that, talking man-to-man so to speak, you're doing all wrong."

Reen glanced around Hopkins's looming bulk to the graffiti on the wall. The spiked letters, like slashes in the plaster from which blood oozed, bothered him more than the oblique message. There was implied violence in that calligraphy.

"Not your fault, of course. But I feel when you have things mixed up, it's my job to set you straight. For example, it's a well-known fact that if you give a woman any power at all, she'll either cave in at the first sign of trouble or else turn into a ball-breaking bitch. Bless 'em, they just can't help it. You understand 'ball-breaking'?" the director asked helpfully.

"Yes," he replied. Hopkins's references to body parts never ceased to fascinate Reen.

"The CIA," Hopkins said. "You have to do something about the CIA. Cole's on the rag, the vindictive bitch. Or maybe she's menopausal or something. You have to back me, Reen-ja. She's ripped the *cojones* right off some of my best agents. Probably made a victory necklace out of them."

Hopkins was so tall that Reen was eye-level with the man's tie. It was a nice tie, done in dark blue with small pink seashells lined up in neat rows across it. The only thing about the tie Reen found bothersome was that the lines were angled rather than horizontal or vertical. Why, he wondered, would the designer want to tip the pattern that way?

"Someday you're going to look up," Hopkins said, "and see she has a pair of gray *cojones* on that necklace, figuratively speaking. You understand the word *cojones?*"

Reen wondered how much the FBI knew about himself and Marian Cole. Skirting Hopkins, he quickly descended the stairs.

The FBI director hesitated a moment before following, Speaker Platt at his heels.

"Cole's got something on you, doesn't she, Reen-ja?" Hopkins asked when he caught up. "You can tell me what it is. Maybe I can persuade the Bureau to help."

Hurriedly, Reen changed the subject. "Why haven't we been able to find out who is painting the graffiti on the walls?" Not much that was human frightened Reen; but the graffiti had him worried. It meant that someone close to him, someone in the White House itself, hated him enough to be a dangerous foe.

"Secret Service have their heads up their collective butts," he said, deftly combining two body parts into a single image. "You know, one time when the downstairs was open, a tourist wandered in on Kennedy when he was having breakfast. Can you imagine?"

"I don't wish to discuss Kennedy," Reen said sharply. He wondered if Hopkins carried a pocket of hero worship in the multizippered, confusing organ that was his human heart. If Hopkins loved the memory of Kennedy, he could be the author of the graffiti. Reen glanced at the director's manicured hands but could see no evidence of paint.

When they reached the bottom step, Hopkins gave a quick, abashed grimace. He was huffing from the unaccustomed exercise, and his jowled face was an alarming shade of red. "Sorry.

Nothing personal. So are we going to get together on this CIA thing?"

Without answering, Reen hurried to the cavernous situation room. The National Security Council had had time to become bored. Vilishnikov, head of the Joint Chiefs, was brushing dandruff from his red epaulets. Hans Krupner, the education advisor, was making an origami giraffe from a paper napkin. Krupner, it appeared, had gotten closest to the riots. His hands were still atremble, disturbing his efforts at folding. There was a bruise on his forehead.

At a corner of the U-shaped table, Marian Cole was carrying on a listless conversation with DiSecco of Finance. When she caught sight of Hopkins and Reen together, she shot the White House chief a suspicious look.

Marian was dressed in brilliant crimson, a color chosen to annoy him. And she was spotlighted by one of the ceiling's recessed bulbs. The light, Reen noticed, was kind. The translucent skin of her cheek glowed pink, like the tender hue of the seashells on Hopkins's tie.

Faced by her silent accusation, Reen hesitated. An instant later her blue eyes darted away, releasing him from the pain of her scrutiny.

Reen took his usual seat at one prong of the U to avoid being bracketed by the taller humans. Platt was standing indecisively, considering the only empty seat: the President's. Finally the Speaker grabbed a folding chair from the wall and, with murmurs of apology, squeezed between Hopkins and an environmental consultant from MIT.

Vilishnikov began pulling papers from his briefcase and setting them on the table. "I have here a copy of the Tariff Regulation Bill. I thought we might go over it point by point. The President has five days left in which to sign. Five short days. Then it becomes a pocket veto, and I assure you, when that happens, Europe intends war."

No one on the east side of the U was aware that the door was swinging open behind Vilishnikov. The west side instantly froze. DiSecco slid lower in his chair, as though preparing to duck under the table.

A marine sergeant in full-dress uniform stepped into the room. "Ladies and gentlemen," he announced, "the President of the United States."

In a show of conformity, the humans all stood, DiSecco having to pull himself up from his crouch. A Secret Serviceman was at the doddering President's elbow. Age and the crush of responsibility had bowed Womack's once ramrod-straight back. The face had withered to a deceptively sweet-expressioned skull. For a moment the Secret Serviceman and the President fought a small war over which way Womack was to turn. At last, gentle but persistent, the agent won; he led Womack to his seat at the head of the table, and the rest of the National Security Council took their chairs.

Reen stared down the table at the only other human he loved. Womack was drooling.

"War in Europe," Vilishnikov continued.

Womack snored once, loudly. Everyone turned to the President. Womack's eyes were closed; his mouth hung open; his head bobbled precariously. Quickly the Secret Serviceman eased him into a position where the presidential face would not drop to the National Security Council table.

"So. War in Europe," Vilishnikov began once more, clearing his throat. "As a precautionary measure I have ordered our troops in this hemisphere to full alert—"

"Why?" Hopkins interrupted. "If the Europeans move, they'll move east. To China. To Japan. To Korea. Who cares? What's important are the disappearances. This month five of Reen's people have turned up missing. That makes twelve so far this year."

Marian Cole put down her coffee cup and smiled at the frustrated head of the Joint Chiefs. Her swept-back blond hair seemed to be rebelling against that morning's hairspray. A lock of it hung above her right eye. "Don't you worry, Arkady, honey. Billy takes over meetings the way a hog takes over an acorn patch. We'll talk about your war if you want to."

Hopkins's small eyes narrowed further, to be nearly buried in frowning flesh. "Maybe Director Cole doesn't want to talk about the disappearances because the CIA's behind it. I suggest we start investigating over at Langley."

"Try it. You talk a good game, Billy, but you're proud-gelded." Marian Cole coolly regarded the ceiling. "The will's there, but the bang's a dud."

Hopkins smacked the table with his open palm. All the members of the NSC but Marian Cole, Reen, and the snoring President jumped in place.

"Two Cousins," said the White House chief.

Hopkins turned to Reen, his jowls shivering, his expression that of utter disbelief.

"Ten Loving Helpers have gone missing this year, but only two Cousins."

"Shit!" Hopkins shouted. "They're still your people, aren't they?"

Reen could not fathom why Hopkins was so enraged. "Yes, but—"

"Billy," Marian said in an indulgent voice, "why don't you just let me handle this? The CIA was taking care of all the alien business before. We have kind of a historical caveat."

"Listen, Reen-ja." Hopkins rose from his chair like a mountain thrust upward by plate tectonics. "The CIA has been working on ways to get rid of your people ever since the Truman administration. You know that. And they would have kept on if the budget had been funded."

Reen took in the appalled faces around the table. Marian Cole was the only one who seemed calm. The lock of hair had fallen another quarter of an inch. There was a smile on her red lips.

"Oh, sit down, Billy," she said with a wave of her hand. "The thing we should be talking about here is what the Cousins intend to do if Europe declares war and if the domestic terrorism isn't stopped. What about it, Reen?" Her denim blue eyes twinkled. "You have the obvious weapons superiority. We're a bunch of wing-clipped ducks in a lake. Why don't you finish us off?"

Around the table a breathless, terrified silence. Krupner spasmed, accidentally decapitating his origami giraffe. He looked down at his guilty hands and the torn paper in dumbfounded woe.

"Jesus Christ," Hopkins whispered to Cole. "Will you shut up."

"Somebody's got to have the balls to say it. What about it, Reen?" Marian asked.

Reen stiffened, feeling the tug of her nearness as a star feels the thieving pull of a black hole. Each time they were together, she stole more and more of him. He was a small creature growing even smaller, a being on the very edge of disappearance.

He fought to keep his treacherous mouth shut. Had they been alone, he would have told her. He would have answered any question, no matter how ugly the truth.

"Come on," she said. "What are you guys waiting for?"

Hans Krupner burst into tears. "We have always the same meetings. Threats. Shouting. Everyone at one another's throats. So this is the peace the Cousins promised us? I tell you, I cannot stand such peace anymore."

At that moment the President rose. The NSC looked expectantly, encouragingly to Womack. Vilishnikov stared at the President with the wonder of a blind man catching his first glimpse of the sun.

Womack fumbled with his fly, took out his penis, and, before the Secret Serviceman could stop him, voided his bladder on the tariff bill. Urine splattered. Krupner forgot his tears and inched away from the spreading wet.

"Meeting adjourned," Reen said, rising and heading quickly to the door. There he stopped and looked back. The members of the NSC were standing, gazing down at the urine-splattered papers. The humans were differing shapes, differing colors. Even in physical appearance they were chaotic. He felt he could read idiosyncratic fears and individual ambitions behind their tiny eyes.

"Does that count?" DiSecco asked. "Listen. Could we somehow construe that as a signature?"

Reen called, "Director Cole."

Marian lifted her head.

She was angry with him, he knew; and that was to his great regret. On the other hand, she didn't have the courage to refuse his direct order.

"I will see you now in my office."

3

REEN WAITED IN THE OVAL OFFICE fifteen minutes before opening the door to the huge reception area to find Marian Cole talking to Natalie as though they were old friends. The two women, one tall and blond, the other short and blond, turned. Natalie, he noticed, had exchanged her irritating blouse for a cream-colored sweater.

"I told you I wanted to see you," Reen said to Marian.

Natalie spoke up: "But you said first thing this morning to hold all calls."

"You might have announced Director Cole was here."

"That would have been a call. You tell me 'Hold all calls' when you don't want to talk to anyone; and then you're supposed to say, 'Hey, I asked so-and-so to come over, so forget the holding-the-calls thing.' That's how you're supposed to talk to a secretary." She rolled her eyes.

"Hold all calls while the director and I are speaking," Reen told her.

Natalie went back to her typing. "Okay."

When he reentered his office, Marian followed. He closed the heavy oaken adjoining door, his claw clicking on the brass knob.

"So. What's Billy Hopkins been saying about me?" she asked.

Reen walked to the windows and peered out. The riots were over, and a sanitation department truck was washing the blood from the streets. "I don't talk about him to you or you to him. That would be disloyal."

"Disloyal?" she asked in amusement. "I thought maybe Billy was babbling again."

He was glad that she was standing directly at his back, right in the sixty-degree dead spot of his three-hundred-degree vision field. He didn't want to see her face. "Angela asks about you."

Behind him there was silence. Reen, who ached no less for Marian's approval than four-year-old Angela did, longed to turn to see if she was smiling or frowning. "It's been nearly a month. I thought we would go see her."

"I'm tired of this, Reen." Marian's voice was so weary that it frightened him. Humans aged in too short a season, like the fleeting Appalachian fall. From the past year to this it seemed that her moistness and energy had gone. There were new lines on Marian's face, more silver in her hair. She was slipping from him too quickly.

Marian moved slightly to the right and entered his peripheral vision. She stood as she stood when they had first met: hands clasped, chin lifted. The other children, stolen in their sleep and awakened to alien surroundings, had screamed. But not five-year-old Marian.

That one, he told the doctors. *I hope it will be that one.*

"Don't fight me, Marian," he told her.

She gave Millard Fillmore an appraising look. "How can I? You always get your way."

He knew he should apologize but didn't. Too many years, too many chances for apologies had passed. He opened the French doors for her, and together they walked to the south lawn.

In the Rose Garden the crisp air held the tangs of autumn and cordite. Down the spread of grass, on the other side of the fence, stood two knots of humans encumbered by still cameras and minicams. Reen would have found it difficult to distinguish reporter from tourist but for the frenzied shouting from the media and the CNN truck parked nearby.

His eye lit on a solitary figure between the throngs: a young man with a purple Vespa and a backpack. For two days now, each time Reen had ventured onto the south lawn, he had seen the boy. And even from that distance Reen could feel the disquieting intensity of his stare.

What could be so important to demand such a single-purposed vigil? The boy's pose was taut, his expression that of barely contained fervor. Reen pictured the boy reaching in the backpack, bringing out a gun, a bomb. Head down, Reen hurried his stride.

Past a knee-high barrier of ornamental shrubbery the ovoid commuter waited as it always did. And there waited Thural, a head taller than the three Loving Helpers at his side. His black eyes were pools of calm. The Loving Helpers' eyes were dark, abandoned wells.

"Cousin Reen-ja," Thural said, speaking quietly in Cousin language. "Jonis went with two Loving Helpers to observe the riot and has not yet returned."

Reen entered the shelter of the ship's doorway, just out of the backpacked boy's possible line of fire. "But the riot has been over for some time."

"Yes, Reen-ja. It causes me to wonder."

"Inform the Community, then," Reen said. "Maybe they can find him. In the meantime we will be taken to West Virginia." He motioned to Marian, who was standing on the lawn, well out of the shadow of the ship's overhang. Well out of the Loving Helpers' reach.

"Keep those things away from me," she said.

After a self-conscious glance at Marian Cole, Thural told the Loving Helpers, "Go." In unison the three about-faced and marched toward the command room, Thural at their heels.

When they left, Marian entered. Reen led her down the right-hand corridor.

"I hate them," she said. "I can't stand the way they move, like little robots. I hate the blank way they look at me. Ninety-three percent of your people. Doesn't that scare you?"

Reen stopped in the middle of the hall and looked back, searching her expression for pity. Her face was hard. "We live with it."

"No, you don't."

Embarrassed, he continued down the hall to the lounge. Marian gave the monochromatic, minimalist room a sweeping glance and then tried to make herself comfortable on a chair that was too short for her legs. Reen perched on a sofa opposite her and contemplated the wall. There was a falling sensation as the ship's gravity changed.

When Reen glanced at Marian, he found himself staring into the side of her cheek.

"I want you to be happy," he told her.

"That's great, Reen. You rape me, then insist I enjoy it."

Humans always muddied the clear water of emotion; and in that murk the handsome, darting shapes of love swam with ugly creatures of lust.

Once she had loved him as a playmate. Then he took the place of her absent father. *I'm going to marry you,* Marian, at six years old, had told him. And the psychologists, accustomed to the caprices of human children, had laughed.

But neither Reen nor the psychologists had been prepared for her determination. It was Marian, not Reen, who always got her way.

Remembering that touch was important to humans, he leaned forward to grasp her beautifully wrought hand. The Cousins, in their twelve hundred centuries of civilization, could have created splendor with hands like those. With their three stubby fingers and claw they had managed only to produce utility.

He noticed the aging lizard texture of her skin and tried, with helpless dismay, to smooth it. His claw gently traced the raised white scars at her wrist, the evidence of her earlier disappointment with her husband. Once, he reminded himself, she had loved Howard, too.

"It's my fault you're so bitter. If I had known that remembering would . . ."

She slipped her hand from his. "You never come by anymore. But you got what you were after."

"Angela." He rolled the name in his mouth like candy. "Wasn't Angela worth it?"

Her eyes narrowed, her lips twisted. The savagery in her face unnerved him. "Women are made to be brood mares, is that what you're saying?"

"No," he replied, wondering what he could do to make things right. He suddenly realized how deluded he had been. And how tragically his experiment was turning out.

Thural poked his head into the lounge to say they had landed. Marian got to her feet.

"You will hug her," Reen blurted.

She looked at him blankly.

"I don't care how you feel about me. And it doesn't matter whether you wanted Angela or not. She is here, and you are her mother. Angela is a mammal. She needs to be hugged. I'm not practiced at touching. And I suspect I'm no good at it."

But Marian knew that, didn't she? Their own shy, awkward embraces had led to—what? he wondered. A sterile thing that surely hadn't been enough for her and had been nearly too much for him. No, theirs had been a laboratory mating, not warm limbs wrapping warm limbs but a petri-dish entwining of DNA.

As he followed her off the ship, he wondered dismally if she needed more and if that was the reason for her anger.

It had snowed in the West Virginia mountains. The sun was struggling to peek out from behind a layer of cirrus clouds. Reen slogged through the drifts on the walkway and kicked his boots clean on the mat before he entered the house.

A knot of gray, large-headed, and huge-eyed children were playing ball on the living room floor. As soon as Marian entered, one popped up from the group and darted her way, as dramatically and hopelessly drawn to Marian as an iron filing to a magnet.

Love, Reen thought. One day his daughter would choose another of the recombinants to mate with, and when they mated, they would do so with love. Perhaps they would talk after the act was over, the way humans so often did. Angela's children would grow up under the sunny indulgence of both mother and father, and her life would be sweeter than Reen's had been.

As Angela hugged Marian's legs, Marian stood immobile, gazing into the distance, seemingly unaware or perhaps embarrassed by the show of adoration. After a heartrending wait, Marian bent, pried the child's grasping hands from her thighs, and picked her up.

Reen relaxed and studied the perfect five-fingered gray hand now clasped in Marian's pink one. Angela's nose was tiny and well formed, her mouth a small bow. On the top of her head was a dusting of hair as pale as the snow on the hills outside. Despite her color, despite her huge eyes, she was mostly Marian's child.

"Reen," Angela said and blinked.

The ice of Reen's earlier annoyance thawed. He put out his hand to his daughter, and she grabbed his claw.

Sandra Gonzales, the caregiver, and Quen, the Cousin overseer, ambled up.

"Such a good child," Mrs. Gonzales was saying. The caregiver had the plump roundness of bread dough. Gray children trailed in her wake like eager gulls behind a tugboat. "Angela's such a kind, sweet little thing, Ms. Cole. She plays with the other children so well."

Marian had not ceased her vague contemplation of the room. Although she held Angela in her arms, she had not once looked at her child. "You should have some colors in the house. Children like bright colors."

"Distracting," Quen said. "They must learn to focus. They are human, but they are Cousin as well."

Marian put the little girl down. "I want to take her outside. Does she have a coat or something?"

Mrs. Gonzales fluttered her hands. "Yes, yes. A coat." She bustled out of the room, the children following.

The two Cousins and Marian Cole stood in uneasy silence until

Mrs. Gonzales came back and began to bundle Angela into a zippered windbreaker. "Your mother wants to take you outside. Won't that be fun? And then you can tell all the other children about it."

"What will she tell them about?" Marian asked sharply. "About having a mother that she knows or about playing in the snow?"

The smile slid like melted frosting from Mrs. Gonzales's sweet roll of a face.

"The other children have no idea who their parents are," Marian said.

"Not important," Quen told her.

Mrs. Gonzales was studying the zipper intently, much more intently than the job deserved.

"Then why is it so damned important that Angela know who I am?" Marian asked Quen with such ferocity that the Cousin blundered backward.

"Why is it so important?" Marian demanded.

No one answered her. Quen stood where his backward flight had taken him, his gaze averted. Mrs. Gonzales, lips puckered, was still fiddling with the coat zipper.

"They're killing us off," Marian told Mrs. Gonzales. "All very quietly. We're being sterilized, lady. Did you know that? Look at the statistics. The birthrate is down eighteen percent, and no one realizes what's happening."

"Not in front of the children," Reen said.

She gave him a brief glance and turned to Mrs. Gonzales. "Can't you see? In a hundred years or so, there won't be any humans left. These children will take over the world."

Quen stiffened. "These children," he said with pride, "will inherit the universe."

Giving the seam of the zipper a last tug, Mrs. Gonzales said in firm, quiet benediction, "There now," as though she were an elderly marzipan queen sending her champion into battle.

The tension in the room evaporated; an inevitable sadness took its place. Marian took her daughter's hand and led her to the door.

"Reen," Angela called, flapping her fingers at him. "Reen."

He followed a discreet step or so behind. Outside, in the wind, a blush rose on Angela's cheeks, pink human color, from either the cold or her excitement.

Reen remained on the porch while Marian walked the child to the edge of the forest. Picking up a handful of snow, Marian packed it into a ball. Her voice drifted across the frozen yard. "Like this, kid. Here."

Quen stood at Reen's side. "Do you not want to be with her, too, Reen-ja?"

"Later." After three unsuccessful tries, Reen finally managed to grasp his own meager clump of snow.

By the evergreens, Marian was bending down to Angela's height. The wind carried Marian's faint voice to him. "Come on. Every kid should know this. Body heat. That's what makes the snow pack down." Whirling, Marian threw the snowball. It sailed across the glade and, before Reen could duck, slammed into his chest, shattering into a thousand glittering pieces.

He staggered back. Quen asked anxiously, "Are you all right?"

"It didn't hurt." Reen brushed the snow from his uniform with his free hand. The snowball hadn't been meant to injure. What hurt were Marian's icy glances, her hard-packed words.

She was laughing. Reen knew enough about human children to realize that, had Angela's mind been as human as her looks, she would have been laughing, too. Instead his serious little girl bent and, dogged as any Cousin, packed her own snowball.

"That's a good girl," came the shadow of Marian's voice. "Now throw it at your daddy. Throw it hard."

Reen stood, an easy target. He would not have moved even if his daughter had been holding a gun. Angela threw overhand as her mother had done. The snowball rolled off her fingers and dropped to the ground a couple of feet in front of her shoes.

"That's okay, kid," Marian was saying. "We'll make another one. You can always make another snowball."

Reen looked at the snow he held. When he relaxed his grip, it slipped through his fingers like sand.

"She knows a great deal about us," Quen said.

Reen nodded.

"Will she talk?"

"No."

In her red dress Marian was a cardinal in the trees, a holly berry among the green of the pines.

"But what if she is not so much under your control as you believe?" Quen asked, skirting the edge of indelicacy.

Reen dusted his hands. "She has revealed nothing important. The programming is working."

But was it? Perhaps her new coldness toward him was the first symptom of rebellion. It had been years since Marian was under the power of the Loving Helpers, and time had a way of blunting things. Probably he should put her under Communal control again, to make certain, but he hadn't the heart. No. He would stand, vulnerable and still, and accept the snowballs of her rage.

Marian, all warmth and brightness, was bending down to Angela, his gray, quiet child. She was speaking too low now for him to hear what she was saying, but Angela was staring into her mother's face as though all the wisdom of the prophets was hidden there.

"But what if that is not enough?" Quen asked. "What if she is capable of breaking the programming?"

Reen's heart, too, had its secret compartments. In the largest compartment lay the Community. In the next, Angela. Marian and Jeff Womack resided in their own places. But Reen knew what should be important and what should not.

"Then she will have to be killed," he said.

4

AFTER LANDING AT THE WHITE House, Reen followed Marian down the ship's ramp to the south lawn. The shouts from the reporters at the fence were a wordless cacophony, distant as Marian's laughter across the Appalachian snow, muted as the cries of the gulls swooping in from the Potomac.

Reen noticed with relief that the boy with the Vespa and backpack had disappeared. And he saw that, near a boxwood hedge, Tali was waiting.

Reen lifted a hand in greeting. "Cousin Brother."

Tali didn't reply. There was something important to be discussed, Reen realized, and Tali wouldn't talk until Marian left.

Reen took a hasty and somewhat ungracious leave of Marian. Pensively, he watched her stride across the grass to her limo parked in the circular drive.

"Cousin Brother Firstborn," Tali said without preamble as soon as she was out of earshot, "Jonis is missing. The Loving Helpers who were with him have been found dead."

Reen regarded his Second Brother, by birthright the guardian of his conscience. "Where were the Loving Helpers found?"

"They were put into trash bags and placed by a newspaper stand on Constitution Avenue."

"Such a thing has never happened before."

"As soon as one human pattern establishes itself, another pattern supersedes it. Therefore we should not trust patterns."

It was Tali's right to give advice to his First Brother, but Reen also had a right to ignore it. "How were the Loving Helpers killed?"

"I thought it tasteless to ask, Reen-ja. Hopkins seemed very distressed at having to tell me, and I myself was uncomfortable hearing the news."

Reen lifted his face to the clouds scudding across the pallid December sky. "Why should that make you uncomfortable? By now the others have all died in captivity anyway."

"But no one is aware of our weakness, Cousin Brother."

"The kidnappers know. Does Director Hopkins have any idea why this crime was different?"

"Hopkins believes something went wrong and the kidnappers were afraid of being seen. That is why they took Jonis and murdered the Loving Helpers. But then he understands these things better than I," Tali said with unconvincing humility. Humility was something Reen's Second Brother had never been very good at.

"Does he have suspects?"

Tali watched Marian's limo nose its way through the iron gates and the barricade. "He says the CIA."

Reen gazed after the limo as it rolled out into the E Street traffic. "Hopkins accuses the CIA of everything, Cousin Brother."

Tali suddenly faced Reen. "You tell her too much."

A fractious breeze shadowboxed with a bed of chrysanthemums nearby, making the heavy-headed flowers duck and weave. Only Tali, Cousin Brother Conscience, had the right to address Reen so sharply, and he exercised that right too often for Reen's taste. "She has been implanted, Tali. She's been under my control since she was a child."

"Control or not, what she knows will make her hate us. Why do you insist on telling her?"

It would have been foolhardy to explain. The fact was that Reen couldn't help himself. Time had knit them. Unravel the thread of Marian, and the weave of Reen's life would fall apart.

"Remember, duty is to the Community, Reen-ja," Tali said.

Reen dipped his head in acceptance of the criticism. "And I realize it is your duty to remind me." Reen made his way to the West Wing, leaving his conscience standing in the watery sunlight by the boxwood hedge, staring after him.

The Rose Garden was littered with wet brown leaves. As he picked his way through the rosebushes, which had been cut back and bagged like corpses for the winter, Reen noticed Hopkins watching from a window. By the time he opened the French doors and entered the Oval Office, Hopkins caught up with him.

"You talk to Cole?" the director asked.

Reen took a deep breath. The Oval Office was redolent with the smells of lemon oil, peach potpourri, and old smoke from the fireplace. "Of course I have talked to Cole. You must have seen us come off the ship together."

Reen felt crowded by everything: Marian, the threat of war, the dark undercurrents in the Congress. And he was terrified above all else of being stalked. His fear made him feel so lonely, he nearly confessed it to Hopkins.

"It'll be all over the six-thirty news," Hopkins complained. "Marian gets all the media attention. How do you think that makes me look? Where do you two go, anyway?"

Reen curtly changed the subject. "Tell me about Jonis."

"Jonis? Oh, the last kidnap victim. Listen, Tali tells me Jonis was in charge of your defense. What if he talks?"

Reen thought of Marian and the flat indicting look in his Cousin Brother's eyes. "He won't talk."

"If the CIA's behind it, Jonis is going to spill his guts."

"He won't talk." Reen pointedly looked away from Hopkins and at an enameled table, a state gift from India.

"You want to give me permission to search Langley?"

"No." Reen strode out of the office, through the reception area, and to the colonnade.

"Well, okay. So don't worry. If he doesn't talk, we're home free. I've got the thing under control."

"If things are under control, where is Jonis?"

"He has to be with the rest of them, right? We're trying to get them back, but solving a kidnapping is slow."

"If solving a crime goes slowly, things are not under control." They entered the main building at nearly a trot. Reen passed the White House pantry where a dark-suited member of the kitchen staff looked at him curiously.

"We're talking to witnesses. That's all we can do for the moment."

In the elevator vestibule Reen paused.

"Where are you going?" Hopkins asked.

The nice thing about the FBI director was that he wore pleasingly dark suits and somber ties. But there were times Reen wished he could replace him. The White House chief tired of the man's inane questions. "Upstairs."

"To see Womack?"

"Is there anyone else upstairs I might want to see?"

"No."

"Then it is obvious I plan to visit the President." The elevator arrived. As Reen stepped into the car, Hopkins put his hand to the door.

"He's losing it bad. He's hired another medium. Did you know that? And his whipping it out in front of the whole NSC . . ."

Reen moved to the back of the small paneled elevator. "The President acts senile, but I know better. Get your hand off the door."

The director shook his head. "Our collective butts are in a sling, and he's not doing a damned thing about it. If Womack had any sense left, he would have signed that tariff bill this morning instead of pissing on it."

"Did you ever stop to think at what point the President upset the meeting? He planned the interruption. Get your hand off the door."

Hopkins pulled his hand away. "He *planned* that? What are you talking about?"

Reen hit the button. "He tells me he's on strike."

5

JEFF WOMACK HAD MADE THE OVAL room on the second floor his study, and through his terms in office he had succeeded in changing its decor to one designed to make Reen's visits torturous and brief.

In the crowded, eclectic room, fleur-de-lis wallpaper did battle with Early American and Santa Fe; and Womack sat in a maple rocking chair, an afghan tucked around his sweat-suited legs. At a heavy table in front of him was a Domino's box containing the messy, aromatic remains of a pizza. Womack's long, lushly wrinkled face was lowered, his chin tucked to his chest. Pink scalp shone through his thinning white hair. He was regarding the floor with dull interest.

"Jeff?" Reen said.

The head snapped up. The brown eyes narrowed slyly. "Hi there, termite. Grab yourself some pizza."

Reen glanced into the box. The pizza was a thick-crusted combination: sausage, green pepper, and black olives scattered at random over the cheese. Reen preferred the dishes that the White House kitchen prepared: asparagus in rows with a neat stripe of hollandaise; circles of scalloped potatoes, all the same size. "No, thank you."

"So how'd I do this morning?"

Reen walked to the President's side. "You annoyed me."

Womack's smile brightened. "Which bothered you more? The pissing or the drooling? I've been practicing, see?" He opened his mouth. A glistening thread of moisture dropped from his lips.

"May I ask you a question?"

"Ask away." Womack wiped the spittle with his sleeve.

Reen took a deep breath. "Does menopause affect women's ability to deal with logic?"

Womack gave him a sharp look. "Knotty problem."

Reen steeled himself for the answer. All morning he had been haunted by Marian's puzzling anger. He had always believed she was intelligent, but females, after all, were females. Perhaps her intelligence was as much of a house of cards as his own.

"Where'd you pick up that idea?"

"Bill Hopkins."

"Hah!" The President lifted a forefinger. "I guessed as much."

Whipping off the afghan, Womack stood, then shuffled quickly to the bar. The President was a tall, frail gnome of a man who, when the mood hit him, could move with alarming speed. He took a cigarette from a crushed pack on the fireplace mantel and lit it, leaning gracefully against the wall.

"I wish you wouldn't smoke."

"Why? You can grow me another set of lungs like you usually do." Womack opened a cabinet, took out a fifth of Wild Turkey, and poured himself a drink. "Grow me another heart," he said grumpily into the glass, "so I can outlive another vice president."

Shifting uncomfortably on his feet, Reen asked, "And as to my question?"

"Hopkins is after Marian Cole again, right? He's jealous. Good. Keep 'em guessing. Just be careful not to show too much favoritism to Marian. If Hopkins discovers you're in love with her, he'll use that as ammunition."

"Thank you. I'll be more careful," Reen said, queasily contemplating the chaos inside the pizza box. "Should I also be careful not to show my love for you?"

Womack scowled. "Do me a favor. You *like* me, okay? You're *fond* of me. You'd like to go *bowling* with me. But let's not have a kid together like you and Marian."

As though Womack had taken a swing at his face, Reen flinched. "You know?"

Womack tapped a finger against the side of his patrician nose. "I make it my business to know things. My old political enemies used to call me a snake. But snakes, you know, they see all the dirt. Don't pay attention to what Hopkins says about Marian. Hopkins is jerking your chain."

Reen wondered how Womack had learned about Angela. A too-talkative Cousin? Or was he simply guessing? The President was superb at speculation.

"Listen, I'm still on strike, mind you," Womack said, "but about that meeting—I thought a little free advice might be in order." He studied the level in the glass before he lifted it to his mouth.

"Yes?"

"Get rid of Krupner. He's going to fold under pressure. Anyone who cries in the middle of an NSC meeting . . . give me a break."

Reen moved to the windows and looked past the Truman balcony's folding chairs to the Jefferson Memorial, a white marble pimple on the chin of the Ellipse. "The Germans want him."

"The Germans want a German. Tell them the problem. They'll replace him. If you want my advice, take it. If you don't, fuck you. By the way, I'm low on booze."

A spot of color near the White House fence drew Reen's attention. That color. That jolly grape–Kool-Aid dot of color. The purple Vespa was back.

"Termite? You listening? My world's crumbling, don't you hear? My liquor's almost gone, and all you can do is stare out the window."

Reen tore his gaze from the scooter and the watchful, motionless figure beside it. "All right. I'll send Thural up. You can tell him what you need."

"Yeah, Thural or Jonis. I like old Jonis. Thural, he just gets one of the Secret Service guys to do it. Jonis is *creative*. There's this bum—I guess the hell *that's* insensitive—okay, a street person. Okay? A homeless son of a bitch. Old Jonis meets him at the fence, hands him enough money to get me and the bum a bottle. Scratches both itches at the same time, Jonis says." Womack lifted his glass. "Great guy, Jonis."

"Jonis has been kidnapped."

The glass paused at Womack's lips.

"Who is the homeless person?" Reen asked.

"Never saw him. Don't know his name." Womack stared bleakly into the fireplace, then threw the remains of his cigarette onto the burning logs. "Poor Jonis. Think you'll get him back alive?"

"If he is not back within three days, we may consider him dead."

The President's intent eyes flicked to Reen. "Why three days especially?"

Reen dodged the questioning look. "Did Jonis have other connections we were not aware of?"

"Oo!" The President clapped a hand to his head. "Oo! I wanted to show you something!" Womack rummaged around in the bar's cabinet. "Shit. Where'd I put it?" Turning away from the bar, he scanned the room.

"What?"

"Something I found in the West Wing." In four rapid, arthritic strides he was at his knotty pine desk. Sliding open the top drawer, he brought out a folded piece of paper.

With one arm Womack swept the Domino's box from the Santa Fe table and onto the floor, sending the remains of the pizza tumbling facedown onto the carpet. He opened the paper carefully. On the white page rested a yellowish translucent cone.

Reen cringed.

"Know what it is?" Womack asked.

"Of course I know what it is."

"Is it yours?"

Reen stiffened. "No! When I shed a claw sheath, I shed it in private. Then I dispose of it, just as any Cousin should."

"Pick it up. Take a real good look at it."

"No. And stop playing with it. You don't know where that's been." But he had already caught sight of what Womack wanted him to see. A raised line ran down the cone's center: the adolescent ridge. There were no more young Cousins, and only one thing left had a claw like that.

"You see?" Womack asked. "How'd *that* get into the White House?"

"It dropped off. The Taskmaster didn't notice—"

"Don't be a dunce! I found it while I was crawling around under the furniture in the West Wing, like I told you. And no one brings Loving Helpers into the building."

"Yes, yes. This is all very interesting—"

"It's a *mystery*," Womack said, a gleam in his eye.

Reen lowered his gaze. "Congress is insisting that you choose a vice president." When he glanced up, he was astonished to see dread shadow Womack's gaunt face.

"There is only so much that regeneration can do. One day you *will* die, Jeff, and we will be unable to stop it." They had been friends for Womack's entire term, fifty-one long years. Never would Reen know another human so well. Despite his special relationship with Marian Cole, never would he love a human so perfectly.

"You said Congress wanted me to. How do *you* feel about it?"

Reen fought the upwelling of resentment in his chest, hoping that Womack, who sensed things so well, would not suspect that he chafed under the congressional pressure. "Something could happen to you."

Again those brown eyes picked him apart. "Could it?"

"I hear you have hired another medium."

"Marian tell you? Or Hopkins?"

Reen raised his head.

"Ah," Womack said with the heartfelt satisfaction of a glutton sitting down before a seven-course meal. "So it was Hopkins. It doesn't matter much, though, termite. As many mediums as I hire, as much as they tell me about the other side, the thought of dying still scares me." He laughed. "It scares me to death."

With his claw and forefinger Reen plucked the sleeve of Womack's velour sweat suit. "The mediums are frauds. No one can call up spirits that way. Besides, the Appropriations Committee threatens to make your expenditures public."

"What? Ted Long behind this? That bastard doesn't scare me. The press is saying I'm senile. The gossip inside the Beltway is I'm dead. So what? I haven't stepped outside this room in three months, and my approval rating's eighty-seven percent. Now *that's* what I call presidential. Let Ted Long shove *that* Harris poll up his ass."

"Jeff, please. What if war breaks out? Can't you just sign the bill and have it over with? Must I bring Loving Helpers here to force you?"

Womack yanked his sleeve from Reen's grasp. His jaws were clenched, his words strangled, his gaze terrified. "Let go of me, you little gray shit!" He lumbered to the rocking chair and sat. "Christ, what a mess. What a bunch of goddamned bad karma. I'm the guy who handed the Earth to you fuckers. Then you stab me in the back."

A chill fury seized Reen by the nape of the neck. "You've never forgiven me for pressuring you to appoint Hopkins. Well, my Brother wanted Hopkins, and it has always been easier for me not to displease Tali. I give you back your own advice: Grow up, Jeff. This is politics."

For a breathless moment the two glared at each other. Reen was aware of the sickly, jailhouse pallor of the President's face, the distinctive garlic and tomato odor of the pizza. Then Womack's expression softened. "Hey. Consider this a learning experience. If you get in over your head . . . well, I have plans. I have agendas. You'll see."

"I hate your agendas." Reen's shoulders slumped as if the weight of the planet had descended on him.

From the rocking chair a contemplative, wry silence. "Don't trust me, do you?"

"You taught me every lie, every trick. How can I help but not trust you?" Reen's voice trembled with the conflict of emotions he felt for the man. Womack had been one of Reen's longest-running trials—the cost, Reen had always figured, of victory. And yet, for all their arguments, he loved him, loved him with the same despairing love he felt for Marian Cole.

"You know, when push comes to shove, termite, you won't have the heart to get rid of me. But your Brother will."

Reen walked hastily out of the room. In the vestibule of the elevator he punched the button hard with his claw. He wanted to get away from Womack, but he wasn't sure what drove him: anger at Womack or fear of the truth.

"Hey, termite," Womack called.

Reen peeked around the corner. The President was framed in the doorway of his study, the pizza at his feet, a monarch amid the ruins of his kingdom. "Okay, so you don't believe in mediums. But you believe in spirits, right? I mean, we picked this spiritualism up from you guys. You're not just jerking me around?"

The elevator opened with a rumble and shush. "Of course there are spirits." Reen stepped into the car and let it take him down to safety, away from the torment in Jeff Womack's eyes.

6

BACK IN HIS OFFICE REEN SAT AT HIS terminal while the shadows of the trees outside lengthened and the day faded to night.

At six-thirty Natalie came in, her coat on her arm. "I'm going."

"Yes." He nodded, barely looking up from his work.

She hesitated at the door. "I mean, I have to go home now, you know? Sam'll want dinner."

He stopped scrolling the report, the cursor blinking on an item concerning unrest in Italy. "I understand," he said, although he didn't so much understand as accept. After years of frustration at his secretaries' holidays and vacations, he'd stopped trying to change them. He'd discarded the idea that humans were lazy. He'd even once, not long ago, taken a sort of vacation himself.

He expected her to leave, but she didn't. She stood with one hand on the jamb. "You want me to turn on the light?"

"No." He went back to his work but then looked up again. Natalie hadn't moved. "Is anything wrong?"

She took a breath to speak, then let out the air and the thought in a barren sigh. "Well. Don't work too late."

"I always work late."

"It makes me feel guilty. Thural's usually with you. I don't feel so bad when he's here."

"Thural is seeing about Jonis." Reen lifted his hands from the computer and set them primly in his lap. The room slowly darkened. The spill of light behind Natalie tossed a rectangle of gold across the carpet like an abandoned evening wrap. "You've worked for me now, what?" he asked. "Two months? When you work here long enough, you'll get used to my hours and the fact that I often work alone."

She scratched idly at the doorjamb with one long fingernail.

With a kind smile he said, "What would I do when I go home other than sleep?"

"You could watch TV. Sometimes they have great stuff on TV. Sitcoms. True-life murder stories. Ought to try it. I'll tell you when something good is coming on, and maybe you can bring in the portable."

"That would be nice," he said vaguely, thinking how distasteful it would be to watch a program on crime. Human life was short enough without other humans bringing it to a premature close. He'd known twelve presidents, had loved three of them, and now had outlived all but one.

"Sam," he said finally, because apparently she was not leaving. "Is that your husband?"

Natalie walked forward. Reached into her purse.

Startled by the unexpected gesture, Reen shrank back against his chair. He thought of the graffiti, of the boy with the backpack, and expected to see a gun in Natalie's hand. Instead she took out her wallet.

"My kid." She flipped open her wallet and held it toward him.

Reen took the wallet and switched on his green-shaded desk lamp. In the photo it was high summer. A blond boy with a smile and a baseball cap stood in the batter's box, bat in hand.

Sam had the doomed, sad beauty of his dying breed. The pool of light under the lamp washed the freckled face with brass. His hands held the bat with nonchalant grace. There was arrogance in the set of his shoulders, a fearlessness in his eyes.

"He's a good kid."

Reen handed back the photo. "Such photos are to be valued." He knew Natalie could not understand what he meant and that she would never be allowed to. One day his own daughter would look at such pictures to remind herself of the debt she owed the past. When the Cousins died out, as they one day surely would, and when Reen, for her sake, made humans extinct, he wanted Angela to remember.

Natalie tucked the wallet back into her purse. "His dad, the son of a bitch, never sends us any money. That's why I got a little upset with you today about the blouse."

Reen folded his hands. "You must have a raise. Thural will see to it."

Her mouth fell open. Even in the dim light of the reading lamp, he could see her cheeks blanch. "I didn't mean—"

"I know. Go home to Sam. Don't worry about me. Mothers and fathers should concern themselves with their children."

"Okay. But stress can get to you. All work and no play . . ." Her voice wavered in indecision or perhaps in futility. Without finishing the thought she turned and made her way from the room. Reen watched her go, thinking of the photo of the boy, of the baseball game.

All work and no play.

He didn't understand the concept of baseball; he didn't understand games. *Take the snow and pack it,* Marian had said. His daughter, so instructed, had thrown the snowball with somber dedication and only because her mother had told her to. Angela had the wide shoulders of a brachiator, the generous musculature of her mother. But Reen knew she would never stand in a batter's box, her face agleam with joy.

All work.

He lifted his hands diligently to the keyboard. After a few moments of reading, his mind immersed itself in the Italian crisis, and

Natalie and her son were forgotten. At eight o'clock a maid wordlessly brought his dinner. By eleven he was so tired, the letters on the screen began to blur. He checked to see that the French doors were locked, flicked off the terminal and the reading lamp, and left his office.

The Secret Serviceman on duty in the colonnade gave him a brief glance. Other than that quick, furtive movement, nothing stirred.

Reen paused at the open doorway of the pool that Roosevelt had constructed, Nixon had made a press room, and reporter-weary Womack had reconverted. The White House was otherwise quiet, but something by the pool was making a sound. He entered. The lights in the pool were on, reflecting blue ripples across the ceiling. The filtration system gurgled. Water lapped the tiles.

On a lounge chair lay a bundle of old clothes, and from it came a noise like a buzz saw. And an arm. The hand, clutching an empty bottle of Mogen David, rested knuckles-down on the concrete.

Reen tiptoed to the guard. "There is a man sleeping by the pool."

"Yes, sir. The President's new medium."

"Why is he sleeping here?"

"Passed out, sir."

The guard looked away. An oppressive silence fell. Reen waded through it to the exit. Outside, the night air was cool, and sparse traffic growled down Pennsylvania Avenue.

Reen walked across the grass, nervously searching for the boy with the backpack. The fence was empty. Beside the West Wing the commuter ship gleamed dully in the full moonlight, Thural a ghost beside it. Reen trudged up the ramp. At the door he paused.

"Jonis bought liquor from a homeless man. Were you aware of this, Cousin?"

Did Thural's gaze shift in alarm? The movement was so quick that Reen couldn't be sure. "Yes, Reen-ja. Although I never personally—"

"Keep this information from the FBI but order the Guardians of the Community to find the man and bring him to me."

"I will give the Guardians his name and description—"

"Good." Reen turned his back on Thural and marched into the ship.

The lounge seemed perversely vacant without Marian there to vex it with her colors. He sat. A few minutes later Thural came to him.

"Reen-ja? We have landed at Andrews, and I have alerted the Guardians about Jonis's human friend."

Reen stared at his feet. Stress will get you, Natalie had said.

All work.

Every part of Angela functioned. Her hands were marvels, her brain clear. But had he made some terrible mistake? Quiet, shy Angela had the strength of a human in her body and the stamina of a Cousin in her mind. How would she handle the stress that was bound to follow her as an unkempt dog its master? As countless parents had before him, Reen wondered whether she would be happy. And if she could not find peace, he wondered, would she ever forgive him?

"Reen-ja?"

Without meeting his aide's gaze, Reen stood and followed Thural down the ramp.

7

WHEN REEN WALKED INTO THE COUS-
in Place, the first thing he noticed was the peppery acid smell of sleep.
The second thing stopped him, brought him up short with a jolt of
pleasure: the blandness of the gray monolithic room. The room was
empty but for one Cousin. The Sleep Master sat quietly, his dark eyes
full of slumber.

Reen, Thural at his heels, turned to enter the right-hand room.

"Wait."

The raspy voice came from behind. Hand to the soft wall, Reen
turned. The Sleep Master's gaze was focused on him.

"You may not go forward."

Reen stood back to let Thural pass. He cast one look of longing
into the chamber, at the Cousins packed quietly into their niches,
before he made his way across the floor to sit at the Sleep Master's
feet.

A light airy silence settled around them like mist.

"I am very tired," Reen said pointedly.

"I know. But you bring humanity with you when you come. Wash
yourself of the humans, and I can allow you in with the others."

Reen fixed his eyes on the curve between wall and floor, willing
his mind blank; but his brain fussed against rest like a recalcitrant

child at bedtime. Gradually he became aware he was thinking again, picking at the problem of Marian, sorting through his worries about Womack and Jonis.

"Even in here, Reen-ja, you disturb the sleepers. I feel them stir."

"Should I leave?" he asked dully, hoping the Sleep Master wouldn't take him up on the offer. His tiredness was ponderous and inescapable, like a weight about his neck. More than anything he wanted to crawl into a niche, feel the stiff embrace of the close walls, and relinquish, for a few hours, the strain of individuality.

"No. Talk to me. If you talk to me, perhaps your mind will not shout."

Reen looked into the Sleep Master's pocked gray face. "What do you wish to discuss?" he asked, wondering if this would lead to another lecture.

"I have found that if you talk about your day, you steal the power from it."

Reen dropped his weary eyes to the old Cousin's black boot. "Jonis has been kidnapped, Europe threatens war with China, and President Womack is still on strike."

"Yes?"

The room was cloying with the spice of sleep, and Reen found himself nearly dozing where he sat. *And I love my daughter and her mother to my own detriment.* "That is all."

"Those are small things to disturb the sleepers so."

"Complications are made of small things."

"Better that you put these small things away to come here."

As though I could put my troubles in a pocket. But the Sleep Master, insulated from human minutiae, could not understand. Reen tried to relax again, his mind peeling away the day in tiny patches, as though it were the clinging skin of an orange. Suddenly his consciousness lay stripped in his palm, tender and naked to the veins.

"Go, Reen-ja. Go before you fall asleep on the floor."

Reen staggered as he stood. He shuffled his way through the chamber door and into the blue-lit niches beyond. Finding a vacant hole, he clambered in and lay down, unblinking eyes to the ceiling, arms rigid at his sides, as comfortable as a larva in its egg.

Angela slept like a human. Standing over her bed, Reen would often marvel at the way her lids shuttered her eyes. Her arms would curl to her side, her legs bend. She would press her head into the pillow and give herself to the dark.

The idea of darkness terrified Reen. It was darkness that bred human dreams. The closest Reen came to dreaming was when he felt the ghosts of long-dead consorts near him and heard their whispery voices.

Reen, the Old Ones said, and he knew he was sleeping.

Reen, you disappoint us.

They didn't speak with the anger he had been expecting but with a serene sort of dismay. Within arm's length of his niche stood three gigantic shadows.

The people are dying, Reen. Who will guard the eggs? Who will guard the sleepers?

Go away. Reen wished that he could sleep as Angela did. He would close his eyes on the ghosts. *We are all dying, and the egg cases are barren.*

The shadows at his shoulder began to dissipate into the gloom. *You are a father. You should understand,* the Old Ones hissed.

"Reen-ja?"

The Old Ones were back again for more of their fruitless lectures, only this time the ghosts were small.

"Reen-ja?"

A curt sound. A *ssst.* "Quiet, Thural," Tali said. "You will wake everyone."

Putting his hand to the close roof, Reen slid himself out of his niche. Thural and Tali were standing in the hazy blue aisle, the Sleep Master behind them, wringing his hands.

"Yes?" Reen whispered, wondering what time it was and whether their interruption of his sleep meant that Jonis and the rest of the kidnapped Cousins had been found.

"The police have discovered a body, Reen-ja," Thural said, keeping his voice down.

"The body of Bernard Martinez," Tali added importantly.

Around the three talkers, Cousins began to wake.

"The homeless man that Jonis often spoke with," Thural said. "He has been found strangled. I think it best you get up."

8

Outside the Cousin Place a rain fine as an aerosol was falling. Lights glistened on the tarmac. To the east a lethargic dawn was bleaching the sky. Tali, Reen, and Thural walked past a mothballed B-1 bomber to a four-seater Cousin craft. As they climbed into the ship, his Brother resumed what must have been an earlier lecture.

"It was embarrassing to the Keepers," Tali grumbled, appropriating the front passenger seat.

Thural plunked himself down gloomily at the controls, leaving Reen the back.

"Involving the police. Looking for a man only to find him recently dead," Tali went on.

The ship, not sensing other passengers, closed its transparent canopy. Thural grasped the control ball and pulled, drawing the craft upward a few feet, where it paused, wobbling.

"I had no way of knowing he had been murdered. And if the Keepers were more skilled at hiding the truth, the police would have never found out we were looking for him." With unCousinly petulance, Thural slammed the control ball right. The craft skipped northwestward like a flat stone across water.

Past the white egg shapes of the Anacostia Cousin Center the

Capitol dome rose through a thorny crown of trees. Beyond that, the Washington Monument stood gravestone sentinel over the Mall.

Tali swiveled toward Thural. "I think you know more than you are telling. That this man was found strangled means the President is involved in a conspiracy against us."

Alarmed by the direction of the conversation, Reen leaned forward, inserting his body between the two Cousins. "You jump to conclusions, Brother Conscience. That there is a conspiracy is obvious, but perhaps the President, not the Cousins, is the target."

"Gullible Reen." Tali's vitriol stung. "You trusted Eisenhower. You signed his silly Vandenberg treaty. And you see how he lied to us."

Reen sat back, perplexed. "Lied to us? Eisenhower might have delayed our landing, but even as he signed the treaty he vowed his people would never accept our leadership. And so it is. It was we with our arrogance who misjudged the situation. The humans are thrown into chaos, Brother, even fifty years after contact."

Tali sniffed. "It is not chaos. It is anger you see. The humans rage as Eisenhower did the first time he saw our ships. The man smiled and smiled, but still he raged."

Reen recalled Eisenhower's fixed, tense grin; how the President's hands, held stiffly at his sides, had clenched with impotent, white-knuckled fury.

The ship banked over the drab Potomac. Ahead of them, a Delta airliner, landing lights blazing, descended from the low clouds toward National.

"But we were the ones who broke the Vandenberg treaty," Thural said. "We allowed the humans to think we could wage war against them."

"It is not our fault they jumped to conclusions. And who broke the treaty first, Cousin, when Kennedy plotted to have Reen killed? In the skill of lying the humans will always have the edge." Tali's gaze fell on his Brother with the finality of a guillotine. "Find us a good man to take over the presidency, Reen-ja. Someone like J. Edgar Hoover. Someone we can trust."

Reen tried to avoid Tali's eyes but was only partially successful. The way the seating was arranged in the ship, it was impossible to turn his back.

"Where are we going?" Reen asked Thural.

"M Street," Thural muttered.

Reen glanced down. The quaint roads of Georgetown were constipated with rush-hour traffic. Ahead, where Wisconsin Avenue crossed M Street, strobes from a group of squad cars washed the morning sidewalk with festive red and blue. Thural inched the ship over the gold dome of the Riggs Bank and to an empty space near the curb.

"Both of you forget Communal Duty," Tali said as the ship settled at a slight angle.

The canopy peeled back. Reen lifted his face to the mist. His Brother's reedy whine and insolent clicks were beginning to tire him, and he was looking forward to the relative peace of talking with the policemen.

As soon as the door spread open, Thural hopped out, Reen at his heels. A frigid breeze from the nearby C&O Canal pressed the fungal scent of river water into Reen's face. Traffic was backing up behind the parked ship, and frustrated commuters were leaning on their horns. A gathering of people at a bus stop turned to eye the three Cousins darkly.

A human with skin the fine texture and rich brown of glove leather approached with circumspection.

"Morning." He scanned their chests. When his eyes fell on Reen's nametag, they widened. "White House Chief Reen. I didn't expect to see you here, sir."

Rain was condensing like liquid diamonds in the man's black curls. He flashed his badge. "Detective Rushing, D.C. police. Hear your people are interested in the victim." Rushing let the sentence dangle, as though hoping Reen might pick up the thread and weave something useful out of it.

An army of policemen were gathered around the door of the old Vigilant Firehouse.

"You've called out many policemen for the murder of an inconsequential homeless man," Reen remarked.

A few yards away a squad car's radio spat static as monotonously as a teakettle on the boil. The huge detective laughed. "Homeless man? Bernard Martinez wasn't a homeless man, sir. Or at least he was homeless by religious conviction. Karma seller. That's what Martinez was." Rushing took a plastic bag from his pocket; a roll of blue tickets was coiled at the bottom like a snake.

Reen took the bag.

"Five-and-dime-store tickets, like the kind you'd buy for a church carnival," the detective explained. "I recognized the victim, but the tickets were the clincher. We've picked up Martinez eight times for airport solicitation."

Rushing plucked the bag from Reen's hand.

Reen walked to the body, which lay under the plaque dedicated to the dead firehouse dog. The wet pulp of a *Wall Street Journal* was pulled down from Martinez's face. The eyes bulged like eggs. Stars of blood marred the whites. The cheeks were chicken-pocked with burst capillaries. The garrote was still embedded in the neck like a vindictive necklace.

"Saint Bernard," Rushing said.

Reen turned inquiringly.

"That's what they called the victim. Saint Bernard. Seems he had quite a reputation among the karma sellers." Rushing's lips stretched into a semblance of a smile; his eyes were quietly observant. "If I might ask the reason you were looking for him, sir?"

On M Street the volume of honking intensified. The detective raised his head and called, "Thomas!"

A uniformed policeman shouted back, "Lieutenant?"

"Get over there and direct traffic."

"Alien ship's in the way, sir. Maybe—"

"Just get the traffic moving! So—" Rushing dropped his voice and looked skeptically down at Reen—"we got a helluva mystery here, sir. A religious corpse with all the marks of a professional hit. You'd be doing us a favor if you could—" The detective glanced over Reen's shoulder.

Reen turned. A green Plymouth compact sedan was making its way slowly down the sidewalk, herding the sullen people at the bus stop to the edge of the curb. The car halted, and four men in dark suits climbed out.

"Shit." Rushing ran a hand through his cap of black hair. "I goddamn don't *believe*—"

"Kapavik, FBI," one of the approaching quartet said, flipping open his ID. "We'll take over the investigation from here, officer." He whirled to a shorter man behind him. "Call the lab to pick up the body."

A metallic crash.

The driver of a cherry red Jaguar, patience lost, had rammed the Cousin ship with his car. As Reen watched, the Jag backed into a Seville behind, then roared forward. Headlights broke with a wind-chime tinkle. The Cousin ship scraped a few feet along the sidewalk.

"Thomas!" Rushing shouted. "Handcuff that man!" Bending to Reen, the lieutenant said, "Maybe you should move your ship, sir."

"They can't hurt it."

A grimace passed over Rushing's face, as though from a twinge of indigestion. Quickly he turned to Kapavik, who was observing with professional interest how the driver was being dragged from his Jaguar.

"The Bureau doesn't have jurisdiction, Kapavik."

The FBI man's eyes were a pale wintry blue. "I believe we do."

Tali caught Reen's sleeve with a claw and pulled him away from the humans. "A karma seller, Reen-ja," he said with breathless alarm. "I begin to suspect terrible things. Was Jonis not aware karma selling is illegal? What could Jonis have been thinking, Cousin Brother? And what other illegalities could he have been involved in?"

More officers had run to Thomas's aid. The owner of the Jaguar was struggling; it was taking three men to subdue him. Reen's eyes met Thural's, and he saw remorse there. "Did you know this?"

Thural wrung his hands. "Cousin Reen-ja, I would never—"

"Did you *know*!"

Faced with the First Brother's wrath, Thural groaned. "Yes. Forgive me, but President Womack is anguished. Jonis felt pity for him and bought him things: karma and liquor and pizza. He arranged meetings with mediums. Cousin Reen-ja, believe me. Jonis was foolish but kindhearted. It was an innocent—"

A glint of grape purple at the edge of Reen's vision. The Vespa was speeding down the sidewalk. Reen sucked in a startled breath and took a quick step backward, stumbling over the bare concrete, over his own mortality.

He tried to shout for help. Only a croak emerged. So stupid. Why hadn't he mentioned the boy to Hopkins? To Marian? They could have stopped it. They could have . . .

At the corner of his vision Reen could see Rushing and the FBI men. They were too far away to stop what had become inevitable, too absorbed in their argument to notice what was happening.

The boy parked and hurried to the trio of Cousins, his stride purposeful, his gaze intent. He was reading nametags.

Less than ten feet away now—point-blank range. The boy took the backpack from his shoulder, unzipped it, shoved his hand inside. Across the black plastic, cheerful yellow letters: GEORGE WASHINGTON UNIVERSITY LAW SCHOOL. Reen's world compressed until the boy filled it, horizon to horizon. The youthful pink-cheeked innocence, the rain-soaked hair, the brown eyes swollen from lack of sleep.

Closer. Close enough so that a weary and unsteady hand wouldn't miss the shot. Close enough to shove the muzzle against Reen's chest as he pulled the trigger. This near doom, a human would have fled. Reen froze. His pulse slowed. His vision blurred.

Through the hum in his ears, a voice, softer and more musical than fate's voice had a right to be: "White House Chief Reen? This is from the Senate Appropriations Committee."

The Senate. Had Reen been wiser, had Womack taught him better, he might have sensed the direction from which danger would come.

"Sir?" The boy again. "Sir? You're required to take this. With all due respect, sir, it's not within your right to ignore a subpoena."

Reen's vision slowly cleared. The boy's hand was outstretched toward his chest. There was a piece of paper in it.

With trembling fingers Reen took the subpoena and stuffed it into his pocket. The boy nodded and trudged to his scooter. Numb, Reen watched him drive off into the rain.

"A subpoena?" Tali's voice dripped contempt. "First Jonis embarrasses the Community, and now you, First Brother. Do you see what your laxity has done? It is your function to lead, and lead with morality. Not—"

Rushing's voice rose in a shout. He was livid. "You are obstructing a homicide investigation."

Kapavik shook his head. "This isn't one of your holdups or drug shootings. This homicide is directly related to a kidnapping, and that makes it a federal matter."

Reen's attention wandered, his disoriented mind still trying to grasp that he was alive.

Then he saw the mob.

They had emerged from their cars to gather on the slick cobblestones. Some were holding folded umbrellas like clubs.

Temper lost, Rushing drove a forefinger into Kapavik's chest. "It doesn't matter if twenty aliens were kidnapped, the stiff is mine."

The crowd was ominously silent. Their eyes were on the three Cousins. The policemen, sensing the crowd's mood, left the irate motorist lying against his Jag's hood and retreated west, toward Potomac Street.

Reen thought it prudent to point out the glowering mob to Rushing. He was opening his mouth to speak when Kapavik snapped, "How the hell did you hear the kidnap victim was an alien?"

A man in the crowd cocked his arm and let fly with a coffee mug, his pitching style even more beautiful and fluid than Marian Cole's.

The mug whizzed through the air, a blur of white. It sped past Reen and, with a meaty thud, knocked Tali off his feet.

"Tali!" Reen cried. He dropped to his knees beside him. "Brother!"

Tali's cheek lay against the sidewalk, his eyes dull and sightless. Reen put his hand to his Brother's back, then jerked away as he touched sticky blood and the ravenous suck of Communal Mind.

Rushing inserted his bulk between the trio of Cousins and the mob.

"Alien down!" Kapavik screamed to his men. "There's an alien down!"

Somewhere from the circle of FBI and police a gun boomed.

"Cousin Reen-ja!" Thural cried in a piping, hysterical voice. "Is he dead?"

"No. Not yet." Frantically Reen tried to drag his Brother toward the ship with his claw. Tali's head lolled; his flaccid arms hung; the body rolled out of Reen's grasp and tumbled heavily to the pavement.

Over the screams of the crowd and the shouts of the policemen, Reen heard the stuttering rattle of a machine gun. One of the FBI agents was firing warning shots with his Uzi. Poofs of dust ran along the wall of the Riggs Bank.

"Help me, Thural! Please! Won't you help me carry him?" Hooking his claw under the seam at Tali's upper arm, Reen jerked the body to its knees. Thural mastered his stunned confusion enough to grab the Cousin Conscience by the belt. Staggering under the dead weight, they dragged him to the ship.

The door parted as they approached. Thural let go of Tali and threw himself into the pilot's seat. Reen eased Tali's slumped form into his lap.

It was as though he were falling into a pillowy well. Reen dimly felt the ship jerk sideways, heard a metallic clunk as it slammed the red Jaguar into the grille of the Cadillac behind. He struggled to think. If he didn't fight the Communal Mind, he would end up as useless as a Loving Helper. "Up! Go *up!*"

Thural pulled on the ball. The ship wrenched itself into the air.

And silently, helplessly, Reen dropped. He fell toward a colorless place where nothing was important: the Vespa, the riot, the coming war. Then Reen's weakening grip loosened even the cherished: Womack, Marian, Angela.

With a moan Reen sat up. The ship was hovering above the Victorian mass of Georgetown Park, quivering as much as Thural himself. "The Potomac," Reen said.

Thural slewed the craft over the elevated Whitehurst Freeway until it was seesawing above the river.

Again Reen tumbled down, down, this time into a darkness where Tali's secret thoughts lurked, an unexpected and unexplored den of monsters. Startled, he pushed away his Brother's frightening thoughts. "Andrews. Get us to Andrews," he mumbled.

"Yes, Cousin." Thural lifted the craft high enough to miss the bumper-to-bumper traffic on Theodore Roosevelt Bridge.

Tali's hand twitched. Thural glanced over in surprised relief. "I think he is coming out of it, Reen-ja."

Tali heaved himself upright in Reen's lap, drunkenly fumbling at the wound on his shoulder. Caught in the undertow of oblivion, Reen held his Brother tight so the childhood comfort of Cousin flesh against flesh would call him back.

"Cousin Conscience," Thural said. "Tali. Listen to me. You must stir yourself. The little death nibbles at you."

A few nonsense syllables dropped from Tali's mouth. Then he said in a muddy voice, "They hurt me."

"Yes. Do you remember now?"

Tali's eyes were suddenly clear, the gaze piercing. He twisted out of Reen's grip and the bonds of Communal Mind dropped away so suddenly that the onrush of freedom made Reen gasp.

"I remember. Get your hands off me, Cousin Brother. We are not children anymore."

He shoved past Reen with such force that he bumped Thural, sending the ship into a brief, alarming dive toward the Capitol. Tali did not notice. Breathing hard, he dropped into the rear seat. "They hurt me."

Reen remembered when they were children—when thoughts were innocent and life was less constrained. Centuries before, he and Tali had touched. Then, when they were grown, touching became taboo. As much as the Communal Mind repulsed Reen, he'd once mourned its loss, and Tali had mourned with him.

Now his Brother sat, arms rigidly at his sides, disgust in his face.

"Are you all right, Cousin?" Thural asked solicitously.

Tali curled his claw underneath the bar of his nameplate and savagely tore it off. The bit of plastic flew past Thural's head and pinged off the canopy. "They do not bother to learn our names."

Reen stared at the rectangle of black plastic lying on the control panel. The hook of the nameplate was bent at a furious angle.

Thural told him, "They don't see as we see, Cousin. We all look alike to them."

The ship swept over the congestion on Suitland Parkway.

"I will never wear the nameplate again. Not ever."

Reen turned to study his Brother. Tali was glaring down at the traffic below as though he wished he were an alien from an old science fiction movie and the scene they were playing with the humans was from "War of the Worlds." He stared down at the pedestrians and the cars like Godzilla, wanting to crush them all.

Reen's heart skipped a beat. "As you wish, Cousin Brother."

9

WHEN THEY ARRIVED AT ANDREWS, Tali, still wobbly from his brush with the little death, climbed down from the ship. On the tarmac he pulled his sleeve free from Thural's steadying claw and marched into the Cousin Place, leaving Thural and Reen standing alone.

Thural said, "It must be a small wound. Tali will be all right, Cousin First Brother."

But would he? Remembering the ugliness he had sensed in his Brother's mind, Reen wondered if the wound was deeper than Thural knew. "Yes, I am sure he will," he told him. "I would like you to take me to the White House now."

As they lifted off again, Reen noticed that some of Tali's blood had splattered on his tunic. He brushed at the stiffening stain, knocking off a few brown flakes.

In a low, diffident voice Thural said, "Cousin Tali is too full of anger, Reen-ja."

"It is wrong to criticize the Conscience," Reen said curtly, hoping Thural would change the subject.

"Yes. Still, the humans have done nothing to us, and Tali has too much anger."

They banked over the Tidal Basin and passed the Washington

Monument. Reen took his Brother's broken nameplate from the control panel and closed his fist over it.

Troops had been called out to the White House. The men by the tanks looked up as the craft passed over their heads. On landing, Reen jumped from the ship without exchanging another word with Thural. As he walked to the West Wing, he slipped Tali's broken nameplate into his pocket.

Hopkins was waiting for him in the colonnade. "Reen? That you?" The man bent over to read the tag on Reen's chest.

"It's me."

The director's beefy face sagged in relief. "Thank God. My guys phoned me to say an alien was down, but they weren't sure which of you it was."

"Tali." Reen strode past the director and down the hall toward the main building.

"Tali? Oh, Jesus Christ. Not Tali. Hey, where are you going?"

"To see the President."

"Oh, that won't do you any good." Hopkins panted as he kept up with Reen's quick pace. "I went up a minute ago to talk to him, and the man was *drooling*. He was drooling all down his shirt. Must be a bad day or something. Say, I'm sorry about Tali. My guys did all they could, considering that—"

"Tali is recovering."

Hopkins put one hand to his chest. "God. The stress, you wouldn't believe. I thought I had my right nut in the wringer."

Near the kitchen was new graffiti.

AT GROVER'S MILL.

BRING CHICKEN POX.

"*War of the Worlds*," Reen whispered.

"Huh?"

"I'm not fond of fiction, but I felt I should study all fictionalized aliens. Whoever wrote the graffiti has heard about the radio play *War of the Worlds*. That should give you a clue about who is doing this."

"Oh." Hopkins squinted at the message. "Grover's Mill. Now I get it. But everyone and his dog's heard about that. Won't do us much good."

From the other end of the carpeted hall Marian Cole called Reen's name.

"Bitch," Hopkins muttered.

She approached at a saunter. "And good afternoon to you, too, Billy. Reen, I know you're going up to visit the President, but I need to talk to you now."

Out of the corner of his mouth Hopkins told Reen, "Watch yourself with her. I don't know what she's got on you, but—"

"Now, please," Marian said, and led Reen down the wide red-carpeted hall to the Map Room. A fire had been banked in the hearth, and a plate of food had been set out.

"Go ahead," Marian told him. "I know you're hungry. If no one bothers to remind you, you forget to eat."

Touched, he sat down. She took a chair opposite and rested her chin in her hand. "Detective Rushing is one of ours. I want you to make sure he gets a good look at the body before the FBI takes over."

Reen cut into a stuffed tomato. "So that's how he knew a Cousin had been kidnapped. Certainly he may have the body, if you like."

"I like. How's Tali?"

He was moved, too, that she asked about his Brother, and pleased that Rushing had been perceptive enough to notice which Cousin had fallen. "Better, thank you."

"Shit," she said with guttural anger. "Rushing told me he was down. I hoped he was dead."

He lowered a forkful of chicken salad. The heavy silverware chimed against the porcelain. Reen looked into her eyes and was cast adrift in the turbulent ocean of their blue. "I have never wished harm on any human, as you have just wished on my Brother."

She took a breath. "Vilishnikov has taken the precaution of calling out the army. You probably saw the troops in front of the White House. We've picked up new satellite data. German tanks are massing on Russia's border with China."

He wanted to touch her. Was afraid to. "Sometimes I wish I had treated you like the others. You could have been any one of hundreds of women, never knowing, never remembering . . ."

"Reen!" Her cheeks were flushed; her tone sharp. "Germany is heading up a European invasion of China. What do you plan to do when the missiles start flying?"

With his claw Reen pushed a potato chip to the side of his plate. "I don't know. I don't know anything. Is it Howard? Is that what the problem is?"

Her laugh was short and ironic. "Howard?"

"Something has happened between us. Are you still in love with Howard?"

"Oh, Reen. Love dies. It's no big deal," she said softly. "It happens every day: People fall in love, they fall out of love. Relationships end."

He clutched her hand. It was warm, warm as the glow from the fire. He squeezed her so tightly, he could feel her pulse. "I don't understand endings."

The room was hushed, the air heavy with the scent of lemon oil and furniture polish. She fought to pull free of his grip. After a moment he opened his fingers and let her go.

"I used to hold your hand and you clung to me. Do you remember?" he asked. "During the experiments, we shared things, as Brother bonds to Brother. Cousins live centuries, Marian. And love is the only neverending thing we have."

He had searched for that Brother union in Marian. Too late, he understood the consequences of what he had done. He made Marian remember the pain so that she would grow to need the comfort of his touch.

"It was a long time ago." She sat back. "What's in your pocket?"

He had forgotten the subpoena. Now he took it out and handed it to her. She read it, chuckled, and gave it back. "Get a good lawyer."

"I've never been before a Senate subcommittee. What will they do?"

Suddenly her smile failed. He stiffened in alarm.

"Reen, you're in danger. So's the President. And Tali's behind it."

Reen made an irritated click-click with his tongue. "Only humans are so fickle."

"Tali's involved. And Jonis has to be found."

She must have noticed him flinch because she asked, "What's the story with Jonis?"

He picked at the gold rim of the plate with his claw. "I was afraid I would find the kidnapper was you."

Love, Reen thought. It was the only neverending thing he had. It didn't matter that Tali gave Reen his disapproval. He also gave him love. As Brothers that was something neither Reen nor Tali could help.

"I didn't take Jonis," she said. "But your Brother knows who did."

He got up quickly and walked to the door, stuffing the subpoena in his pocket.

"Reen? Your Brother knows who did."

As he left, his hand touched the edge of his Brother's nametag, and he fingered it thoughtfully.

10

BEFORE GOING TO SEE THE PRESIDENT, Reen went to the West Wing to order the FBI to hand over Martinez's body. On his way out, the House majority whip waylaid him.

"Do you realize how hard it was to get that bill passed?" Barbara Yates was not much taller than Reen. Eye level. Her anger was visceral and barbaric.

"The Eastern bloc outnumbers us two to one. The Chinese delegation is so big, most of them have to vote electronically. Do you realize how many arms I had to twist? We're in a recession. This bill could get the economy moving. When does the President plan to sign?"

"I'm sorry." He was sorry about Marian's bitterness, about the impending war. He was sorry for it all.

"I hear you were served the subpoena. Six days from now the hearing will be broadcast live on C-Span. It'll be picked up on the networks. Womack's too popular to target, but *you* . . . You're dead meat. That black budget of Womack's—you know how much he spent this year? Two million! What in hell is he doing that costs two million dollars? And what's important enough about his veto to make our boys go to war?"

"I don't know. I don't—"

"Well, you'd better just find out, hadn't you. And you'd better be ready to answer, or you'll be found in contempt of Congress. And tell Womack to stuff his executive branch power play up—"

Reen fled. Barbara Yates's shouts followed him out the door.

Hopkins had either given up waiting for Reen or had decided, uncharacteristically, to go back to work. Reen passed a Secret Service agent standing at wordless attention in the cross hall and took the elevator to the second floor.

In the presidential study a fire was lit against the chill of the misty day. Womack and a weak-chinned, bespectacled man in a T-shirt were seated at the Santa Fe table having coffee.

"Hi, Termite," Womack said. "Meet Lizard."

The man lifted an emaciated arm in greeting. Lizard had horn-rimmed glasses and the sort of skin that looks as though it can be used for polishing silver.

"Can we talk in private?" Two million dollars for mediums. The sum sounded exorbitant.

"You can talk in front of Lizard," Womack said.

Reen shook his head. "I would rather not."

Lizard tucked his thumbs into his belt and slumped with insolent indifference.

"What'd you want to talk about?" Womack asked. "Go ahead. Don't mind Lizard. He's dead."

Lizard nodded sagely, his glasses glinting in the light. "Laid my hog down in 1972 doing eighty-five on Highway 20. So I don't have no stake in no live people shit."

Confused, Reen took a seat close to Womack. "Bernard Martinez was found strangled."

"Oh, bummer," Lizard groaned. "Me and Bernie were tight." He shoved an entwined fore- and middle finger into Reen's face. "Like fucking brothers. I mean, even though Bernard was shitting corporeal and all."

"Why don't you call Bernard and see who killed him?" Womack suggested.

Lizard's eyes rolled back into his head. Reen sat selfconsciously, watching the bloodshot whites. Finally the medium's irises returned to their normal position and he gave Reen a lupine smile. "Bernie ain't talking, man. He's ascended, you know. An important fucker in the spirit world."

Reen glanced down at Lizard's torn jeans. Little of the two million, apparently, had been spent on clothes. A tab of blue protruded from a begrimed pocket. Lizard must have bought his karma tickets the same place Bernard had.

"How well did you know Jonis?" Reen asked the medium.

Lizard darted a glance at him, then looked away. "Man, *everybody* knew Jonis. Jonis got around." After a pause he said softly, "Some shit happening in the basement of the West Wing. Heavy shit. While Jeremy was sleeping it off by the pool, he heard something."

"Who's Jeremy?" Reen asked.

With a wave of a gnarled hand Womack motioned him silent. "Jeremy's the medium. Lizard's the spirit guide. Let him talk. Go on, Lizard."

Lizard's eyes were the still, muddy color of algae in a shallow pond. "He heard something he wished he hadn't, man. And then he drank and hoped he'd forget it. Hoped God would forgive him for getting shit-faced, and prayed nobody'd seen him there."

"What'd he overhear?" Womack asked.

"Heavy, heavy shit."

Weary of this, Reen turned to Womack. "Thural tells me Jonis arranged to buy karma for you, Jeff. Who else was he involved with other than the karma sellers?"

Instead of Womack, Lizard answered. "Wasn't no karma sellers who offed Jonis. And they didn't mean to ice him."

"Why do you think Jonis is dead?"

Lizard turned those hazel eyes on Reen. The pools were muddier and deeper than he at first imagined. If he fell into Lizard's eyes, those dank waters would close over him. "His ghost comes to me, man.

That's how I know. He says they was real surprised how easy you guys die."

A thrill of fear ran down Reen's back like a rivulet of rain.

"You want to talk to him?"

"No," Reen said sharply.

"Funny. Jonis wants to talk to you," Lizard said. "He keeps trying to get your attention. Wants to apologize, he says. Wants to warn you. But he says you only listen to those old farts. The big shadows."

Startled, Reen blundered up from his chair. He was sure he had never described the Old Ones to Womack.

Womack caught Reen's wrist. "Remember what I found in the West Wing, termite? The thing that had no business being there?"

Reen pulled out of Womack's grip.

Lizard said, "They killed Bernie but not before he found out what they was doing. And they kidnapped Jonis because Jonis knew it all."

Womack leaned over the table. "It's coming to a head. I can feel it. Teddy Roosevelt tells me so. Cut your losses, termite. Get people close to you that you can trust. Fire Cole and Hopkins before it's too late."

Reen jumped to his feet and ran for the elevator, Womack following in his fast old-man shamble. "Reen! Reen!"

Reen plunged into the safety of the car, but before the door could close, Womack slapped a hand on the jamb. "Get rid of them, termite."

Reen pounded the row of buttons frantically, by accident setting off the alarm. Womack stepped into the elevator, and the car started its descent. "You'll have the Secret Service crawling all over us."

Reen turned his back.

"I know you don't want to hear it," Womack said.

Reen concentrated on the whirls of the wood paneling, how they nested into one another, shape into shape, like waves seen from a height. He lost himself briefly in the comfort of its pattern.

The elevator stopped. The doors rumbled open. A worried voice: "Sir? Is everything all right?"

"Elevator goes up," Womack chirped in his official-idiot voice. "Elevator goes down."

"Yes, Mr. President."

The doors rumbled closed. The car lifted.

"Are you still talking to me?" Womack asked.

"No."

"You trust people too much, termite."

"You and my Brother should get together, since you both enjoy lecturing me."

The door opened. Reen walked out of the vestibule and headed to the stairs.

"Your Brother's in the middle of it," Womack said, grabbing his arm.

In the study Lizard was sitting calmly in his chair, drinking his coffee. Their gazes met. Lizard's eyes had the tranquil self-assuredness of a man twice his size.

The President marched Reen back to the elevator, pulled a key from his pocket, inserted it into a brass plate, and turned. The car stayed put; the doors stayed shut.

"Did you hear me?" Womack asked.

"Yes. But I don't believe you."

The President leaned back against the wall, crossing his arms. "I'm scared to death, termite."

Reen was frightened, too. Frightened by the voices the medium had heard in the night; by Womack's lunacy.

"Get rid of Cole and Hopkins. They're spiders. You can't walk around Washington without getting a faceful of web."

"But only you can fire them."

"Forge my signature like you usually do."

"If you're so worried about them, why don't you abandon your strike and fire them yourself?"

"You took my office."

"I will give it back."

"No thanks."

Ordinarily Reen liked tight places, but the small elevator car was beginning to suffocate him. Womack was close enough for Reen to feel the heat of his body.

"You fire Krupner yet?" the President asked.

"Do you think he's in on it, too?"

"Not Krupner. But you'd better fire him all the same. It'll give you some practice. Never fired anyone before, right? Okay. First, you go in and sit on his desk. He sits in his chair. That gives you the advantage of height. Then you say something like, 'You know we're all fond of you, Hans.' That way he won't be able to bitch about it being personal. You tell him, 'But lately you haven't been pulling your own weight.' You with me so far?"

"You haven't been pulling your own weight," Reen repeated dubiously.

"That's the way. Then you say, 'We need a good halfback, someone who can carry the ball. You just haven't been advancing the offense upfield.' Understand?"

"No."

"Doesn't matter. You tell him. He'll get the idea. Then you call the Germans and tell them you fired Krupner. Don't tell them before. Work from a position of strength, otherwise the bastards will think they can yank your dick every time you turn around."

"Are you sure it's wise to make the Germans angry right now? An army is mobilizing on the border of China, and the CIA says the Germans are behind it."

Womack clapped his palms together with glee. "That's perfect! If the Germans are planning to invade China, they won't dare give you any grief over Krupner." The President took the key from its plate and pocketed it. Before he left, he leaned toward Reen, his eyes abnormally wide, mouth pursed, forefinger to his lips. "Shhh. Don't tell anyone what we talked about. It's dangerous."

Reen wondered which was more dangerous, Womack's paranoia or discussing Womack's paranoia with a third party.

In the hall he paused, undecided. In the fifty years since the landing, Jeff Womack's guidance had been invaluable, consistently astute. But Reen was beginning to see it was now necessary to separate the President's kernels of reason from their demented chaff. Firing Krupner seemed logical when Womack had first suggested it. Now Reen wasn't so sure.

"May I help you, sir?" the man on duty asked.

Reen ignored him and walked to the West Wing.

Once in the first level of the basement, Reen looked for Krupner's office and found the nameplate, HANS KRUPNER, EDUCATION COUNSEL, at the end of a dark corridor next to the bathrooms. He opened the door. Krupner's tiny office was a riotous origami zoo.

"Dr. Krupner?" Reen called.

Past a barrier of varied animals on the desk, a voice answered: "Yes?"

As Reen approached, Krupner's balding pate came into view, followed by his round, questioning brown eyes. Reen searched for a place on the desk to sit, failed, and at last took a seat on a steel folding chair.

"Hans," he began, peering over a spread-winged eagle. "We're all very fond of you."

Brows rose over Krupner's bonbon eyes. "Yes?"

Reen, leaning forward to bring more of Krupner's face into view, nearly crushed a paper horse. "But I've noticed lately that you're not pulling weight."

Krupner's face became very still.

Reen blundered on. "We need a good half to carry a ball. You don't advance the field."

Blood had drained from Krupner's cheeks, leaving them the color of paper, as if the man had become an origami self-portrait. A line of perspiration salted his upper lip.

Reen wanted more than anything to flee from the tiny office and Krupner's agonizing stare. It hadn't been his intention to hurt the man's feelings. He had expected that Krupner would protest the firing, would perhaps indignantly resign. Instead the silence in the room was a soft but inescapable pressure, like a pillow forced against the face.

The corners of Krupner's mouth trembled. He was bent forward, straining; but Reen couldn't tell what exactly he was straining for. Could the man be in pain? Could he be—God forbid—voiding his bowels in the chair? Then the answer hit Reen. What he was seeing was intense confusion. "*Bitte?*" Krupner asked uncertainly. "I'm sorry. I don't—"

"You're fired."

Tears sprang to Krupner's eyes. His head dropped into the cage of his hands. "*Gott in Himmel. Gott sei dank,*" he said. "I'd thought—"

Reen backed quickly to the door. "Have your resignation on my desk in an hour."

Up and down went Krupner's head. Up and down. He stared around the room, as though already planning how to pack his animals.

"I'll call Germany for you."

"*Ja, ja,*" Krupner agreed in a lackluster voice.

Reen hurried upstairs to the Oval Office. The House majority whip, he noticed with relief, was gone. "Call Germany," he ordered as he passed the reception area where Natalie sat reading a novel.

Still clutching her book, finger marking the page, she stood and followed him. "Do you realize what time it is there?"

"Call the governor—what's his name?—at home."

"All right," she replied doubtfully. "Werner Hassenbein."

"What?"

"The governor's name is Werner Hassenbein. You should at least know his name if you're going to get him out of bed. You know, it'd be better if this could wait until morning. The Germans have been real agreeable. No sense pissing them—"

"Just place the call." Reen sat behind the uncluttered rosewood expanse of his own desk.

"Videophone hookup?"

"Yes, yes." He waved her out.

As she stalked from the room, he heard her mutter, "Your

funeral," and he wondered what she meant by that and if he should be afraid of her, too.

A few minutes later Natalie's voice came over the intercom: "Hassenbein's on hold."

Reen swung around to his credenza and tapped a command on the AT&T unit. REFUSED VIDEO SEND flashed across the screen.

"Governor Hassenbein?" Reen asked.

A mumble came over the receiver. "Yes?"

"I have just fired Hans Krupner."

"What?" The governor was awake now.

"I must ask you to arrange a replacement for him immediately."

"Oh." There was a long pause. "All right. Nothing scandalous, I hope."

Reen thought hard, wondering what the Germans would consider scandalous. Invading China? "He just wasn't . . . pulling his weight."

"*Ja, ja.* All right. Yes. These things happen."

The intercom buzzed. Natalie said, "Call on line two."

Reen ignored her. "When can you send a replacement?"

"Well . . ." Hassenbein said judiciously, as though he were counting the days on his fingers.

Natalie: "Emergency call, sir."

The governor said smugly, "We have, you know, a pool of good applicants to choose from."

"Yes, I'm sure. Let's set up a time. I can send one of my ships to get you. There is a great deal I wish to talk to you about. The tanks you have sent to Russia, for example—"

"What?" Hassenbein blurted. "What tanks?"

A burst of static from the intercom. "Quen on line two, sir. He says there's a medical emergency in West Virginia, and you're to pick up the line immediately."

"What ta—"

Reen punched the red square at the edge of his phone, neatly clipping the end of Hassenbein's question. Hand shaking, he pushed the pulsing light on two. "Quen?"

The Cousin Caretaker's voice was frantic. "Angela is sick, Reen-ja. Very sick. You must come to West Virginia at once."

"She—"

"*Now*, Reen!" Even over the phone lines, Reen could hear the hysteria in his Cousin's voice. "Come quickly."

Reen was out the door and halfway across the anteroom when Natalie called, "Governor Hassenbein's still on hold. What should I tell him?"

Cold terror rose in Reen's chest like water from a broken pipe. Distantly he wondered if the little death was coming for him as it had come for Tali.

"Sir?"

He turned blindly to Natalie, for a moment wondering where he was and what he had been about to do.

"Sir?" she asked in a hushed voice.

He remembered. Angela. Angela needed him. "Tell him anything," Reen gasped as he ran to the ship.

11

QUEN MET HIM AT THE DOOR TO THE children's house. "Oh, Reen-ja," he said, wringing his hands. "She is very sick."

Reen brushed him aside, ran past a clump of wide-eyed children entranced by a puppet show, and burst through the doorway to the female dormitory. Angela's bed was empty.

Some part of him had always known it would happen. The combination wouldn't work; the mixture of genes would be unstable. A few years of life, and some unseen mistake, some fatal error in planning, would kill her.

"Reen-ja," Quen said, his voice thick with pity.

Shut up! Reen's mind screamed. If Quen didn't speak, Angela would still be there. She would come running to him the way she always did. Reen stood frozen, one hand on the door, his disbelieving eyes on the barren bed, the vacant pillow, the way the late afternoon sun cast a river of brass across the empty floor.

Quen touched Reen's sleeve with a claw. "Reen-ja," he whispered sadly. "She . . ."

Reen's mouth widened until he felt it had opened a tunnel through his chest. He should have known never to fall in love with anything so fragile. "Shut up!"

In the living room the high silly voice of the puppet hushed. The children, startled by the shout, began to cry.

Warm human fingers grasped his shoulders. "Sir," Mrs. Gonzales said quietly. "She's in a room by herself. We're keeping her away from the other children."

Reen found himself being pulled around. He tripped over his numb feet. Behind Mrs. Gonzales's doughy bulk stood an assembly of curious, large-headed children and Quen, his black eyes wide.

"Are you all right?" Mrs. Gonzales asked, steadying Reen with a strong hand, a hand made for cooking gingerbread and wiping children's greedy faces.

Reen didn't have the strength to answer.

"It's just the flu, sir," she told him in her soothing voice. "Here. Let me take you to her. She's been asking for you."

Reen let her lead him down the hall and through a door. On a twin bed Angela lay inert and unmoving, her huge eyes closed.

"Her fever spiked," Mrs. Gonzales was saying. "We had a little convulsion and it alarmed Quen, but she's all right now. We gave her an alcohol rub, and her temperature's down."

Reen walked through the fog of Mrs. Gonzales's voice and looked down at his daughter. Her face was pinched. There was a hectic flush high on her cheeks: twin spots of clown color. Her mouth was open, her breathing labored.

"Seizures happen to small children with high fevers sometimes." Mrs. Gonzales's calm voice brushed at Reen's sticky anxiety. "It's frightening to watch, but nothing to get alarmed about."

Tentatively, Reen touched his daughter's arm. The skin was hot and dry, as though banked coals were baking her from the inside out. Quen was right: His daughter was very sick, and Mrs. Gonzales, as all humans eventually did, was lying to him.

Angela's eyes opened a slit.

"Your daddy's here, Angela," Mrs. Gonzales said. "See? Your daddy came to see you."

"Daddy." Angela grabbed Reen's hand. He lightly squeezed back, fearful of injuring her. Suddenly her face drew up into a mask of misery, and she was crying. "Hurts. It hurts, Daddy."

Reen whirled to Mrs. Gonzales. The caregiver was smiling and checking her watch. "She seems to do well on Tylenol. Let's give her another child's dose and some orange juice. Her throat's been bothering her." Mrs. Gonzales made her way from the room, shooing away the inevitable crowd of children.

Quen walked in. "She believes it is a minor human disease, Reen-ja, but I am not so certain."

Reen turned his back on Quen. If Mrs. Gonzales said it was a minor disease, that was the explanation Reen chose. He would hold that explanation and wring sugared comfort from it.

But Quen was a Cousin, and Cousins weren't given to lying. And he was a scientist; he should know. As Reen gazed at his daughter, sour anxiety came oozing back.

"Hurts," Angela said in a demanding pipe, as though she expected her father to send the pain away as easily as he might order a junior senator to leave the room.

"Mrs. Gonzales has gone to get you Tylenol," he told her helplessly.

Mrs. Gonzales came in with the Tylenol bottle and a glass of orange juice. "Here, sweetie." She put two tiny pink pills on Angela's tongue. "Raise her head," she told Reen.

Putting a hand behind the child, Reen gently lifted. Mrs. Gonzales slipped the end of a straw into the child's mouth. Angela took a sip but then wrenched her head away. Orange juice dribbled onto her pajamas. "Hurts."

"Children always get a little cross when they're sick," Mrs. Gonzales said with a forbearing smile. "Come on, sweetie. Just a little more."

"If it hurts her . . ." Reen said, unsure. Angela pressed her face protectively into his arm.

Mrs. Gonzales ignored him. "If you drink your orange juice, honey, you can have some ice cream."

Pouting, Angela turned to Mrs. Gonzales. When the caregiver put the straw back into her mouth, Angela drank almost half.

"Good girl. Quen? Why don't you go get Angela a scoop of ice cream. Chocolate. She likes chocolate."

With a glare, Quen left.

Mrs. Gonzales pulled Reen aside. "Quen may be the geneticist," she said firmly, "but I'm a pediatric RN. I know children. Angela's going to be just fine."

Reen wanted to believe her. But when Quen brought the ice cream, Reen noticed that Angela ate only a few spoonfuls before becoming weepy and demanding again. Mrs. Gonzales put a palm to the child's brow. Then she took Reen to a rocking chair in front of the window and set the blanket-wrapped Angela on his lap.

"Hold her," she said.

Reen cautiously slipped his arm under his daughter's head. Unlike Tali, nothing moved in Angela's mind, neither dark, hateful creatures nor ghosts of the Community.

"If her fever climbs," she said, "call me."

Angela filled Reen's arms with warmth. Outside, a gunmetal sky was sifting a fine snow that obscured the gray winter hills. "Snow," Angela whispered before lolling her head against her father's shoulder and drifting into an uneasy sleep.

Awkwardly, wishing he were more practiced at embraces, Reen rocked his daughter as the day blurred into night. On his lap Angela twisted and whimpered. In the main part of the house Reen could hear the sporadic laughter of children, could smell dinner on the stove.

It was dark when Quen made his way quietly into the room. "Reen-ja?" he whispered. "Will you be staying the night?"

Reen shifted his weight to ease a cramp in his leg. Angela stirred restlessly. "Yes."

Kneeling at Reen's side, Quen studied the little girl. "It is interesting that she called you Daddy when she hadn't before."

"Yes," Reen said faintly. "Interesting." He'd never demanded that she love him, never encouraged her to call him anything other than his name, but the fact that in her misery she had acknowledged him as her father brought a raw ache to his throat.

"There are niches," Quen went on. "Not so many Cousins as in Washington, but enough to sleep well."

A cold draft from around the windowpane caressed Reen's arms and face. "I will stay here in her room." He gently wiped the glaze of perspiration from his daughter's forehead. Her skin was like and yet so unlike his own: gray, but supple and moist as a human's. Her curled hand was a marvel of engineering. Miraculous, dusky eyelashes shadowed her cheeks.

"But Reen-ja . . ."

"One night won't hurt me."

In the darkening bedroom there was a quiet sound, the sound of Quen's sigh. "Should I stay with you?"

From his tone Reen could tell that Quen hoped his offer would be refused. "Go sleep."

"If you tire, Cousin . . ."

"I know," Reen said curtly.

After a moment Quen rose and padded away, leaving Reen holding his daughter. In the glow of the outside lights the snow drifted, settling on the gentle curve of the ship, on the branches of the trees. Several times Reen felt himself dropping off to sleep, but then some unexpected movement of the snow or of the wind-nudged trees would wake him.

Around midnight a cramp seized his right arm, and he carefully moved Angela's head to his left shoulder. At three in the morning, by the luminous numbers of the digital clock on the bedstand, the snow stopped. In the hush a raccoon, foraging for an early morning meal, trundled through the pool of light between the house and the ship, the wind ruffling its thick fur. Pausing just at the edge of the light, the raccoon turned its bandit eyes toward the window where Reen sat in silent vigil over his daughter.

Reen dozed and was roused by the low, mournful hoot of an owl.

As dawn broke vague and blue, he stretched his shoulders to ease the ache in his back.

At six-thirty Mrs. Gonzales came in the room and stood in the pink sunrise from the window, looking down at Reen and his child. Angela's smooth face was still. Reen couldn't remember when the feverish twitching of her body had ceased.

"Her fever's broken," Mrs. Gonzales whispered. "She's fine now." Reaching down, she lifted Angela from Reen's arms. The child muttered in her sleep.

"We'll put her in her own bed. Are you all right?"

"Yes," he said, but when he stood up, he nearly fell. He was weak. There was a hot ache from his neck to the middle of his back. His left leg was numb. Holding on to the wall for balance, he limped out to the common room where Quen and Thural were waiting.

"Reen-ja," Thural said anxiously. "You didn't come to the niches."

"I know." Reen tried to bring his Cousin's face into focus.

"Will you sleep now, Reen-ja? A few of us will go back with you to make a Community."

Reen lifted his hand in negation, then let it drop as he forgot what the gesture had been for.

"Reen-ja. You will become ill yourself," Quen said sharply.

Thural said, "He becomes stubborn, and there is no way to deal with him. Let me take him to the Cousin Place at Andrews. Once he smells sleep he will go into a niche soon enough."

Reen knew he should be irked by what was said, but the moment the words were uttered, he tried and failed to grasp them. They drifted from his clutch like leaves in a stream.

"Come, Reen-ja." Thural grabbed Reen's sleeve with his claw. Obligingly, like a large, dimwitted dog, Reen let himself be led out of the children's house to the ship.

12

As Reen walked into the Cousin Place, the odor of sleep hit him, and he started to sag. Thural grabbed his tunic and tried his best to hold him upright without coming in contact with his body.

"Reen," the Sleep Master said.

Bleary-eyed, Reen turned the old Cousin's way, wondering what was wrong.

"Repeat the first covenant."

Thural nudged Reen against the wall with his boot and hooked a claw in his sleeve to prevent him from sliding to the floor.

For convention's sake Reen kept the irritation out of his voice, but it annoyed him that the Sleep Master would choose such a time to review catechism. "Work," he replied.

"And work's brother is?"

"Sleep," Reen said dully.

"Humans often ignore both, Reen-ja. Cousins cannot afford to. There is too little time left us for work, and too great a price to pay for forgoing sleep. See that you remember that."

When the Sleep Master turned again to gaze at the wall, point apparently made, Thural guided Reen into the chamber.

Reen straightened his body against the hard confines of a vacant niche. The interlocking plates in his back relaxed. Now that it was permitted, he pulled the edge of the Communal Mind up to his neck like a secure blanket, and in a few moments he was asleep.

Thural woke him. "Reen-ja?"

Reen inched himself onto his side and saw his aide, a specter in the hazy blue of the aisle.

"Have you rested enough, Cousin?"

Reen wasn't sure. No time had seemed to pass from the instant he had lain down to the instant he had awakened. "What is it?"

"Hans Krupner is missing."

Reen was fully awake now. He slid out of the niche and was suddenly aware that Thural wasn't alone. Tali was standing by the door. "Kidnapped also? When?"

"I think not kidnapped. But I should tell you all of it, Cousin," Thural said. "While you were asleep the Germans called. I was training Sidam to replace Jonis as your second aide, so I took the call and spoke to Werner Hassenbein. He says they received a fax from Hans Krupner, a fax of an interoffice departmental study of baby food production at Gerber. He asked me where all the strained peas are disappearing," Thural said, twisting his upper body miserably, "and I did not know how to answer."

Reen looked at Tali, but his Cousin Brother was giving no hints. "Strained peas?"

"Missing food, Cousin, between the raw ingredients bought and what appears on the shelves. I told the Germans to delay their flight, but they are on the Lufthansa supersonic to Washington. Hassenbein says he will call you over the Atlantic. I fear they may have caught on at last, and I believe Hans Krupner may be hiding from us."

"Call Michigan and tell—"

"Yes, Cousin," Thural said breathlessly. "Already done. He is on his way."

Grumbling, Reen padded through the doorway of the baths to wash the gummy residue of sleep from his skin. While he was changing, the Sleep Master came in.

"Your mind becomes glass while you sleep, Reen-ja," the Sleep Master said. "I look through the glass and see the torment there. So do the other Cousins, and it robs them of their rest."

Reen lifted his arms into the sleeves of his uniform and caught a whiff of the tannic acid the bathwater had left on his body. "What should I do, then, Cousin, when work is the first covenant and torment is part of my job?"

"It is not work that causes your torment, Reen," the old Cousin told him, "but the love you feel for strangers."

"Humans," Reen corrected him. "We can't call them strangers anymore."

"They do not share the Mind when they sleep, Reen. Therefore they will forever be strangers."

It was quiet in the baths except for the splash some awakening Cousin made in the pools beyond the doorway. Reen dropped his dirty uniform near the bench for the Loving Helpers to pick up. As it hit the floor, something rustled. The subpoena. He bent, grabbed the paper, and shoved it into his pocket. Then he sat on a bench and pulled on his boots, hoping the Sleep Master would go away.

"I have spoken with Tali of the matter," the Cousin said.

Reen muttered, "As though he would understand love," and jerked his right boot on angrily.

The Sleep Master apparently decided to ignore Reen's rudeness. In a tolerant voice he said, "The sleep grows weak, Cousin First Brother. The female should be bred. Eggs would soothe her and help the Community sleep better. Tali agrees."

Reen stood and stomped his left foot into his boot. "There are too few of us left, Cousin. I will not choose one to die simply because the female should be happy."

"Tali suspects the breakdown in DNA can be reversed and that we should try breeding again."

The smell of tannic acid and moisture lay heavy in the room. Reen turned his back on the old Cousin and rummaged around in his locker until he found an extra nametag. "The DNA inviability cannot be reversed. If it could be, the humans might then undo what we have done. We use the breakdown as a weapon, Cousin, and both we and the humans now die of the same malady. No race has lived as long as we. All species run to extinction. That we have run more slowly is a lucky thing that should be celebrated and not mourned."

"You give all our worlds and goods to these mongrel children, Reen-ja."

Angry now, Reen snapped his head around. "They are our children! The only children we will ever have."

"They are not Cousins. We should try breeding again."

Reen made a derisive click-click with his tongue. "The geneticists all agree that if we breed now, we will only breed more Loving Helpers. We might find ourselves in the unenviable position of having to destroy the larvae."

Behind Reen came a sharp gasp. When he turned, the disgust in the old Cousin's eyes hit him like a blow.

"Tali is right. You *are* a monster."

"I am a monster for loving; and Tali is not a monster for his hatred. Perhaps you could explain the ethics of that." Hands shaking, Reen fumbled at the nametag, pricking himself with the pin. In frustration he threw the tag to the floor. "Tell me. When Tali comes to the Community, do you see the ugliness behind his glass mind, Cousin Master of Sleep? Because Tali carries much ugliness in him."

The Sleep Master stared back impassively. Controlling himself, Reen knelt and picked up the nametag.

"Tali puts his untoward thoughts away for the night, as a good Cousin should," the Sleep Master said. "You might learn that from him. But perhaps you are too mired in strangers' lives to learn anything."

Reen rose to his feet, studying his finger. A bead of dark brown blood welled from the wound. "If you are displeased with me, take your displeasure to the Community."

"I have."

For a moment Reen fought to breathe.

"The Community is tearing itself apart very quietly, Reen-ja. I will not permit it. Perhaps one day you will wish to enter the chambers, and I will turn you away—you and Thural and the others who care too much for strangers. Then you can make your own Community where you can sleep and share non-Cousin things."

Who had the Sleep Master spoken with? Reen wondered as he pinned the nametag unsteadily to his chest. And who had agreed with him? "Tell me if you decide this," he said with careful, artificial calm. "But let me know ahead of time so arrangements can be made."

He dared not look at the Sleep Master as he hurried from the room. Instead he looked at his own chest. His nametag was crooked.

13

WHAT HE HAD LEARNED IN THE BATHS
so disturbed Reen that he hoped his Brother wouldn't accompany
him to the White House; but accompany him Tali did. He sat with
Reen in the lounge. Instead of preaching more Communal law, he
kept silent; and Reen was too angry to ask him what he had told the
Sleep Master. Normally silence between Cousins was comfortable.
This was torment.

When they sailed over the tanks gathered at the fence and landed
at the side of the West Wing, the trio of Cousins followed Reen to
the Oval Office. As soon as they entered, Natalie started reading
nametags. "Oh. The whole group, huh? Hi, Thural. Welcome back,
Sidam. The job training couldn't scare you off yesterday? Listen,
Reen. Governor Hassenbein's been calling every five minutes. What's
going on?"

Reen opened his mouth to answer, but Tali snapped, "Go back
to your work immediately. There is nothing here you need to concern
yourself with."

Natalie's face shut down. Her eyes scanned Tali's nameless chest
as though wondering who he was and if he had the power to address
her so curtly.

"It's about the firing yesterday," Reen said, hoping to defuse a showdown.

Luckily the buzz of the phone drew her attention. "Chief of staff's office," she said, picking up the receiver. There was a pause. "Just a minute, Governor. I'll check." With one red fingernail she hit the HOLD button. "It's Hassenbein. You in?" she asked Reen.

Tali, who had not yet learned the wisdom of silence, said nastily, "Of course he is in. Are you blind or merely stupid? Do you not see him standing in front of you?"

Thural and Sidam exchanged winces.

"Look, mister whatever the hell your name is," she told Tali, tapping a fingertip against the desk for emphasis. "Unless you sign my paychecks—"

"Thank you, Natalie. Tell him I'm here," Reen said hurriedly. "I'll take it inside."

At his desk Reen engaged his speakerphone. Natalie put the call through. He could hear the rumble and whine of the supersonic's engines. "Governor?"

Hassenbein shouted over the plane's noise: "Reen? I received a most interesting fax last night."

"Ye—"

"And it causes me to wonder, *ja?* So many tons of peas to Gerber Foods in Michigan, so few bottles of strained peas on the shelves. Production of bottled peas, of *bottled* peas, you understand, has dropped from one and a half million per day to merely seven hundred thousand over the last three fiscal years, yet the production of product, that is to say, the strained peas themselves, has remained the same. I was hoping you could clear up this discrepancy."

Reen waited a long time to answer. As he waited he cast a worried glance at his Brother who, head cocked, was listening intently to the conversation.

"What do you suppose this means?" Reen finally asked.

At the other end he could hear chimes and a garbled announcement from the plane's loudspeakers. The Lufthansa flight was descending, and the passengers were being called to their seats. "It must mean something, yes? For Dr. Krupner to fax me the information."

"We were having a few problems with Krupner. Emotional problems."

"Ah, of course. But still it is an interesting development. Where do these strained peas go? We land in an hour. Perhaps you can find out by the time you pick me up at the airport. I would prefer to be picked up in the White House Mercedes. Your ships sometimes cause me to be . . . indisposed."

Reen looked at Tali. His Cousin Brother was standing rigidly, as Cousin custom dictated, his expression carefully blank. "This Gerber question, Governor Hassenbein. Are you using it to lure my attention away from your plans to invade China?"

A cough. "As much as the deregulation has hurt our manufacturing base, we have no plans to invade China."

"But—"

"Who told you that? The CIA? I have it on good report that your CIA cannot be trusted. And after this Gerber development, I must now be suspicious of you as well."

"I don't understand why developments at Gerber would trouble anyone but an employee of Gerber. Do you see it otherwise?"

He said, "I think maybe I do."

With a click the line went dead. Reen leaned back in his chair and sighed.

"You see what I am talking about, Cousin Reen-ja?" Thural said. "They apparently have discovered something. I fear they have found the component, and if so—"

Reen's intercom beeped. "The CEO of Gerber Foods is here, sir," Natalie said with a huff. "I tried to explain to him that without an appointment—"

"Send him in."

Before Reen could reach the door, Oomal was already entering, one hand burdened by an attaché case, the other outstretched in welcome.

Instantly Reen recoiled. "Oops," Oomal murmured and slipped the offending hand behind his back. "Good to see you, First Brother."

Reen shut the door. "I think the Germans have caught on to what is happening," he said, not bothering to keep accusation from his voice. "They talk about discrepancies with production, but—"

"Oh, that. *That's* no surprise. It's like trying to hide an elephant in the middle of a party, you know? The humans were bound to catch on sooner or later."

At this bombshell the other Cousins froze.

Oomal looked around the room. "Why don't we all sit down? I've been running around the home factory all morning."

Tali turned to the two aides. "You will not be needed in this discussion, so it is best that you go to the ship."

Thural was astonished. Sidam, though, simply turned and left the room. After a hesitation Thural followed him.

"So, Brother," Oomal said to Tali when the two aides had left. "How are you doing? And where's your nametag?"

"You wished to sit," Tali said. "So we will sit."

"Fine with me." Oomal threw a questioning glance at Reen.

Reen sat down in his swivel chair; Oomal slumped into the Louis XV antique and regarded the standing Tali.

"You know, if you hate keeping up with that nametag, Tali, you ought to have this done." Oomal ran a finger lovingly across the gold-embroidered *Oomal* above his left chest. "A little place up in Chicago sews these for me. Here." He pulled a wallet out of his pocket. Under a corporate Visa Oomal found what he was looking for: a blue-embossed card. "They ship UPS."

Tali reluctantly took the card and scowled at Oomal's diamond pinkie ring. "Reen-ja is right to accuse you, Third Brother." He took a chair a few feet to Reen's left and regarded both Brothers with poorly concealed contempt. "He believes you have been left too long to your own devices and that you have failed our trust. He is sure this has put the entire Community in danger."

Reen winced. He hadn't meant to accuse Oomal at all. Polite

inquiry would have been enough. But the Brother Conscience was giving him no way out. Tali wanted to see Oomal's blood on the floor, and he expected Reen to inflict the wound. Reen linked his hands and sat back, trying to decide what to do.

Oomal tapped his claw against the chair's cherrywood frame. Tick-tick went the claw. Tick-tick. "Failed? What makes you think that?"

Oomal was sprawled, legs apart. Tali's back was straight, several inches away from the human comfort of the cushion. Reen studied their different postures for a moment, until he became aware of his own. He was leaning back in his leather chair, rocking slightly. He stopped rocking and sat up.

"We now have a ninety-eight and a half percent birthless rate among women under the age of twenty-four," Oomal went on. "And human science and technology are pretty much at a standstill. You must have seen the reports."

"The Firstborn agrees with me on all Community matters, and he wishes me to warn you: This new generation of humans may be incapable of reproduction and may be partly under our control, but they understand what is happening to them," Tali said. "That is the danger."

A tense silence was broken only by the tick-tick of Oomal's claw. Reen studied the body language, the tiny annoyed gestures, the candid disdain on Oomal's face. Confronted by the censure of both First and Second, a Third Brother should have been humbled. Oomal wasn't. Reen was surprised how human Oomal had become during his years in Michigan. And confused to find that he admired him for it.

Tick-tick. "They don't understand, Brother Conscience. They don't understand anything. They see their engineering is fifty years stale, and they see the drop in the birthrate, sure. Only we make certain they can't think about it very long. We stopped the statisticians' reports at an eighteen percent decline. As far as any humans know, that's bottom line, okay? Listen. Humans under the age of twenty-four used to breed like rabbits, so I have to juggle catastrophic drop-offs in the use of hospital maternity wards and soothe pediatricians and ob-gyn people. It's hard. And nobody's screamed yet. So, Cousin Brother, don't give me this 'they understand' crap. The truth is, you can only hide an elephant so long at a party. You can see that, can't you, Reen-ja?" Oomal turned to his First Brother for help.

"What was Hans Krupner doing at Gerber?" Reen asked mildly.

"A report on preschool nutrition. He came up to Michigan and went over our home office facilities for about a month."

"And you let him?" Tali asked.

"Why not? We're proud of our quality control. Besides, it's not as if we have problems at Gerber with corporate espionage. It would have looked suspicious if we refused."

Reen asked, "What is all this talk about the strained peas?"

"We buy more raw material than we need, and the excess production is sent via orbital mass driver into the sun. At Gerber," Oomal said solemnly, "we're environmentally correct."

Oomal, noticing Tali's disapproval, went on: "Look. You have to see the big picture." He leaned back and described an arc in the air with his hands, as though painting a rainbow. The diamond on his finger flashed. "We have a responsibility to the consumer, and we have to be careful the ingredient won't show up in FDA tests. Compassion Comes First, remember? Remember that ad campaign?—Those warm, fuzzy commercials showing us donating product because Cousins hated to see little babies starve? God! Was that high concept or what?" Oomal saw Reen cringe, and his delight floundered into embarrassment. "Well. So. We're not completely insensitive. The birthrate might have plummeted, but the infant mortality rate did, too."

"About the peas," Reen prompted.

"I'm getting to that, First Brother." Oomal set what looked like an attaché case on the desk and popped the snaps. It was not a briefcase, Reen saw, but a laptop computer.

Oomal was pleased by Reen's interest. "Nice, isn't it? My employees gave it to me for Christmas last year, along with a Roach Motel as a gag gift. They're a lot of fun, my employees." The Toshiba laptop beeped as it automatically booted its program.

"I fail to see the humor in a Roach Motel," Tali said.

Oomal gave him a long, steady look. "Well, Cousin Brother Conscience, I guess you would." Hitting a key, he brought up a bar graph. Reen's interest wandered to Oomal's Piaget: the soothing pattern of diamonds around the bezel, the distressing clutter of the nugget band.

"Production," Oomal said, turning the screen so Reen could see it and pointing to the tallest bar. "Profits." He pointed to the smallest. "We're going to need more price supports, Reen-ja."

"You should simply close the factory," Tali said.

"What?" Oomal turned to Reen in horror. "Reen-ja! You're not thinking of closing Gerber!"

Tali said, "The Brother Firstborn sees the problem as clearly as I do. It is illogical to continue throwing money into a dying company."

Oomal made an exasperated hand motion. "Look. Neither of you knows anything about economics, but let me see if I can put it in terms you can understand. First of all, Gerber's not a dying company. In the third quarter of the fiscal year, when the bottom literally dropped out of baby foods, we diversified into frozen tartlets aimed at the adult consumer. The peach and apple were hits, although I'll admit the strained pea frozen tartlets and the strained carrot surprise didn't move well. But we're doing a brisk business with our strained veal and chicken pâté, which comes prepackaged with a cracker assortment."

Reen saw, next to Oomal's keyboard and *Forbes* magazine, a half-finished Snickers bar. The tough cartilage that served the Cousins for teeth was adequate to chew most foods, but Reen found himself wondering what Oomal did with the peanuts.

"Second, Cousin Brother Reen," Oomal said, "Gerber has a Japanese-style management. The employees think of the company as their home. We do not, as a corporate rule, lay off. I have a hundred thousand employees, sixty-eight plants. If I close them, I put family farmers all over the world out of business." He pulled his wallet out again and shoved pictures across the desk: Oomal in a hard hat smiling amid grinning humans with hard hats; Oomal shaking hands with a pudgy, balding man. "That's Harry Bell, salesman of the year. Harry's a great guy, a real company man. Old Harry could sell diets in a famine. He has three kids and a mortgage. Look at that face, just look at it. How could you put that man out of a job?"

Reen studied the photo: the human hand grasping Oomal's own; the broad grins on both faces. His Third Brother seemed to have overcome the Cousin aversion to touching. Handing the picture back, he asked, "But what can be done?"

"It's simple, Cousin First Brother. We all know the free market economy will eventually go belly-up, and I've done a feasibility study in which I outline the problem we'll have when the zero birthrate hits home. I believe I've found the answer." Oomal gave Reen an unCousinly smirk.

Reen leaned his elbows on his desk. "And what is that, Brother Economist?"

"Bring back communism," Oomal said. "The object of capitalism is to capture market share, anyway. The Cousins will simply become the ultimate multinational corporation."

"And the goods?"

Oomal shrugged. He returned his wallet to his pocket. "We sell what we can and discard the rest. The worst part of the waste will peak inside another fifty years. At that point we can retire the few workers left, give them lake cabins and motorboats, and allow them to enjoy the remainder of their lives."

"Yes. That sounds perfect." Reen had always pictured himself as the benevolent caretaker of the last of humanity.

"I see no point in wasting resources," Tali said. "I suggest we begin the process of euthanasia."

Oomal clapped his palm to his brow. "God, Tali! How can you say that?"

"Before we landed, the First Brother gave us a promise—did you not, Reen-ja?—that if the situation began to get out of hand, the viruses would be used. The situation is now deteriorating."

"Oh, come on," Oomal said. "Reen was pandering to our xenophobia. Those viruses were never intended—"

Tali leaped to his feet. "Do not listen to him, Firstborn! See how he has become human himself! And this has gone too far! Your first responsibility is to the Community, Reen-ja. Must I remind you of that?"

Reen was startled by his Second Brother's vehemence. Oomal simply groaned, "Tali, Tali. Haven't you seen enough murder?"

Tali was apoplectic. "Murder! Third Brother, how do you accuse me of murder?"

"Our ancestors," Oomal said, "wiped every sentient race but the humans off the face of the galaxy."

Tali said heatedly, "The Community expanded, yes. It is in the nature of the Community to expand. Do you have a problem with that, Cousin Brother Economist?"

Reen studied his hands, imagining blood on them. He, like Oomal, had always disliked Cousin history. Reen's people were cowards, but in the depths of their fear cowards could be deadlier than heroes.

"Of course I do. Don't you?" In a quieter, more reproachful voice Oomal asked Reen, "Cousin Brother Firstborn, don't you?"

Reen had no answer. Perhaps his ancestors had been right. Contact was a perilous thing—Reen had never before realized how perilous. Other cultures were so alluring. Tali's humanity was more subtle than Oomal's, but it was there nonetheless. At M Street, Reen had felt a very human darkness in Tali's touch. He could now sense hidden agendas in his demands.

Had he made a mistake by landing? Reen was young when he first met Eisenhower, barely out of the Communal attraction of adolescence, that time when he and Tali and Oomal and the rest of his Brothers slept side by side, locked in shared thought. When he was a child, Reen had only to lift his hand for the others to lift theirs, too.

That was when the fraternal bond had been made. Now Third Brother argued with Conscience. Conscience forced decisions on First.

Oomal said, "Our ancestors murdered without cause. Those other species didn't even get a chance to protest. Bang, and they were gone. Just like that." He snapped his forefinger and claw together. Reen knew Oomal had practiced diligently to get that gesture right. "What our ancestors chose to do is done, but we have a chance to make amends. We'll eradicate the humans, fine. Since they're a warlike species, I can see the reasoning in that. But if we want to have our children's respect when we die, let's please get it right this time. Because our children are half human," he said quietly, "and they will judge us."

Slowly, reluctantly, Tali took his seat. Into the abrupt and unsettling quiet Reen wondered aloud, "In the meantime what do I tell the Germans?"

Oomal snapped his eelskin case closed. "Put something else on the plate." He noticed Reen's confusion and explained: "Find something else to talk about. Accuse them of something. When in doubt, attack."

Reen nodded slowly. "They *are* planning to invade China."

"That's wonderful! Hit them with the invasion of China! And if the production discrepancy comes up, blame it on me. Tell them you have a Cousin up there running Gerber who doesn't know his ass from straight up. Tell them Cousins aren't used to money. Tell them you think Gerber will be run into the ground inside of three years and that corporate raiders are circling over the bones. Next week sometime I'll get the governor into one of our ships and explain to him just how uninteresting strained peas really are."

Oomal started for the door but paused in the center of the presidential seal to give Reen an encouraging look. "Don't worry. I'll take care of everything, Cousin Brother Firstborn. Hassenbein will forget about the strained peas."

Then with a wry smile and a shake of his head he told Tali, "And, hey. Call the toll-free number on that card, Second Brother. Tell them I sent you. And lighten up, okay?"

14

When Oomal left, Tali turned to Reen. "Behold the danger of consorting too much with humans, Reen-ja. You see how the Cousin Brother Economist has given in to slothful habits of speech and thought. He has copied the body language to make the humans accept him more easily. They probably trust him, yes, but only because they no longer see him as Cousin."

Reen ignored him.

"It will ruin our race," Tali said with a Cousinly gesture of his hand which, after Oomal's expansiveness, seemed awkward and self-conscious.

Reen said firmly, "What is there left to ruin, Cousin Brother? Aren't we the last of our kind? It seems to me that Oomal finds enjoyment in acting human, and I for one am glad for him. We must all find our solace where we may." He hit the intercom button. "Natalie. Have the Mercedes brought around. I'll be going to Dulles to pick up the Germans." Then he asked Tali, "Will you come with me, Brother Conscience?"

Tali's curt, negative reply was the best news Reen had had all day. "No. Thural will take me to Anacostia in a few minutes, Reen-ja. Go ahead."

But there was something in the way Tali lowered his eyes that caused Reen to wish he could stay and see what business Tali had at the White House while he was gone. "I will walk you to the ship," Reen offered.

"Oh, I am in no hurry, First Brother," Tali said in a pitiful attempt to sound casual. "Do not fret about me."

"As you wish." With a final backward look, Reen proceeded to the anteroom where Natalie was standing, a mink-collared pink coat over her shoulders.

"Let's go, sir. The Mercedes is in the driveway."

Had she actually said, "Let's go?" Reen looked at the briefcase in her hand. It was a tattered brown thing, an old government issue that even the seal of the President of the United States couldn't make respectable.

"*You* can't go!" Then he softened his tone. "Hassenbein and I are going to be speaking about sensitive issues."

"I'm not letting you out of my sight. You have a whole stack of documents to review and sign, and you were gone all morning. If you insist, I'll take a taxi back from Dulles after you pick up the Germans."

"All right."

Natalie prattled all the way down the hall and through the exit. "I mean, it'd be an inconvenience to get a taxi, but if that's what you want. . . . Don't forget, though, I have the highest security clearance. Probably higher than the governor himself. Who types your memos, anyway?"

The limo was poised like a slick black cat in the afternoon light. Reen walked past the juniper border and climbed in without answering. When Natalie was seated, too, the chauffeur shut the door, sealing them into a leather-scented silence.

As the limo purred around the circle and down the drive, Reen looked out the window at the lawn made an eerie chartreuse by the bulletproof glass. Beyond the army troops at the gate the limo picked up its police escort.

The speaker at Reen's shoulder gave a spit of static. "The sirens bother you, sir?" the chauffeur asked. "You want the radio on?"

"No, thank you."

The click of the snaps on Natalie's briefcase brought his head around. "Here," she said, putting a two-inch stack of papers in his lap.

He switched on the reading lamp and began at the top of the first page.

Pursuant to the agreement made April fifth was as far as he got before the rushing of the scene outside and the slower movement of his eye over the page began to make his stomach churn. He returned the page to the stack and pulled down the blind at his window.

Natalie reached over him and raised the blind. "I'm claustrophobic."

"Oh." After an uneasy glance at some gawking tourists near the ramp at the Roosevelt Bridge, Reen wondered what time it was and checked his watch. He always wore the Rolex that Oomal had given him, but he wore it more for memory than as a timepiece. It wasn't a digital, so he had difficulty deciding whether the little hand was closer to the two or the three. The three. Three forty-five.

On Route 66 the limo speeded up. Reen slumped back into the leather seat and thought about his visit to Michigan, how the few Cousins there had fit into the company party Oomal threw like round pegs nestled happily in square holes.

It had been a nice party, Reen remembered, much more festive than what he was accustomed to in Washington. The humans wore blue jeans and, after a great deal of beer and barbecue, laughed very loud. And when Oomal handed Reen the pretty package and explained to the humans in such a simple way that Reen was his big Brother whom he loved very much, one of the women cried. "That's so sweet," she said. "Isn't that sweet?"

Sweet, he thought, staring at the Rolex and wishing he had made a note of the time Hassenbein had called.

As the limo leaned into a long right turn, Reen saw that they were exiting onto the Dulles Access Road. He would probably be early.

Natalie asked, "You going to sign those or what?"

"I can't read them in the car."

She snatched the top inch of papers. "Pursuant to the agreement of April fifth," she began.

With a stomach-lurching jolt the limo braked and veered. Reen heard the crunch of gravel as it slowed to a stop.

Natalie punched the speaker button. "What's going on?"

With a hum the tinted glass between driver and passenger compartments began to lower. Reen saw the usual sparse traffic on the Dulles Access whipping by and noticed that the motorcycle escort had parked their bikes on the shoulder.

The policemen were walking toward the car, their guns drawn.

The chauffeur was facing Reen, his elbows planted on top of the opposite seat. "Get down on the floor," he said.

Reen's attention snagged on the chauffeur and the silver revolver in his hand. He couldn't believe it. The man was pointing a gun at him.

"You, too," the chauffeur said, waving the black well of the barrel in Natalie's face.

Reen decided it would be wise to comply with the chauffeur's wishes. The man's expression was inflexible. But Reen couldn't get his body moving. The policemen were very close now, and they looked remarkably like real policemen.

"Get *down*!" the chauffeur bellowed. Reen jumped.

Something shoved Reen in the back and toppled him to the carpet. "The man said down, sir," Natalie said sharply. "Didn't you hear him?" To the chauffeur she said, "Listen. You're kidnapping us, okay? But I'm dying for a cigarette. You got a light?"

Reen was on the floorboard where Natalie had pushed him, and her shoes were in his face. New shoes, he thought stupidly, wondering if she had bought them with the White House credit card. They were navy high heels with small gold bows. Natalie was rummaging in her purse. It was a big beige purse and it didn't match the shoes. That wasn't at all like Natalie.

"On the *floor*!" the chauffeur shouted.

Three popping sounds, one right after the other. Natalie bounded to the opposite seat and wriggled through the partition. The limo jerked forward, the sudden acceleration pushing Reen's shoulder into the upholstery behind.

Clunk, clunk, clunk went the limo as it slammed into metal. The motorcycles, probably, judging from the way the big car bounced.

He heard a hum and sat up. The partition's opaque glass had been raised. The Mercedes was rushing up the Dulles Access, weaving in and out of traffic.

"Natalie!" Reen cried, punching the intercom button.

No one replied. He hit the lever to lower the partition's glass. Nothing happened.

Reen lay down on the floorboard again. The Mercedes was so heavy that, without looking at the gray screen of winter trees rushing by the window, he might have thought they were gliding along at a sedate twenty.

The car slewed. Brakes screamed. Reen was flung toward the door. There were four jarring bumps as the big car mounted the curb, and four more as it dropped to street level again.

Reen sat up and saw they were headed in the opposite direction from the airport. The Mercedes skidded across three lanes, cutting off a green pickup. Ahead was the red-striped toll barrier and a small gesticulating figure in a booth. With a muted bang and a shudder, the Mercedes plowed through the barrier, knocking it several feet into the air and over the car. Reen looked out the rear window and saw it lazily falling, a candy cane from heaven, before a thicket of leafless hickories hid it from view.

They whipped through a residential section of Tyson's Corner and took Chain Bridge Road toward Wolf Trap, weaving in and out of traffic, running red lights. Somewhere near Vienna they turned west onto a winding lane with woods on one side and pastures on the other. Then they were deep in Virginia horse country.

Reen punched the intercom button. "Natalie?"

The limo was flying down the secondary road, going much

too fast for him to jump to safety, even had his paralyzing fright allowed.

"Natalie? Are you there? Please. Are we going back to the White House now?"

The ammoniac smell of urine and the copper-penny smell of human blood spread through the heating ducts like a contagion.

"Natalie?"

Reen sat back, linked his hands in his lap, and, to keep the little death from taking him, began frantically thinking of pleasant things: Oomal and the party. Oomal handing him the present. Reen not knowing quite what to do with it because no Cousin had ever given him a gift. He remembered his Brother saying gently, "Open it, Reenja." How the humans and Cousins had gathered around, the woman crying, "How sweet." And Oomal, because he could not embrace him, had hooked his claw into Reen's sleeve and asked, "Do you like it?"

Reen looked long and hard at the Rolex. *My big brother whom I love.*

The Mercedes squealed to a halt. The door opened. A man in a white hard hat reached in and grabbed Reen's arm. The workman was huge, his hands enormous. Reen found himself being dragged from the Mercedes, and he hit his side painfully on the green phone receiver the man wore at his belt. The workman slammed the Mercedes door and gave the side a sharp slap.

The limo sped away. In horror, Reen watched it disappear around the next curve.

Feeling the man's grip momentarily relax, Reen tore himself free and ran across the road toward the woods. He was thigh-deep into a patch of thorny blackberry bushes when the man flailed in after and grabbed him again. Reen struggled. The man fought to hold on. The subpoena dropped from his pocket.

"Come on, sir," the man said as he grasped Reen about the waist and pulled him to a white and green Chesapeake Bell panel truck.

The man threw Reen facedown onto the truck's carpet. The rear doors banged shut, and a moment later they were speeding down the road, the opposite way the limo had gone.

Huge hands grabbed Reen and pulled him up onto a cushion. "How many fingers?" the phone company man asked, holding three stiff fingers before Reen's face.

Reen looked away. If he had to die like Jonis and the rest, then he would do the best his small courage allowed and at least keep silent.

The man sat back, sighed, and unfastened a walkie-talkie from his belt. "Domino's delivers," he said into it. Then he crawled away and sat with two other phone company men who were checking their Uzis.

Yes, Reen decided, the best thing to do now, the easiest thing, was die quickly before they caused him pain.

The three linemen were too alike to tell apart, all broad-shouldered with slim waists. Their hard hats hid their hair. One of them crawled forward and held four fingers up to Reen.

"How many fingers, sir?"

Reen turned his head away. Right now they were elementary questions; later the questions would get more difficult. *Why are you here? What are your plans for us?* And then would come the agony. To protect the humans, Reen had hidden his suspicions from the Community. In fact, his suspicions were so terrible, he himself had dismissed them. The kidnapped Cousins had not died gently in those three allotted days. Reen knew they had died tortured.

"You hear me," the man said. "I know you can hear me." The man went back to the others. "I think he's okay."

No, Reen thought, seeing his death as clearly and as close as the carpeted wall before him. *I am not okay.* When they had held him long enough, they would see his life seep from him, and they would wonder. With perverse satisfaction he wished he could see the astonishment on their faces.

The truck braked. Reen heard the slam of the driver's door. He glanced warily at the three men in the back, but they were intent on their guns. The door slammed again. The vehicle inched forward and stopped.

Reen's heart faltered. If only he had been able to overcome his own squeamishness and bring some Loving Helpers along. The Helpers, condemned to a life sentence in Communal Mind, were an uncomfortable reminder of the ancient Cousin past, the declining Cousin future; but a touch from them could send human consciousness to a place where free will did not exist. Reen loathed the panic he had seen on human faces when they found themselves sinking into that dark well of compliance. At this moment, however, he would have given anything to see his kidnappers wearing that same powerless look.

Someone flung open the rear doors. They were in a barn. Late afternoon sunlight streamed through weathered slats. Reen took a breath and smelled the dry, prickly scent of hay, the earthy aroma of long-vanished horses.

A man dragged Reen out and unceremoniously dumped him on a pile of straw.

Reen sat quietly, watching the bars of sun slant through the gaps in the wood. He listened to the ticking sounds of the van's engine, the quiet murmur of the kidnappers' voices. Then a man threw a blanket over Reen's legs and set a chilled can of Coca-Cola beside him.

After a brief hesitation Reen picked up the can and popped the top.

"Don't give him that," another man said, knocking the can out of Reen's hands, spilling cold, sticky Coke over the front of his uniform. "I thought I told you not to bring any carbonated drinks."

So they knew something about Cousins, Reen thought in disappointment as he watched the remainder of the Coca-Cola Classic being taken out of his reach.

The man came back with a bottle of orange juice, which Reen ignored.

"He wanted the Coke," the first man said.

Reen watched as the second man poured the contents of the can into the hay. "Carbonation kills them. He was trying to commit suicide. If you have any more carbonated drinks, get rid of them now." Then he called over his shoulder, "A helluva painful way to go, sir."

Oh, but nothing was painful to a Cousin for very long. In that, Reen had the advantage over a human. He had seen humans die.

He looked at the kidnappers, wondering if they would end up screaming in hospital beds or bubbling their lives away in car crashes. Better to be a Cousin, he thought, and die without much pain. Better to be fragile and long-lived. The Sleep Master was a four-century Cousin; Reen himself had seen two centuries pass.

When Reen died, the Earth Community would never be the same. The Cousins were scattered in sparse knots across the galaxy, with not enough firstborns to send, as Reen himself was sent when Thural's First Brother had died. No, the Community on Earth would not recover from the shock, and secondborn Tali would hold a precarious and uneasy dominion.

He waited for the men to begin the torture, but instead they sat down, took fried chicken from a cooler, and started to eat.

"You hungry, sir?" one of them called.

Reen turned his head away to stare at the back of the old barn and the shafts of dying sunlight. It was the last he would see of Earth, he figured, and the sight was a good one—not as good as the Rockies would have been, or Angela's face, but under the circumstances the dust motes dancing like gold flakes in the sun were enough.

There were things left undone. For one, he wished he could keep Tali from Community rule. But the humans and Cousins would have to fend for themselves now. Reen had lived long enough to see his child born, ensuring some sort of continuation of his species. There was no sense at this late date in accepting any more pain than he had to; no point in struggling, as a human would, to persevere. After all the intrigue at the White House, his life had suddenly become very simple. Sighing, almost content, he sat back against the straw and watched the evening taper into night.

15

OUTSIDE THE BARN, THE SUN SET IN shades of pink and violet. The dust motes gave one last glimmer before they turned to ash. The kidnappers lit a Coleman lantern, and by its acidic glow three played a card game while the fourth sat watch over Reen. At either six forty-five or seven forty-five by Oomal's Rolex, Reen heard the sound of a car. Blinding white light blared through the boards at the front of the barn like the loud opening chord of a symphony.

One of the men threw the barn door open, and a BMW drove inside. Reen sat straighter.

The interrogator had arrived.

Shielding his eyes from the headlights, Reen watched as the car door opened and a figure emerged. Self-assured footsteps swished on the straw as they approached; the weighty sway of a full-length mink coat; the smooth curve of legs in nylon hose.

"Hi, Reen," Marian Cole said.

Heartbroken, he turned away, putting her in that blank spot in his vision, the place where he wished he could now send her forever.

The straw rustled as she sat. "Not going to talk to me?"

He would have talked to her without this, and she knew it. But perhaps she wanted the witnesses Reen had never allowed her to have.

There would be no torture, Reen realized with a sinking sick sensation. Marian wouldn't need it. She would simply ask him the questions over and over until love pried his lips ajar and he began to speak.

"Well, at least look at me, okay? It's hard talking to your back."

He couldn't.

"Please," she said softly.

Without wanting to, he whirled. "Why did you do this to me, Marian?"

The men by the Coleman lantern had turned to stare.

"Shhh, shhh." Marian trailed cool fingertips across his mouth. "Don't."

With a furious jerk Reen turned his back on her again. "Is this what you meant by endings?"

She fumbled for his hand. He tried to snatch it away, but she held him tight. "Shhh. Don't be afraid. Isn't that what you used to say to me when I was the one who was helpless? God, Reen. Do I have to be a Cousin before you can trust me? Natalie was one of ours. Since I've been director, all your secretaries have been agents. And their only job is protection. I knew your Brother and Hopkins were going to make their move, and once Jonis was kidnapped, I knew they'd do it soon." She tugged at his hand. "Come on. I want to talk to you in private."

She pulled him, his reluctant feet stumbling, toward her car. Once in the backseat, she closed the door, fumbled in her purse, and took out a pack of cigarettes.

"I gave these up three years ago; did you know that?" She fished a Carlton out of its box with her fingernails and lit it. The warm glow from the lighter washed her face free of the small wrinkles around her eyes, making her seem, for an instant, magically young. Flicking the lighter closed, she took a drag. The enchantment ended. Age and worry claimed her face again.

"Natalie called just after she handed you off. That was the last we heard from her before she headed to the safe house. They must have gotten to her a little after that. We found the Mercedes. There was blood on the front seat. We don't know yet if all of it came from the chauffeur."

Chagrined, Reen mumbled, "I'm sorry about not trusting you. And no, you don't have to be a Cousin for that. I trusted you before, but lately . . ."

"Just listen." She tapped the cigarette against the ashtray, dislodging a small column of ash. "Two hours ago a bomb exploded at Gate Six at Dulles. The Germans were killed instantly. Whoever arranged that meeting set you and Hassenbein up for murder."

"Krupner told them," Reen said. "He sent a fax—"

"Forget Krupner," she said with such confidence that it gave Reen pause. "He works for the Germans. We've known that for a long time. Poor Hans wasn't much of a spy. No, this was bigger than Krupner. The usual White House chauffeur was called by someone posing as the head of the serving staff and told not to come in today. Right now we're looking for the police escort, but the cops who were assigned to you have vanished." She took a deep breath. "There's something else I need to tell you."

There were two deep furrows on either side of her mouth. Her lowered eyes were lusterless. Was it about Angela? His heart skipped a beat. No, that was impossible. None of the West Virginia Cousins would have told her anything about Angela. "What?"

She took another drag before replying. "This afternoon, just about the time the bomb went off at Dulles, the White House commuter fell into the Watergate Complex and exploded." Leaning forward, she tapped the ash into the ashtray. "Nobody on the ship survived." After a pause she asked, "Who was on board?"

"Thural," he whispered. Cousin Thural, almost close enough to be Brother.

"I'm sorry."

"And Tali," he remembered. Odd how he had thought of the Cousin first and the Brother after.

"I ordered this made for you. Here."

She pressed a hard rectangular piece of plastic into his hand. A nametag. He opened his fist and read the letters: TALI.

"No one knows who was on the ship so we're going to a party. In separate cars, of course. I'm leaving in a few minutes to pick up Howard. Tali wasn't invited, but if he shows up, the hostess won't make a fuss. It's very *in* to have a Cousin as a guest."

His Cousin Brother was dead, and Reen was being asked to impersonate him. He wasn't sure he could.

Marian reached over and unpinned his nametag. "Keep your ears open for anything anyone tells you. Act like Tali if you can. Pretend you have a rod up your ass. Don't talk much, and when you do, don't, for God's sake, be your usual charming self."

Taking Tali's nametag from his open palm, she replaced his with his dead Brother's.

He looked up at her. She was staring at him strangely, as though trying to memorize his face, as though picking out the tiny differences between his features and the cookie-cutter features of the others.

Warm human hands on his neck pulled him close. A kiss on his cheek.

"I got lipstick on you. Here." She scrubbed her thumb over the spot her lips had touched.

Stunned, he lifted his hand to his face.

Her laugh was smooth cream with a bite of lemon sorrow in it. "Just like a kid, you know that? Sometimes you're just like a little kid."

Grabbing his hand, she took an unsteady breath, then reached across him and opened the door. He would have fallen out if she hadn't still had hold of him. "A car's here for you, and a chauffeur. Don't speak to me at the party. Tali and I hated each other."

He stumbled away, and she slammed the door. Her chauffeur jumped up, got behind the wheel, and backed the BMW out of the garage.

Reen watched the car pull onto the farm-to-market road. He stood there long after she was gone.

16

THE PARTY WAS HELD IN ONE OF THE larger houses on Georgetown's Q Street. When Reen rang the bell, a butler answered and was obviously nonplussed to see a Cousin standing on the stoop.

His eyebrows rose. "Whom may I announce?"

"Tali," Reen replied, feeling a pinprick of guilt for having momentarily snatched his Brother from an untidy grave.

The eyebrows rose another, seemingly impossible notch.

"Tali, sir? And will that be all?" he asked with the air of a man accustomed to royalty.

"Second Brother and Conscience to White House Chief of Staff Reen."

The brows lowered. "Very good, sir. Please come this way." With a bow he ushered Reen into the marble foyer. There was another hesitation as the butler scrutinized Reen's small body to see if he was hiding a coat.

From a wide, arched doorway to the right came the sounds of a Brahms sonata nearly drowned out by the strained gaiety of party conversation. Disconcerted by Reen's lack of an evening wrap, the butler paused at the entrance, Reen just to his back.

"Tali," the man announced. "Second Brother and . . ." He cleared his throat and continued gamely, but as though suspecting he had it wrong, "Conscience to White House Chief of Staff Reen."

The babble stopped. The pianist missed the next bar of music. In the back of the huge room, his bulk competing with the Steinway grand beside him, William Hopkins stood with Speaker Platt. The FBI director's mouth was agape; a canapé was crushed in his startled fingers.

Reen trudged down the steps, wading into the pool of stunned guests.

"How nice to see you," a woman corseted in a beaded dress exclaimed as she unfroze from her confusion and sailed across the carpet to greet him.

The hostess, Reen assumed, wishing Marian had thought to give him her name.

"And what a *surprise!*"

Had Reen been there as himself, he would have inquired whether the surprise was pleasant or unpleasant, and had he any suspicion of the latter, he would have stayed only long enough to make his exit less obvious as an escape. But he was Tali now, and Tali never used social graces when rudeness would do just as well.

The woman approaching was tall and broad. Reen received a too-complete view of her décolletage.

"Yes," he said sharply and swiveled away.

And found himself eye-to-eye with Hopkins, who had circled from the piano to make a flank attack. The usual smile was absent from the FBI director's face. He was staring fixedly at the nametag on Reen's chest.

"Mr. Hopkins," Reen said. "Is there something you want?"

Hopkins gave him a flat smile. "No. Nothing," he replied before gravitating back to the small Speaker of the House.

Reen stared hard at the director's broad shoulders, his mind turning that smile over and over, as his hands might have toyed with an interesting objet d'art. Cousin ships had too many fail-safes for the crash of the commuter to be an accident. Sabotage, then. And if

Hopkins had been behind it, he would know the Cousin at the party wasn't Tali.

A passing waiter pushed an ornate silver platter into Reen's face. Reen admired the orderly rows of canapés for a moment, then selected a shrimp on toast, the only food he recognized.

"What about that Gerber?" a voice asked from behind Reen.

Reen nearly dropped the shrimp. The questioner was a pudgy man, his black formal dinner jacket spread wide to either side of his ample belly, as though he were offering his gut up for sacrifice.

"Who are you?" Reen asked.

"Ralph Bitterman, CEO of Heinz," the fat man said. "I remember when you guys undercut us and Beechnut out of the baby food business."

"And?"

"Running it into the ground, I hear." The man, Reen saw with dismay, was quite drunk. Bitterman pulled a stray guest into the conversation. "Say," he said, gloating into the captured woman's face, "did you hear Gerber's going broke? The White House is supposed to hold a news conference about it tomorrow."

A waiter lowered a tray of drinks into Reen's view. Without thinking, Reen took one.

"Now why do you suppose the only baby food manufacturer still in existence is going broke?" the fat man from Heinz asked the woman.

Reen glanced at the stemmed glass and noticed it held champagne. He toyed with the idea of drinking it down and ending all his troubles quickly. No one had told him about a press conference.

"What about it, uh . . ." Bitterman leaned over drunkenly to read the nametag. "Tali? Eighteen percent decline in the birthrate. Cousins buying up and ruining baby food manufacturers. Hey. There has to be a story there somewhere."

Reen remembered Oomal's metaphor about the elephant at the party. He looked numbly around the room to see if there was anyplace to hide.

"You going to answer me, or what?" Bitterman asked, switching from boisterous to pugnacious without any transition. He reached out and grabbed the front of Reen's uniform. "Are you going to answer me?"

At the head of the stairs the butler cleared his throat. "Marian Cole-Franklin, director of the CIA," he announced, "and husband, Dr. Howard Franklin, professor of biology, Georgetown University."

As the hostess moved across the carpet to greet her new guests, she slid between Bitterman and Reen, adroitly plucking the CEO's fist from Reen's uniform. "How *nice*, Marian! And don't you look *lovely!*"

Foiled, Bitterman slunk away and was soon engulfed by the party. Marian stood with her husband at the top of the stairs. Howard's handsome face was slack, his nervous laugh too shrill, his eyes glazed. He had been drinking again.

And Marian. Marian. The butler had taken her mink. Her dress was a filmy white thing that reminded Reen of lilies. The color in her cheeks was high, her mouth curled in welcome. She kissed the hostess's cheek with vacuous duty as her gaze swept the crowd, resting on Reen for a moment in pique before it moved on.

Then Marian's blue eyes widened on something pleasant a few yards to the right of Reen. Her arm rose in greeting. A bright smile spread her lips. "Director Billy. Get me a drink, will you?"

Reen watched her leave her husband and stride across to the fireplace, to the now-solitary Hopkins, who was either playing a part like Reen or was genuinely delighted to see her.

"Bourbon straight up?" he heard Hopkins murmur intimately as he ran a possessive hand down her bare back.

Resentfully Reen watched them disappear into the adjoining room. Vilishnikov appeared from the same open doorway, clutching a mixed drink with a cherry in it. Reen, relieved to catch sight of someone he knew, almost waved but stopped himself in time.

Vilishnikov set out toward him anyway. A few feet away he halted in surprise. "Oh, Tali," he said. "I am thinking you were your

Brother." The head of the Joint Chiefs was wearing his dress uniform, and the weight of his medals seemed to make him list to one side.

"I was wishing to speak to Reen about Krupner."

Reen was so startled that he almost took a sip of his champagne. When the drink waiter passed, he rid himself of the glass and picked up a tomato juice with a celery stick buried in its heart. "What about Krupner?"

"I am not, as you may be aware, happy at the Pentagon," Vilishnikov said. "Such a bad commute. Perhaps now that he has disappeared, I may have his office?"

"Ask Reen."

Vilishnikov, rebuffed by the sharp answer, lifted his chin and began searching the room for possible deliverance. Apparently he saw someone familiar because his smile widened. Intent as a heat-seeking missile, he made for the French doors.

At the Steinway the pianist thundered into a loud piece which Reen, whose musical knowledge began with Bach and ended with Beethoven, didn't recognize. He admired the skill of the pianist, however, and there was something disturbingly familiar about the man's face.

Reen caught a snippet of conversation next to him. "So nice to hear a composer play his own work," a woman in pink said, touching the hostess's arm.

"Yes," the hostess murmured. "Rachmaninoff has always been one of my favorites. He does Pavarotti with lesser success, you know. Something about the vocalization."

They wandered away toward the room with the bar.

Glancing around, Reen saw that Marian was back with her elegant gray-haired husband. The lids over his large brown eyes were at half-staff. ". . . that lard-assed Hopkins's hands on you," he growled. Suddenly he reached out to grab Marian's arm. She pulled away, hissing something Reen couldn't hear. She had a fixed half-smile on her face and her blue eyes were hot with embarrassment.

Howard's voice, thick with self-deprecation, rose over the crowd:

"No, I don't think I've had enough. I never get enough. Poor Howard doesn't get anything anymore." He turned to a man beside him and brayed a laugh that turned heads. "She's in love with a dickless gray alien."

People froze. Marian's tense smile disappeared, and for a moment she stood as Reen himself stood, alone and defenseless in the turmoil of the party.

Abruptly the embarrassed gathering shifted. One man in the crowd turned to another. "So," he said, "what's new over at Justice?"

Reen ducked and weaved his way through to the open bar. As he passed the piano, the pianist finished the piece, stood, and shot his sleeves. Their eyes met.

"Hi." Rachmaninoff suddenly wasn't as self-assured. The man seemed to have shrunk inside his formal attire. "I'm Jeremy Holt." He offered his hand.

Reen regarded the hand dubiously. "Holt? I thought you were Russian."

The refused hand jerked back to the safety of the suit and dallied around a pocket for a moment before deciding on a few simple twitches at the man's side. "Oh, no," the pianist said with an edgy squeak of a laugh. "I'm the President's new medium."

Reen took a step back to study the horn-rimmed glasses, the chamois-soft skin.

"I sleep in the Lincoln bedroom. He drops in on me every once in a while to see how I'm doing."

"President Womack?" Reen asked.

"President Lincoln. I sort of met your Brother, but I was someone else at the time. I wanted to tell him that I'm available for funerals and weddings and bar mitzvahs."

Reen looked at the business card Holt thrust into his hand and wondered how he could steer the conversation to the karma sellers without making the man suspicious.

Holt laughed again, his chortle going over the heads of the guests like a wayward fly ball. "You want a composer? A rock star? A dead president? I can be anybody you want. It's because I have a go-between like Lizard. Lizard's great. When he asks spirits to come through, they don't refuse."

"The karma sellers . . ." Reen began.

But abruptly the hostess was there, taking Holt's arm and propelling him away. Her voice trailed behind her like strong flowery perfume. "Marvelous, darling. For the rest of the evening, how about Van Cliburn?"

Abandoned, Reen meandered past the open bar and found a door that led into the refreshing chill of the backyard. Following a curved path through ornamental shrubbery, he came to a gazebo. There he sat and nursed his tomato juice. Earth's moon, pale and wan, topped the roofs of the nearby houses.

So far the party had been useless, except for Hopkins's odd smile and the news of the press conference. That information, Reen thought glumly, might have waited until the morning. A few hours from now he would have to return to the Cousin Place, and the Sleep Master was sure to sense the anxiety in him.

"Tali," a voice whispered from the bushes.

Reen stood and looked around but saw nothing.

"Listen and don't talk," the voice said.

The bushes stirred in the night wind. The noise from the party was as faint as memory. Dead moonlight iced the flagstones, frosted the redwood railing and the evergreens.

The whisper was cold. "We fucked up getting your Brother today, but we'll try again."

There was a rustle of branches. A shadow separated itself from a tree trunk and, hidden by the night, left the garden.

The voice wasn't Marian's or Bill Hopkins's. It didn't belong to anyone Reen knew. He longed to run after the speaker, to ask how Tali could have betrayed him. He didn't dare. Not now. Not when everything, in its own way, had been settled.

From the house came the bell-like tones of a Beethoven sonata. A broken fragment of cloud scurried over the moon. Reen put his hand over the nameplate and felt the sharp edges of the letters. Tali. Dead Cousin Brother. Tali, who had wanted Community rule so badly, he had been willing to do the human-thing and kill to get it.

Reen sat down, upsetting his drink. Tomato juice spread like thick human blood over the gazebo's planked floor. He would leave the party now and go to the Cousin Place where Thural and Tali were not and never would be again.

He rose unsteadily. As he exited the gazebo, he heard a man weeping. The sounds were labored, as though the man were trying to bring to the surface a grief that had long ago congealed.

A dark form sat on a bench, its face in its hands. Reen passed without being seen. The man on the bench was Howard.

17

THE CHAUFFEUR DROVE REEN NORTH, away from the White House, taking winding residential streets to Rock Creek Park. Back and forth they threaded past thickets of trees and bicycle trails until Reen thought to check his watch, saw it was nearly midnight, and began to wonder whether he was being kidnapped again.

Fifteen minutes later the chauffeur pulled the Buick over to a wooded copse and stopped by a parked BMW. Marian, a phantom in the moonlight, got out of her car and climbed into the backseat with Reen. Wordlessly the chauffeur left the car and stood by the fender.

Marian's dress made a slithering sound against the leather seat as she moved toward him. She smelled of perfume and cigarette smoke. "Have fun at the party?" she asked.

"No. And you?"

"It was all right."

Reen gazed out the window into the moon-dappled shadows under the trees. Far across the park, streetlights gleamed in shades of topaz and aquamarine. "You were talking to William Hopkins, I noticed, and you seemed friendly."

"Jealous?"

Marian was a pale blur next to him: the glimmer of her dress, the glint of her blond hair. Was she smiling? "No. But it causes me to wonder."

"Billy and I keep friendly pretenses up. It's expected at parties."

Friendly pretenses. Was it only that? Reen asked himself again if it was sex she wanted. For him, Marian's company was enough. Still, the idea of her and Hopkins together was painful in an apprehensive way, like the beginnings of an inflammation beneath the skin.

"Did you find out anything?" she asked.

Reen was looking at the trees again. Under the streetlight a few stubborn leaves gleamed on dead branches like silver coins. "No."

He had learned nothing that would help Marian. His Conscience, the betrayer, was dead. During the drive through the park Reen had made peace with his Brother. Tali had plotted against Reen not for power but for sad, misguided duty to the Community. Reen could forgive him that.

"Too bad." Leaning over she unpinned Tali's nameplate from his chest and replaced it with his own. She was a warm shape in the dark, as nebulous and emotionally charged a presence as the Old Ones.

"I love you," he said.

Her form wavered. "What brought that on?"

Howard's words, he realized. The idea of sharing Marian with Hopkins.

"If you want someone else," he said, "I'll accept that. After all, I didn't stand in your way when you decided to marry. What I cannot understand is why you stay with Howard after the way he . . ." Reen stopped himself.

A suck of indrawn breath. "I don't want anyone else."

So Hopkins wasn't the usurper. Her tyrant was Howard. After all these years, still Howard.

"Why bring Howard into this?" she asked, suddenly irate. "Haven't you done enough?"

So what she felt for Howard was guilt, not love. Reen wondered which emotion was the stronger and which one she would heed.

"Oh, shit." She swiped at her eyes. "Poor, dumb Howard."

"What do you want of me, Marian?"

"Let's buy a house in the country, all right?" She laughed. "Maybe some horses and some dogs. Let's retire there. At night you can tie fishing lures. I can knit. At eleven o'clock we'll climb into bed and watch the news on TV. Forty-seven years, Reen. Don't you think you owe me that?"

He squeezed her hand. "I'm sorry."

"I know." She pulled away, opened the car door, and was gone.

"I'll take you back to the White House now, sir," the chauffeur said, getting into the front seat.

Reen didn't answer. He watched Marian's BMW disappear around a curve.

The Buick executed a three-point turn and headed south, taking Reen around the darkened zoo and down a nearly deserted Connecticut Avenue toward the White House.

They were stopped at the gate , and an army officer leaned into the car. "Yes, sir? Who shall I— White House Chief Reen! Sir!" he said in surprise, seeing Reen's nametag. "Everybody's been worried about you. Go ahead." He gestured to the marine guard in the gatehouse. With a buzz the gates slid back, and the Buick purred around the drive to the West Wing.

A commuter ship was parked at the side of the building, Reen noticed as he stepped from the car. Head down, he walked toward the Cousin who was standing at the door. The Cousin unexpectedly trotted down the lawn to meet him.

"Reen-ja!"

Reen's steps faltered. It was Thural standing there, elation in his ebony eyes.

Reen's throat spasmed. No words emerged. He walked to Thural's side and snagged a claw in his sleeve, pulling him as close as Communal law allowed. "Cousin."

Thural hooked the side of Reen's uniform, and Reen could feel the cold, welcome press of his claw. For a moment the two simply stood, holding on to each other as the early morning traffic rumbled down Pennsylvania Avenue and the moon set behind the buildings.

To Thural's back another Cousin emerged from the ship. Stunned, Reen watched his Brother Conscience approach.

"Reen-ja," Thural said. "The commuter ship crashed with Sidam in it. It might have been Tali and me, but at the last minute Tali had business and sent the ship on."

What sort of business was that? Reen wondered as he watched his Brother stride across the lawn to them. *Was it accidental business or planned business that saved him?*

"Where were you?" Thural went on. "We were so worried when the bomb went off at Dulles and you did not return."

Ah, but was everyone worried? Reen felt the pull of his Cousin's claw as Thural gently prodded for an answer; but Reen only had eyes for his Brother.

When Tali stopped on the grass beside them, Reen's sharp gaze never left his Brother's face.

"Someone tried to kill me," he said.

18

FOR THE RIDE TO THE COUSIN PLACE, Tali chose to sit with Thural instead of with Reen. Reen lingered a while in the ship's lounge, then wandered to the circular hall and peered out the windows as the craft rose from the lawn. When they had gained some height, Foggy Bottom and the Potomac came into view. The searing halogen floodlamps that had been set up for rescue work were so bright that even at that distance they made Reen wince.

There was not much to rescue. One entire side of the Watergate was rubble, and what was left looked like a ruin awaiting demolition.

As the ship sailed east, the lights of the rescuers grew smaller and smaller until Reen couldn't pick them out from the blazing clutter near the river. He looked down at the Capitol, an illuminated pastry set on the dark starry tablecloth of the Washington streets. Over Maryland, the lights were sparser, with busy little angular embroideries at Woods Corner and Camp Springs.

When they landed, Tali hurried off the ship as though fleeing his Brother, fleeing the truth. Reen pursued him. By the time they reached the Communal chamber, the Brother Conscience was already heading for the niches.

Reen halted in the center of the room, glaring at Tali's retreating back.

The Sleep Master rose from his bench. "*Out!* Get out of here immediately!"

Tali paused at the door and turned—the Brother who plotted treachery with humans but chose to be, among them, the Cousin without a name.

Without a name. Reen suddenly understood the smile he had seen on Hopkins's lips.

"When I left for Dulles, you remained behind to talk with Hopkins, didn't you, Tali? You plotted with the FBI to murder me."

With a gasp Thural reached out and hooked Reen's sleeve. Reen flung his arm up, away from his Cousin's restraining claw.

The Sleep Master roared: "Get *out!*"

Reen faced the old Cousin. "Sidam died today! A Cousin is gone! Won't you feel that vacant place among the niches? Let us speak the truth, then, in the sleep place where the law forbids lies to hide. That ship was sabotaged." He could see fear in Tali's black eyes. "Why did you put a bomb on that ship, Cousin Brother?"

Something knocked Reen off his feet. He looked up from the floor of the chamber. The Sleep Master had butted him with his claws.

No Cousin strikes another, Reen thought. *But, then, no Cousin murders another, either.*

The Sleep Master leaned over him, claws held as though he wished to hit Reen again. "Leave! You walk through filth and then track it into the chamber!"

Thural interposed himself between them. "Reen-ja is tired, Cousin Master of Sleep. I will take him outside for a bit." And without waiting for the Sleep Master's reply, he pulled Reen up and marched him to the door.

Outside the Cousin Place, the damp air haloed the lights, and the breeze smelled of snow. Thural eased Reen onto the steps and sat beside him. Reen pulled his legs up and rested his arms on his knees. He stared at the tarmac, his rage gradually subsiding.

After a while Thural said quietly, "Tali is sometimes difficult to deal with, but he is still Brother. You do not really believe your Brother plotted to kill you, Cousin Firstborn."

"I refused to believe it before, but I have reason to believe it now."

Resting his back against the smooth wall of the building, Thural contemplated the line of scrapped American warplanes. "Tali did talk to Hopkins. How did you know that, Reen-ja?"

Reen gave Thural a human shrug since no Cousin gesture seemed appropriate.

"I sometimes wonder about Jonis, First Cousin." There was a pensive, contrite look on Thural's face. "There was a time before he was kidnapped that Jonis no longer spoke to me, and we were Brothers, as you know. Why should a Brother stop speaking to a Brother?"

A pale blur of movement beyond the row of planes. A quartet of guardian Loving Helpers was making rounds about the perimeter, a Cousin Taskmaster at their heels.

And Reen thought of Tali. "Because of shame."

As though he had called him forth, the door spread open and Tali walked into the damp wind. Across the tarmac the first flakes of snow began to fall.

In his black uniform Tali was merely a floating head and bobbing hands. "I could not sleep," he said, "without making my peace with you."

"Sit, then," Thural offered when Reen refused to speak.

With a sigh not much louder than the falling snow, Tali sat on the stairs. "It *was* Hopkins I visited, Cousin Brother." The landing-strip lights were reflected in his huge eyes. "But we spoke only of his worry that Marian Cole steals too much of your confidence. This is all we spoke of, nothing more."

"Is it your right," Reen asked, "to judge my actions in the presence of humans?"

"It is my right to judge you at all times," Tali retorted, sounding more like himself. He shifted his body on the steps. "I come to make my peace with you before sleep, Brother, not to be told my duty."

"Let us have peace, then," Thural said, holding a hand toward each of them as though he feared they might begin tussling on the ground like humans.

Reen looked away. Snow was falling faster now, and the wind drove the flakes around the lights like a horde of moths.

"Hopkins is a good man," Tali went on, "but a man of many words when just a few would do. The hour became late, and Sidam was tired, yet Hopkins talked. I sent Sidam on and kept Thural, who did not then need sleep, with me."

"You did not want to tell me you were meeting with Hopkins. You were ashamed to admit it." Cousins weren't bothered, as humans were, by small changes in temperature. But Reen felt cold. He hunched his shoulders and pressed his hands together in his lap to protect them from the wind.

"Yes, Cousin Brother Firstborn." Tali's voice was subdued, earnest, and uncharacteristically contrite. "I was ashamed."

Of course Hopkins had known the Cousin at the party was an impostor. By that time he knew Tali no longer wore a nametag. And he knew that the Cousin who had died was Sidam. But, then, who had whispered to Reen from the bushes? Perhaps someone sent by Hopkins to make Reen distrust his Brother.

"I forgive you," Reen said shortly.

"Then we will go inside, yes, Reen-ja? Yes, Cousin Conscience?" Thural asked. "It is getting late."

The three rose and walked into the warm, spice-scented chamber together, making their way to the niches. The Sleep Master glared at Reen but didn't stop him.

19

THE NEXT MORNING REEN SAT WITH Thural on the flight to the White House. A gray sky, soft as a goosedown comforter, was spread over the city, and from it a few flakes of snow still fell. It was the kind of day Reen liked, one in which sharp edges were softened, harsh colors subdued.

"You should not press Tali so, Cousin Firstborn," Thural said as they passed over the Tidal Basin.

Reen gave Thural a quick, searching look, but his aide was intent on the instruments. "Did you hear the conversation between my Brother and Hopkins?"

The Washington Monument loomed out of the mist. Below stretched the fog-swaddled lights on Constitution Avenue.

"No, Cousin. But I know they talked. I saw Mr. Hopkins and Tali go into a room together. They were there a long time. And it is true that when Tali came out, he looked at Sidam and me, saw that Sidam was tired, and told him he could go home."

They swept over the tanks, the south lawn, and Thural lowered the ship to its pad.

"He thinks your leadership is unsuitable, Reen-ja," Thural said before they disembarked. "And if he can, he will banish you from the Cousin Place. Do what you must, but guard your temper. If you do not guard it well, others may turn from you as the Sleep Master has."

Reen nodded. The door spread apart, and the pair wordlessly trudged through the snow-dusted grass to the building.

When Reen entered the reception area that led to the Oval Office, Thural at his heels, a black man stood up behind Natalie's desk. He was clasping a steno book to his chest. "Good morning, sir. I'm Bobby Pearson, your *temp*-orary. I just can't tell you how delighted I am to be working in the White House."

Reen paused before the painted oak doors and gave the slender Pearson a once-over look. "CIA, I suppose."

Pearson waggled a brown finger in front of Reen's nose, and his pursed mouth delivered a string of tsks. "Now, now. That's supposed to be a secret. But since you guessed!—Well, not only am I proficient in Word Perfect and take dictation like a dream, but I also have a black belt in kar-*at*-e. And with a nine-millimeter automatic I can snuff out a candle at thirty yards. So"—he flipped open his steno pad—"I suppose we should get down to business. You have a news conference scheduled in an hour."

Reen's shoulders slumped. He had forgotten the strained-pea crisis. "Where is what's-his-name, the press secretary?"

A frown drew down the edges of Pearson's mouth. "What's-his-name, the press secretary, quit."

"Well, call my Brother Oomal in Michigan. Tell him to get down here right away. I have enough to worry about, and I refuse to face this press conference by myself."

Pearson lifted a finger to his lips. "Oomal in Michigan. Yes, I do believe I have that number." He was still flipping through the Rolodex when Reen went into his office and slammed the door.

"Do not fret, Cousin," Thural said in a soothing tone. "Oomal will know what to do."

"He'd better. If the humans learn the truth, there is no telling what will happen."

Pearson stuck his head through the right-hand doorway. Reen

stepped back guiltily from Thural. "Your Brother's on his way, sir. Says he'll be here in less than thirty minutes."

"Mr. Pearson," Reen said, recovering himself. "Don't ever barge into my office again. Use the intercom."

As quickly as he had materialized, Pearson vanished.

Thural shook his head and sat down on one of the two loveseats by the fireplace. "If the humans discover the truth, Reen-ja, there will be riots that will make the riots we have now seem small. And the Community will insist on euthanasia."

"It will be a great massacre, Cousin, one way or another." Gloomily Reen sat at his desk and booted his computer. But his anxiety made the words on the screen blur. After a few minutes of pointless scrolling, he turned off the IBM and sat on the loveseat opposite Thural. Hands in his lap, he listened to the pop and sizzle of the fire.

Secrets. The Cousins had so many of them. The secret of how vulnerable they were; the secret of past genocides. Cousins were made up of secrets. And the biggest secret of all was that they were taking humanity with them in their fall into oblivion, a little company for the end.

Pearson, ignoring Reen's previous order, bustled into the room unannounced, a tray of coffee and croissants in his hands. "Marian insisted I feed you. She says you always forget to eat."

Reen watched as Pearson buttered a croissant and handed the plate to him.

"Eat up," the man chirped.

Reen sat, limp pastry in hand, until the secretary left the room again. "I fear for us, Thural," he said, putting the croissant down.

"I fear for us, too," Thural said glumly, pouring himself a cup of coffee, which he then ignored.

Outside the French doors, snow gathered in the Rose Garden, drifted on the walk. Thural's nervous fingers tore a croissant into greasy golden crumbs. Reen checked his watch, then checked it again.

Twenty minutes later the intercom buzzed. In his eternally cheerful voice, Pearson announced, "Mr. Reen? Your Brother's here, sir."

Oomal burst through the door, a gray Mighty Mouse with an attaché case in his hand. "Press conference? Let me handle the whole thing. I can do a press conference, Cousin Brother."

He took a seat next to Reen. "I've been giving this some thought during the trip back to Washington, Brother Firstborn," he said, grabbing Reen's forgotten croissant from the plate. "And I think I've come up with an angle."

The fire snapped. A spark sailed like a meteor toward the blackened bricks.

"Trouble is, we have to come off that eighteen percent decline to make it work." Oomal spoke through a mouthful of pastry. "Here's the deal. The eighteen percent was a noncrisis figure. It's zero-worry level in human terms." He gestured with the croissant. "Twenty percent, that's the discomfort zone, because to a human twenty percent is close to twenty-five percent, and that means an entire quarter dropoff. We've done research."

Reen watched his Brother stuff the rest of the croissant into his mouth and wash it down with Thural's coffee. "Cold," Oomal said with a shudder, giving Thural an accusatory glance. "Okay. So here's the angle." He wiped his hands on the linen napkin that had been placed beside a crystal rose vase. Then, thoughtlessly, he tossed the napkin down, destroying the harmony of the tray. "We come off the eighteen percent and bring it up to twenty-seven percent. Get some anxiety going. There's no way to hide it, Cousin Brother. The shit's going to hit the fan. The thing to do is micromanage, micromanage, micromanage."

Reen stared bleakly at the crumpled napkin, wondering how far the situation would deteriorate and how close lay the brink of no return. The huge room was silent as Oomal poured himself more coffee.

From the intercom a shrill "Five minutes, sir."

Oomal stood up, adjusted his tunic. "I look okay, Cousin Brother?"

Wearily Reen stood up with him. "Can you handle it?" he asked, studying his Brother's face.

"If I can handle stockholders, Cousin Brother, I can handle reporters."

Leaving Thural behind, Reen and Oomal hurried from the West Wing and through the colonnade. At the main building Reen considered taking the elevator, decided against it, and walked to the stairs.

On the steps Oomal fell behind. He was clutching the ornate brass railing and wheezing a little. Reen looked back in alarm.

"You're walking too fast, Cousin Brother," Oomal said wanly. "If I'm going to field questions, at least let me catch my breath."

"What's the matter with you?"

Head down, Oomal told him, "Just a little stage fright, Reen-ja. Not to worry. I always get it, and then I'm always fine."

How could his Brother handle reporters if he was stricken by stage fright? To escape the oncoming disaster, Reen bolted down the steps. Oomal snagged him with a claw.

"Get back up there, Reen-ja, and introduce me. I'm fine. I'm just fine."

Reen hesitated. Oomal looked deathly ill, but he whispered, "It's not as easy as I make out, dealing with what I have to do, Cousin Brother. But my shame is no concern of yours. Go introduce me."

Reen, before any second thoughts could stop him, strode quickly around the door and into the blinding glare of television lights. He groped his way to the lectern, hearing the crowd noise subside into a low expectant grumble.

When his eyes adjusted, he saw that the reporters had dressed themselves, for Cousin notice, in shades of brown and gray. Looking past the television cameras to the anemic light that seeped through the tall windows, he cleared his throat. "I know you are here today about the situation at Gerber—"

A shout from the crowd: "Sir! Sir!"

Shielding his eyes with one hand, Reen peered out into the seated throng and saw a woman on her feet. He glanced nervously behind him and saw Oomal, his expression still numb and heartsick, waiting on the red carpet just past the door.

"Sir!" the woman called.

"Yes?" Reen would have to answer the strained-pea question himself or call the stricken Oomal from the wings.

"Bambi Feinstein, *Havana Libre*. I have a question and a follow-up, sir. Why did the commuter ship crash yesterday?"

Reen stared helplessly at the woman. What should he tell her but the truth? The crash was obvious sabotage. Every Cousin knew that. Yet if he admitted it was sabotage, who should he say was responsible?

The FBI? Because Hopkins had known enough to keep Tali from boarding. His Cousin Brother? Because even though Tali had denied having anything to do with it and even though Brother had a difficult time lying to Brother, Reen still distrusted him.

A murmur spread through the crowd. They were waiting for an answer. But, then, so was Reen.

"We're looking into it," came a whisper to his back.

On the other side of the doorway Oomal was motioning to him. "We're looking into it," he repeated.

Reen lowered his mouth to the microphones. "We're looking into it."

"Second part of my question, if you don't mind, sir," the woman from *Havana Libre* went on, leaving Reen stunned by her acceptance of his nonanswer. "The Watergate is of immense historical value. Are you planning to commit funds for rebuilding?"

"Yes," Oomal hissed.

"Yes," Reen said, glancing at Oomal, who seemed to have recovered and was anxious to get to the microphone. Ignoring the raised hands, Reen blurted, "The CEO of Gerber Foods is here and will answer your questions."

He stepped off the wooden box that had been positioned at the lectern for Cousin convenience and took his first deep breath since facing the television lights. Oomal bounded to the vacated box and gave the press as wide a smile as a Cousin could manage.

"Good morning. I have bad news and some not-so-bad news."

Chuckles splattered around the crowd like sporadic rifle fire.

"Okay, the bad news," Oomal went on. "According to our studies at Gerber, human births are down a full twenty-seven percent."

Hands shot up. Oomal disregarded them. "The decline is highest in developed countries. At Gerber we believe there are two reasons for this. Number one, a decline in native births seems to follow a first contact. Why, we don't know. It may have something to do with stress in the native population. Second. Second," he said more loudly over the clamor, "we believe that Earth may have reached its optimum population level. Now, species don't simply get to that level and stop, you see." He marked an arbitrary boundary with his hand. "They surpass it"—his hand went up a notch—"and then experience a sharp decline in births." The hand lowered two notches. "A nonsapient population is naturally culled by lack of available food, but sapient species seem to work on a deep psychological level, a level we don't completely understand. After some study we have come to believe that Earth may be slightly overpopulated at the moment, and a decline in births is simply your way of dealing with it. Now I'll answer questions."

Reen stared up at Oomal, suddenly realizing how brave his Brother was and how schizophrenic the job he managed. It was clear now why the little death had brushed Oomal the moment before he took the podium.

"David Ching, CBS News," a tall Asian said, standing. "When you first took over Gerber fifty years ago, were you aware that such a drop might occur?"

"The possible drop in births was of some consideration in the buy-out, and it has given us the chance to monitor it closely."

"Do you have any plans to correct it?" Ching asked quickly, before any of the other reporters could break in.

"Correct it?" Oomal cocked his head. "You know, only mistakes need correcting, David. This may be a natural process. We'll continue to monitor the situation, however, and if it appears that humanity is reaching the danger level, we will certainly do all we can to promote fertility. Yes?" he asked, pointing.

A familiar woman jumped up from her chair. "Harriet Standifer, *Washington*—" The *Post* reporter's question died in her throat. She was staring wide-eyed at a spot behind Oomal, as though God and a retinue of His archangels had materialized there.

Wheeling, Reen came face-to-face with Jeff Womack. The President winked at his chief of staff and tucked his tie into the jacket of his pin-striped suit. "Excuse me." Womack nudged Oomal from the stand.

"No, no, Jeff," Reen whispered, waving his hands.

But Womack kicked the box away and leaned down into the microphones. "Good morning, ladies and gentlemen."

The crowd came out of its trance with a thunderstorm of applause. Womack beamed into the cameras. Hands were shooting up all over the East Room.

Womack bent forward, and the audience went breathless with quiet. "I am pleased to announce that, at seven-thirty this morning, Eastern Standard Time, I signed the Tariff Deregulation Bill into law."

"What is this?" Oomal hissed, turning to Reen. "What's he doing?"

Reen was too stunned, too terrified to answer. The President was a loose cannon, and the Cousins were trapped with it on a small boat. One roll the wrong way, and they would be crushed.

Womack waited for the excited whispers to die down. "And I have another announcement, one of great historical importance."

Reen wondered frantically how he could remove Womack from the lectern. Did the President know about the sterilization plan? And if so, had he picked this moment to tell Cousin secrets? Reen and Oomal would be murdered where they stood. Not even the Secret Service would intervene to save them.

"I've served without a vice president for two years, and the time has come to correct that. Right now," Womack went on, checking his watch, "the Senate is voting to approve my choice for a new vice president, and I would like to take this opportunity to introduce him."

Reen gasped. Someone was standing in the shadow beyond the door.

"He is a man with a great deal of political experience," Womack continued, "and someone I'm sure you will all recognize." He swept his arm to the side. "The spirit of John Fitzgerald Kennedy."

Bursting into the East Room, Jeremy Holt, the medium, held his hand high in greeting. Womack patted him on the back. The medium, needing no encouragement, bellied up to the microphones.

With a boyish, disarming smile Holt said, "Ah, thank you," even though no applause, not even a murmur, had been offered. "It's nice to be back."

Reen took in the broad Bostonian accent and the twinkle in the eyes, and even though it lay a century away, Camelot came rushing back. Of all the presidents he had known, he hated Kennedy the most. Dangerous Kennedy with his smiling eyes.

Those mannerisms: the tip of the head, the casual grace that only long-standing wealth could buy. Kennedy stood in Jeremy Holt's body. Kennedy, the once and future king.

"I've, ah, been privy to some interesting information on the other side."

Dizzily Reen felt Oomal grab his sleeve. There was a humming in his ears, a prickly dryness in his throat. He felt his mouth open and wondered if he was about to say something or simply scream.

"Ah, first of all, there *was* a gunman on the grassy knoll," Kennedy said with a pleasant smile. "The FBI marksman beyond the fence was put there by J. Edgar Hoover, while Lee Harvey Oswald, like Sirhan Sirhan later, was under total alien control. My brother's death was a payoff, ah, to the FBI for helping the aliens get rid of me. Now, I thank President Womack for his appointment, and I promise to bring myself up to date on some of the history I've missed. I'm sure you, ah, have a great many questions, so I will take them now."

Except for an annoying buzz from one of the kliegs, the East Room was silent.

In the back of the room a hesitant hand rose.

"Yes?"

The reporter stood. The crowd craned their necks. "Uh, Gordon Appleton, *London Times*."

"Yes?"

Appleton took a deep breath and brought his question out in a stammer: "S-sir? Is it true about you and M-Marilyn Monroe?"

20

As Kennedy answered questions, Womack turned and quickly left the East Room, Reen at his heels.

"How could you do this to me?" Reen cried.

On the steps Womack paused, his hand on the banister. "Everything's coming to a head, termite. There's blood on the floor in the basement. Watch your back."

Womack continued his climb. Reen followed. "You tell me to watch my back and then you nominate Kennedy as your vice president? You know when he was president I had him killed. How could you do this?"

"No time, termite. No time." Womack topped the stairs and scurried for his suite.

Pewter light from the high windows flooded the huge room. On the desk a McDonald's Happy Meal sat half eaten.

"You know I'm in danger," Reen protested as he watched Womack rummage through the dry bar's cabinet. "I was kidnapped yesterday. Don't you even care? A bomb went off at Dulles right where I was supposed to be. The commuter ship was sabotaged. You were the one who told me to fire Krupner. I cannot help but wonder what the Germans would have told me had they lived. I have been called to appear before a Senate subcommittee. The subpoena is lying in a blackberry bush somewhere in Virginia, and you appoint *Kennedy*!"

Womack turned, a pistol in his hand. Reen staggered backward. His hip collided with the open door.

Womack's preoccupied eyes swept past him as though Reen were too insignificant to register. Turning to the mantel, he set the pistol on it. "Forget about the subpoena. I signed the tariff bill. They're not after you now. Besides, the Senate's not the problem. Something big is going on. I always tried to do the right thing. Well . . . nearly always. Do you think history will realize that?"

Although the President seemed to have forgotten about its existence, Reen stared at the pistol. "What are you doing with a gun?"

"Oh, God! I know too much, Termite!" Womack cried. His skin was taut over the bones of his cheeks. His eyes were so wide, Reen could see the halo of white around the irises. "All I wanted was gossip. You know how I love gossip. Now they're all after me. They know I have proof. So I had to choose a vice president, you see? There's danger ahead: bogs and quicksand and knee-deep shit. I mean, there comes a time when you have to put politics away and think about duty and morality and all that crap, you know? Jesus. I took an oath, didn't I? Nobody has the political skills to take my place but Kennedy." He cocked his head and said wistfully, "I always pictured myself as being a little like Kennedy, you know."

Reen approached Womack, holding wary hands up. "Sit down, Jeff. Let me call a doctor. Getting upset this way . . ."

Head still cocked, Womack asked, "Tell me, termite. All in all, don't you think I was a little like Kennedy?"

"I hated Kennedy," Reen moaned. "You know that. I can't believe you'd betray me like this." Tali. Womack. The Sleep Master. Everyone was turning on him.

Womack looked around the room.

"What are you looking for?"

"I forget," Womack said vaguely, patting his pockets. "I lose things. My ballpoint pens. My mind. My soul." He chuckled. "They'll never find it. They don't know where to look. But they know I have evidence. Records. Pictures. I've got it all. So I have to keep the gun handy, termite. Maybe I'll kill a few of them first. Tell me, do you think life's worth living anyway? Listen." He bent down and whispered into Reen's ear. "The Secret Service can't be trusted."

Reen stiffened in alarm. "Do you think that is how the graffiti got on the walls? The Secret Service? Of course, you must be right. How else could someone have written that without being seen?"

Clapping his hands to his cheeks, Womack gave Reen a long-suffering sigh. "I mean they've gotten to the Secret Service. That's what I mean! I tried to tell you! I tried!"

"You tried to tell me what?"

"Shhh!" He put a finger to his mouth for emphasis. "There's bugs in the walls. Bugs in the walls. And they're listening through the window. They have stuff that can do that, you know."

"But who wrote the graffiti?"

"Jeee-sus! Important things are going on. Will you forget about the graffiti? I was the one who wrote the damned graffiti."

"You?" Reen asked dumbly. "You did it?"

"Get with the program, termite! Start thinking bad guys, okay? Start thinking assassinations."

Reen's indignation gathered. He could feel its chill weight at his neck. He backed away from Womack. "You no longer exist," he hissed, giving the President a level, malicious gaze. "You are in that place where the eye does not see."

Womack looked startled, but there was no way for him to fully understand what this meant. Only Marian could know. Marian, who understood endings.

"Come on. Don't be a jerk," Womack told him. "The graffiti—the Secret Service knew all about it. And we had a good laugh. I was messing with you, okay? I was getting under your skin a little, that's all. It's fun to get you rattled."

Reen would never forgive the President's treachery, just as he would never forgive his Brother's; but it would have taken a Community decision to do with Tali what Reen was doing now with Womack. "I cannot identify your face. I do not recognize your voice." Reen turned and stalked from the room.

Womack's apology trailed after him down the hall. "I said I was sorry. You wishing I was dead or something? Come on, Termite. You sound like a three-year-old."

It would not be as if Womack was dead but as if he had never been. Even as Reen shoved that love away, he could feel it tugging at his sleeve, demanding attention.

"Reen!" Womack called.

Head high, back rigid, Reen walked to the stairs.

Womack hobbled after, threw himself in front of Reen. "I'm sorry, okay? I've got my sad face on, see?"

Reen stepped around him.

"Termite?" Womack's voice was thick with hurt.

Reen turned the corner and started down the stairs. His knees gave out, and he huddled there, mourning his loss.

Below, the press conference was breaking up. Jeremy Holt, Kennedy still occupying his body, swept down the hall at Reen's feet, a broad white grin on his lips. The rectangle of light on the carpet blinked out as a cameraman in the East Room extinguished the kliegs.

A moment later Oomal emerged, paused in the corridor, and looked up the steps. "Reen? Are you all right, Cousin Brother?"

"No," Reen replied. "Thural warned me of my temper, and he was right. My anger has caused me to do something stupid."

Oomal came and sat down beside him. "Tell me."

With a catch in his voice Reen said, "I threw Jeff Womack away, Brother, and I don't know how I will be able to bear it. From now on he will talk to me, and I can no longer hear. From now on I will look at him and no longer see. Our friendship is over." Reen peered through the brass banister rails to the floor below, imprisoned by his own decision.

"It'll get better as time goes on," Oomal said softly. "You'll get used to it. Can I do anything?"

"Leave me alone," Reen whispered.

Oomal hesitated, then got to his feet and padded quietly down the carpeted steps.

Love dies, Marian had told him. She was wrong. Love never died. Only relationships. And they left love festering behind.

He could hear the chairs in the East Room being folded for storage, the podium being put away. Soon the room would be cleared. Sitting, staring between the bars, Reen carefully folded and put away one by one the memories of Womack.

Jeff, a young President just two months in office, standing in the hot, whipping wind of the Vandenberg base, the aftershock of having learned of aliens and secret treaties still trembling in his face. His hand coming forward, a whispered word from an advisor, and the hand jerking back nervously to his side. Reen looking up at this new President and wondering how they would get along.

Fists pounding the table eight months later, Jeff's red-faced shouts of "No! No! You don't have the right!" and Reen telling him mildly that treaties were worthless and their landing inevitable. How much younger they had both been: Reen, unused to humans, pushing too hard; Jeff, unused to Reen, glaring at him as though he were a monster.

Less than a month later both of them facing each other across the oval doughnut of the UN's National Security Council table. The banks of cameras, the hush, the other members fearful and silent in their knowledge that the Cousin ships could outfly a plane and send conflicting messages into the brain of a missile. Reen, Loving Helpers around him like a living wall, because if a gun was fired, they would die for him—ten, twenty, a hundred, a thousand of them, if need be. Reen watching Jeff calmly as the new President shouted, "Why should these nations give up their sovereignty? It isn't in the interests of the united states that they become colonies." And Reen, who had learned to see behind human words into that dim region of what was left unsaid, recognizing the President's dark mirth.

A little show for the cameras. Jeff had taught him that. "Wave at the cameras," he said a year later as they stood on the White House portico. And in the Green Room, before the fireplace, the crumbs of their finger sandwiches dusting their empty plates, the remains of brown coffee ringing the bottom of their cups, Jeff pointing to Reen's chair and telling him about all the heads of state who had once sat there.

Jeff was a student of history, a pupil of human nature, a scholar of vice. Jeff had taught Reen well.

Thinking back, Reen couldn't remember when partnership became love. Affection entered as stealthily as a cat into a strange room, until without warning there it was in Reen's lap, purring and warm.

Now he stood and brushed at his legs, as if shooing it away. Below him, the East Room was silent. A maid, dustcloth in hand, passed across the hall on her way to the pantry.

Jeff, slapping Reen lightly on the arm and laughing at something he said that he hadn't meant to be funny. Jeff, poking him lightly, playfully in the side with his finger and for the first time calling him termite.

When had that been? Reen wondered. The years flowed into each other like rain into a calm sea.

Upstairs, a clap—loud and sharp. Reen lifted his head curiously and heard swift footsteps from the elevator. Another clap, different from the first. The slam of a door. A slight clank as the elevator descended.

Somewhere in the quiet building a maid was running a vacuum cleaner. The smell of frying green peppers drifted up from the kitchen.

The elevator clanked again, once, as it ascended. More footsteps, slower now, but determined. A door above opened with a squeal of hinges.

Whispers, murmurs, a choked "Goddamn."

A thunder of steps, and a Secret Serviceman rounded the top of the stairs at a dead run. He nearly fell over Reen. His face was pale. His forehead and upper lip glistened with sweat.

"Go to the West Wing desk immediately, sir!" The man took Reen's arm forcefully, nearly pulling him off his feet. "Find Miller. Can you remember that? Agent Miller. Stay with him until we have the situation under control."

"What is it?"

"The President's been shot." Suddenly the man was gone.

Reen stumbled up the stairs.

In the study two men stood staring down at Jeff Womack. Jeff lay in that place where the eye did not see and yet, in the light from the windows that was the color of old silver, Reen saw everything clearly.

Jeff was sitting in the rocking chair, his neck crimped back hard against the rest. The McDonald's Happy Meal scented the room with onions; Jeff scented it with blood. His eyes were open, and he was regarding the ceiling with surprise. Behind him on the cheerful yellow carpet was a feathery spray of brains.

"Have somebody call the Senate and see if they've confirmed," one of the men said, glancing at his watch.

The other man hurried away. A doctor and a nurse ran in.

"Let's get him on the floor," the doctor said sharply, grabbing the President by the front of his jacket and pulling him out of the chair.

Jeff punching Reen in the side and calling him, for the first time, termite. Jeff tumbling bonelessly, heavily to the carpet, the back of his skull staining the yellow red. Jeff with the doctor tearing his shirt open, buttons flying, one button bouncing like popcorn off the gun that lay a few feet away.

"Get me an airway."

Brown eyes as wide and unblinking as a Cousin's. Hands curled, the palms perfect and pink as shells. The long, groaning, hopeless sigh from the dead chest as the heels of the doctor's rhythmic hands compressed the lungs.

"What time do you call it, Doctor?" the man in the suit asking.

The doctor snapping back, "I haven't called it yet."

"His goddamned brains are all over the floor."

The doctor, kneeling, pushed at Jeff's chest. But couldn't he tell that that wasn't what needed attention? Jeff's pink brain was pushing through his white hair as though some deformed creature were squirming its way to birth.

Put it back in, Reen thought. *Please put it back in.* They should, all of them, find the pieces scattered on the rug and put them back inside the splintered bone where they belong.

More footsteps pounding. A breathless voice. "Confirmed fifteen minutes ago."

"Shit." The man turning, fists raised impotently.

Reen could not see; but he did. He saw Jeff's blood on the floor. He could not hear; but he heard Jeff laughing in the Green Room, talking about history.

Suddenly Oomal and Thural were at either side of Reen, claws digging into his sleeves so hastily that they left stinging scratches. "Come away, Reen-ja," Thural said, tugging.

Reen felt his feet trip over each other, felt himself falling. Thural sucked in a breath as they collided, and for an instant both touched the oblivion of Communal Mind.

Thural struggled to get away, but Reen seized him around the waist, tumbling him to the floor where dim light and purposeful dark waited, where the young were in their nests and Brothers crawled unthinking through the smooth, cool tunnels of childhood.

"Reen!" Oomal was dragging him back. Thural was scrabbling across the carpet to escape Reen's grasping hands. The humans were staring.

Jeff was staring, his sightless eyes still fixed on the ceiling as his cunning, wry mind leaked across the floor.

Reen lay on the carpet, Thural crouched before him, the gaping hole of the pistol's muzzle a few feet away. One of Jeff's buttons lay near Reen's outstretched fingers.

He pushed himself unsteadily to his feet, and Oomal stepped back.

Quieter footsteps this time, hesitant footsteps. Men entered the room with a stretcher and a long green plastic bag. They looked curiously at the Cousins and somberly at the dead President.

The doctor, still kneeling, looked up at the men with the stretcher. "A suicide," he said.

21

REEN WENT DOWN TO THE GROUND floor and sat in the Vermeil Room, his Cousin and Brother sitting silently by him but not too close lest he touch them again.

The ambulance left, lights winking, siren off. Thural walked to the kitchen and brought back a late lunch.

"You may return to Michigan if you wish, Brother," Reen offered finally, looking at his untouched food.

Oomal pushed his empty plate away. "I'll stay awhile, Reen-ja."

When dusk was settling across the lawn, Reen, without a word to the other two Cousins, left and made his way up the two flights of stairs.

Jeff's office was a yellow hearth of light kindled against the icy evening. A wall-to-wall strip of carpet had been pulled up, exposing the dun pad underneath. In the fireplace was a humped grave of smoldering ash. Jeff's rocking chair was gone.

Reen walked to the bar and stared at the half-bottle of Wild Turkey lying on the counter, the used glass beside it.

Jeff, eyes twinkling over the rim, telling him of Harding's mistress; of Brezhnev's scantily clad masseuse; of broken treaties and purposeless wars.

Jeff, too, had become part of history.

Among the row of books on the shelves above the dry bar, Sandburg's *Lincoln* and Kennedy's *Profiles in Courage* were upside down.

Someone had been searching the room.

Behind Reen came the sound of a drawer slamming shut. He pivoted. The door to Jeff's bedroom was slightly open. Quietly he went to the crack and heard the sound of shoes on carpet.

"I still can't believe the Senate confirmed him," a voice said.

There was a click, like a small box closing. A feminine sigh and a familiar voice, "Last night Womack telephoned all one hundred senators. He traded the signing of the tariff bill, and the vote passed by acclamation. You always underestimated him. I didn't. Womack was a devious son of a bitch."

The quick triple-pump of Reen's heart was so forceful, so loud, that he was certain the people on the other side of the door could hear it. He crept backward, bumping into a small table and catching a vase before it could fall.

Marian Cole was searching for Jeff Womack's evidence.

Reen tiptoed down the hall, down the stairs. He had known Jeff better than anyone, and he knew that if Jeff wanted to hide something, he would have been cleverer than to hide it upstairs.

He would have hidden it where he thought no one would look.

Reen passed the pantry and the Secret Service room at the end of the corridor. The colonnade was silent except for the gurgle and lap of the pool. Reen stole into the West Wing like a small gray wraith and turned left to the Oval Office.

The reception desk was vacant, with a single lamp left burning. The door of the dark office gaped like a mouth. Reen walked in, flicked on a light, and began his search.

It was behind the portrait of Millard Fillmore that he found it, taped to the canvas with black electrician's tape: a fat manila envelope. He tore it from its hiding place and spilled its contents on the desk.

Enough photos to fill an album. Neatly typed memoranda. Notes crumpled by nervous, sweaty hands. And a folded slip of paper with a blue karma ticket stapled to the top. Reen picked that up and opened it. The paper was dry and old, and made a sound like dead leaves when he pulled the edges apart.

Under the blue ticket was the Xeroxed typewritten suggestion: WRITE YOUR SIN BELOW.

Under that was a Cousin's scrawled and difficult handwriting:

> May God forgive us
> for Killing you —
> Jonis

Reen's fingers began to tremble. Paperclipped to the karma ticket was a typed note:

Jonis now an asset.   —Bernie

Poor, deluded Jonis, whom guilt could not release. Reen traced his Cousin's painful scribbles with a numb finger. No wonder Jonis had avoided Thural. It was so hard for a Brother to hide truth from a Brother. And treason was so alien a concept that not even Thural would have understood.

Reen's eye lit on a slender manila folder marked TERMINATION PLAN. Inside, just under the heading CARBONATED DRINK, was a large cheerful yellow Post-it Note:

Eliminating Reen too precipitous. And too much bad karma involved. Advise first step putting Gerber out of business. See historical references re Tylenol Scare.   —J.W.

J.W. Jeff Womack. So the President had known all along what the Cousin plans were, knew that Reen had deceived him. And he evidently was aware of the doomsday virus.

Setting the folder down, Reen forced himself to sort though more evidence. A photo this time. A happy group of scruffy people around a barbecue pit. The karma sellers at a picnic. Bernard Martinez smiled into the camera. His arm was around a huge man with a beard, knit cap, and smooth brown skin. To the photo was paperclipped a note:

> To J.W. Bernard M. frightened. Claims mole in organization. No
> proof this is true. Essential Martinez not flee from D.C. Advise fun-
> nel more money through Jonis to keep karma sellers fat and happy.
> —Agent Miller

Bernard Martinez, a grin on his face, terror in his eyes, his arm around the disguised Lieutenant Rushing. Reen let his breath out in a long sigh.

Quickly he leafed through the rest of the papers. An autopsy report and three postmortem pictures, photos so ghastly that Reen nearly flung them away. Then, above the bloodied, shattered jaw Reen recognized the corpse's eyes. Le Doux. Gentle, quick-witted Le Doux, easy to laugh, eager to please. A month earlier the Secret Service agent abruptly left White House security. Reassigned, Reen had been told when he asked about his absence.

The soles of Le Doux's feet were burned black. Welts lay in a houndstooth pattern across his legs, his chest. On the autopsy report the grim notation:

> Burns caused by application of electrical current. Cause of death:
> gunshot wound. Bullet entered medulla and exited center of man-
> dible.

The letters blurred, an order from Reen's mind not to read further. An autonomic demand of blind love.

With the autopsy report was a Post-it Note:

Landis compromised. Fingered Le Doux. If they shot Le Doux, he talked.

Reen laid the autopsy report down and waited until his vision cleared. Humans were a mix of cold murder and warm laughter. Cousins walked a tepid middle path. It was Reen's own fault that he had underestimated them. Human violence had always seemed newspaper-story distant, television-drama unreal. Now he knew how sheltered the walls of the White House had been and how brittle and breakable they could become.

He forced himself back into the search. More photos. Grainy black-and-white photos taken by security cameras. Photos of Hopkins and Tali. Tali and Loving Helpers entering the Secret Service office at the end of the White House's cross hall.

The pictures halted Reen, his mind balking before the insurmountable barrier of Tali's own treason. Then he was searching hurriedly again, picking up memos, discarding them, their messages barely registering.

Joint Chiefs at Langley 1/17, 1/19, 1/28, 1/30. Miller

Jonis scared to death. Afraid Tali has caught on. Bernie

Don't you people understand? Look what you let happen to Jonis. Someone's following me. The last time I slept was in the Greyhound bus station three nights ago. I have to get out of town NOW. Get me some money or I'll go to Hopkins. I'll tell him everything. I'm not kidding. —Bernie

On the third page lay a wrinkled, unattached piece of paper. Reen opened it carefully. It was even more fragile and brittle than Jonis's petition had been. In Jeff Womack's slanted handwriting, a cryptic series of numbers: 7039713991.

Folding the page carefully, Reen gazed around the oval room. The logs had burned themselves out, and the fireplace seemed to be sucking warmth from the air.

He put the papers back into their envelope, hopped up on a chair, and taped the envelope again to the back of the portrait. Then he walked down the hushed corridor and the quiet stairs to the office of White House security.

He twisted the knob and pushed. The hinges creaked. The room, which should have been manned, was dark. Patting the wall to his right, he found the light switch and flicked it on.

On the worn carpet by the file cabinet Reen found three dime-sized drops of dried blood and four bloody parallel grooves in the beige paint—grooves that human fingernails must have scratched. *Landis compromised. Fingered Le Doux.* But before he gave in to the Loving Helpers, Security Chief Landis had fought.

"You found it, didn't you?" a voice said.

Reen turned and saw Pearson. Pearson who knew karate, who with a nine millimeter could put out a candle at thirty yards.

"The documentation, I mean." Pearson's dark eyes were somber, his voice shorn of its cheerful lilt. "Where is it?" Pearson oozed around the door and shut it behind him.

Reen stepped back.

Pearson's eyes tracked him. "What did you find out?"

Reen forced his dry lips apart. "Are you going to kill me?"

As though surprised, Pearson lifted his eyebrows. He seemed to be gauging how much force he would need to wrest the truth from Reen. How much torture it would take.

Reen said, "Do something, Mr. Pearson. Either kill me or let me go."

The dark eyes shifted in indecision. Then the agent stood away from the exit. Reen rushed past him and out the door, up the stairs, and into the dark, haunted colonnade, where the tingling smell of chlorine seeped from the open doorway of the pool.

In the Vermeil Room, Oomal and Thural still waited, talking in low tones. When Reen entered, they stood.

"What is it, Cousin Brother?" Oomal asked, seeing the look in Reen's eyes.

"Get a Taskmaster and three Loving Helpers," Reen told them. "Bring them here now."

22

WHEN REEN PUSHED JEFF'S BEDROOM door open, the light from the study revealed the figure of Marian Cole and the large hulking form of Lieutenant Rushing. The pair froze.

"Reen," Marian said, pressing a hand to her neck. "You scared me."

The half-light was kind to her face. She didn't look much older than she did at the time of her first rebellion, when she had run away to marry.

"Bring them," Reen said. Behind him was the patter of the Loving Helpers' soft boots, the heavier tread of the Taskmaster. When Marian saw the Helpers, she shrank back against a dresser, hitting her shoulder with a bruising thud.

"Don't, Reen. Just listen for a minute. Jeff was murdered." She eyed the Helpers who had drifted like ghosts into the room. "That was no suicide. The nitrate test on his hand came up negative. The autopsy showed two bruises on his jaw where someone held his head, and two chipped teeth where the gun was shoved in his mouth."

Jeff, his laughter ringing out from the Green Room, a sound as unforgettable as the clap of his death.

"I found Jeff's evidence, Marian," Reen said. "And I read it."

Her face, burdened by the weight of the inescapable, sagged. "What did it say?"

"That Detective Rushing murdered Bernard Martinez. That you knew all the time that Jeff was using the Secret Service and the karma sellers to spy on you and the FBI. Is that why you killed him?"

Rushing edged toward a window. "We didn't kill Womack. Hopkins did. Hopkins was behind it all: Jonis, the attempt on your life, all of it."

In a lockstep that was very much like the lockstep of their minds, the Helpers walked toward Marian.

She held her hands palms out, as though she might find the strength to push them away. "Reen! Please! Hopkins made plans with Tali. He traded your murder for the assassination of Womack. Hopkins figured once Womack was out of the way, Speaker Platt would become president. He squeezed Platt with one hand, Tali with the other."

The Loving Helpers stepped forward. Marian slid to the floor, hysteria constricting her throat. Her cry was that of a naughty little girl who has caught a glimpse of her father's punishing belt. "No! Listen! Hopkins snatched Jonis, and he wanted to take Bernard Martinez, too. Jonis wouldn't have talked, but he worshiped Martinez. He would have told Hopkins everything to save Bernie. I had to order Martinez killed before he gave himself up to the FBI. I *had* to."

"Don't let those things touch her," Rushing said. "Jesus Christ! Can't you see how scared she is? Can't you see that?"

The Helpers stepped forward again.

Rushing reached under his jacket. He drew his gun and pointed it at Reen's chest. His hands shook. "Order them back!"

Reen's heart galloped for an instant before going numb and still.

"No!" Marian rose to her feet with a scream. "No, Kyle! Don't shoot him!"

The gun barrel wavered. "How can you let him do this to you, Marian? You know how he hurt you. How he—"

"Goddamn it!" Her face was tight with anger. She was breathing hard. "What happened between the two of us is none of your business. Put the gun away *now*!"

With a brusque gesture Reen ordered the Taskmaster and his trio of Helpers back.

Rushing slowly holstered his pistol. His voice was a low growl. "She could have had you killed a hundred times, but she didn't. Tali and even the Secret Service wanted to get rid of you. She stopped them. Didn't you know that? Don't you know how she feels about you? Goddamn. And haven't you hurt her enough?"

Marian slumped to a sitting position on the floor. Reen knelt beside her, so close that he could feel the heat from her body. "Do you know where Jonis is?" he asked.

Her knees were drawn to her chest, her skirt a waterfall around her legs. "Buried at Camp David."

Reen reeled back.

"I didn't do it. It wasn't me." Her words stumbled over each other. "I told you: Billy did it. We found out where they took the body. I got to one of his agents."

Her eyes met his. He wondered how he had ever thought they had depth. The irises were as blank as blue paper cutouts.

"Oh, God, Reen," she moaned. "Didn't I tell you that your Brother knew? Didn't I tell you we had to find Jonis?"

"Did they torture him?"

Her breath was moist and close against his skin, like an exhalation from a greenhouse. "Hopkins couldn't get Jonis to talk. He was getting sick, and Hopkins got so scared that he made a move to snatch Martinez. That's why Rushing had to terminate Martinez. Hopkins didn't understand Cousins. When Martinez was killed, he thought torture was his last chance. It confused Hopkins when Jonis died."

Reen stood. "We will get his body."

At his feet, Marian looked up. "My people are already there. We were going to find him and hide him again, hide him better. I was afraid the other Cousins would find out. Hopkins is stupid," she said bitterly. "He thought Tali had told him everything. He didn't know about the doomsday virus. Poor Martinez. He was harmless, really. I didn't want him killed. But he should never have converted Jonis; and the President shouldn't have tried to play detective. Womack was getting too close to the truth."

"And Tali?" Reen asked, gazing down at the top of Marian's blond, disheveled head.

"Your Brother knows about Jonis," Rushing answered. "Hopkins told him. Tali might have gone to the other Cousins for help, but he found out the FBI could prove that the Loving Helpers had subverted the Secret Service and that Tali helped plot your murder. Tali didn't dare turn the Loving Helpers against Hopkins. Too many in the FBI knew. Still, Hopkins was scared shitless when Jonis died. He went to Tali and confessed. Your Brother promised he'd protect him. See? He knew who got to Jonis and why, and he just didn't care. To Tali, man, once Jonis had converted, he was just another human. And your Brother, he doesn't like humans worth crap."

Reen straightened, gazed at the misty cobalt square of window to Rushing's right. "Let's go to Camp David," he said.

Rushing nodded. "We'll drive you."

"You drive," Reen told him with a heartsick sigh. "We'll go in the ship." He looked down at the crouched and terrified Marian. "And we'll take the Loving Helpers with us."

23

"I HAVE LOST THE ONLY TWO HUMANS I ever loved," Reen told Oomal as he watched Marian's car roll through the barricades, past the waiting tanks, and out into the dark rush-hour street.

Oomal gave him a sidelong glance.

"So now there is no reason I cannot out-Cousin Tali," Reen said.

"If that's your goal, you'd best forget it." Oomal seemed amused. "Nobody can out-Cousin Tali." The BMW disappeared down Pennsylvania Avenue, into the river of red taillights. "Let the Helpers take over her mind, Brother. Let me ask her some questions. There are things she's lying about."

"I can't, Oomal." Reen spread his hands and looked at them: the chubby fingers, the stubby claw. No wonder guilt-ridden Jonis hadn't been able to manage a better penned note of apology. "I've begged her to let me prolong her life the way I did Jeff Womack's, but she says she would rather die than have the Helpers touch her. I can't put her under control again."

"I'm gentle with them, Cousin Brother," Oomal replied. "You know I'm gentle."

Reen nodded. Oomal was the gentlest of Brothers, making the descent into Communal Mind a cushioned fall. Yet during that fall, even with Reen holding her hand, Marian had wept. Communal Mind was deep, much deeper than the shallow graves of Marian's eyes—its depths without light, its sides without handholds.

"So a karma seller converted Jonis? No shit," Oomal said in wonder as they started for the ship. "Poor Jonis. There *is* something seductive about the humans, you know. Give us a couple more generations with them, if we had them to give, and Cousins would start wearing three-piece suits and driving Volvos. Maybe Tali knows that. Maybe that's why he's playing Super Cousin. And," Oomal said, giving Reen a knowing glance, "maybe that's why he thinks you're dangerous."

"If he did not think like a human himself," Reen grumbled, "he wouldn't have plotted to kill me."

"Just my point." His Brother paused at the lighted ramp. "Another generation. That's all it would take. Two cultures don't merge without one coming out the winner. Some of us would be driving Volvos, all right, and some would be driving Chevy pickups with guns under the seat. Now I see why our ancestors acquired the bad habit of genocide."

Oomal tapped the shocked Reen playfully on the arm.

"Remember when we first landed and it looked as though things were going to go the other way? Remember you were on the *Today Show,* and you said the Old Ones spoke to you? Overnight it seemed as if every human became a damned spiritualist. That's where this karma seller stuff all came from, you know—that *Today Show* interview fifty years ago. I'll bet you anything that Womack was trying to call up the Old Ones and turn them against us."

Reen looked at his Brother with such shock that Oomal laughed.

"Trying to hook up an AT&T long-distance link with the Old Ones. Come on," he said, snagging his Brother's sleeve, "what do you expect? We took all Womack's power away. But screwing around with cardboard ghosts isn't important. What bothers me is what Marian said about Tali. And how Tali's been acting lately. As if he has a bug up his ass. It's only a matter of time before the Community finds out what Second Brother was up to. And if Tali's panicking, Reen, we have a problem."

Thural came out and stood in the lighted rectangle of the ship's doorway. Reen trudged to him, and the three walked to the navigation room.

"How many humans do you figure know about the sterilizations?" Oomal sat down and hooked an arm over the back of his chair.

Reen fell heavily into his seat. Marian. The Secret Service. Certainly Bernard Martinez had known, and anyone else Jonis had confessed to. There could be hundreds.

"And when do you suppose the balloon's going to go up?" Oomal asked.

Reen looked worriedly toward the tanks surrounding the White House. He didn't reply.

"Maybe we ought to start making contingency plans, Reen-ja," Oomal said.

"Why hasn't someone leaked it already?" Reen wondered aloud. "Why aren't we seeing stories on the news?"

"They're too afraid of that doomsday virus. And so am I," Oomal muttered. "Come on. Let's get out of here. I want to follow that car and make sure they don't duck out on us."

Obligingly Thural took the ship up. Extinguishing the outside illumination so they would not be seen, they located Marian's BMW by its hidden beacon and tagged after the twin cherries of its taillights.

Cottage-cheese clouds sailed across the moon. The road below was a necklace of tarnished silver that some careless hand had tossed on the black, rumpled bedspread of the Maryland hills. Intent on his flying, Thural hunched over the controls. In a gesture copied from the human pantomime book, Oomal pretended to straighten a crease in his skin-tight pants and then crossed his legs.

Humanity was so seductive.

Reen looked down at the faint red dot-dot-dot tracer of the car's lights as it shot past the trees. Marian had deceived him with her strength, her warmth. But Reen had deceived her first.

Come along, the Cousins had told her when the Helpers took her hand and dragged her to the ship.

We won't hurt you.

The murmured assurances of a nurse with a needle to a frightened five-year-old.

Just a little sting, and it will all be over.

Marian, naked on the table, the robot arm digging into her flesh as tears leaked from her eyes. The genetic combination had been so hard to get right. Ten, twenty, thirty years. And each year the same empty promise.

Rape. Yes, it had been something like that.

How fortunate, the Sleep Master's First Brother had written nearly three hundred years before, *to have found a species our ancestors ignored. With the decline in our own population, it may be that we can lift genetic material from them to strengthen our race.*

But Reen had taken that dream a step further than the Sleep Master's First Brother ever intended. Reen had created not stronger Cousins but Cousinly humans. Humans who would live four hundred years and breed like animals for the sheer exhilarating pleasure of it. Angela would probably live long enough to see her progeny cover the galaxy like a blanket.

By then, surely, the new species would find some way to defeat distance, and it would spread to the Magellanic Clouds, Andromeda.

Yes. If the purpose of his rape was Angela, Reen would choose Marian's suffering again even though he knew she still needed pills to sleep.

By the time she reached fifteen, he understood why she kept the lamp burning at her bedside, why she was afraid to be alone. And yet he went on capturing her, a fox mouthing a speechless, terrified rabbit.

He couldn't help himself. From the moment he first saw her he knew that he wanted his child to have her courage. And once he had lost his heart, once the decision had been made, he kept to it through Marian's tears, through her pleas, through her bad marriage and attempted suicide.

There was no good reason why Marian should ever trust him, Reen thought as the ship now passed over the high fence of Camp David and flew over a group of humans gathered under a sparse forest of floodlights. Absolutely no reason.

Thural landed in a darkened, deserted part of the complex.

"You really want to do this?" Oomal asked, leaning over and laying a claw on Reen's arm.

Reen nodded.

"You sure? It's one thing seeing what humans did to Womack, Brother. It will be another to see what human has done to Cousin. As long as I've lived among them, as much as I like them, there are still some things about humans that I—"

Angrily shrugging off Oomal's claw, Reen stood and walked out of the ship. The air was calm, prickly with frost and the smell of pine. Above his head, clouds made a banded halo around the moon.

The Taskmaster herded the trio of Helpers out of the lounge and down the ramp. Oomal glanced around as though counting heads. "Okay. Let's go," he said quietly.

They made their way through the trees.

In the glare of the halogens Marian and Rushing were watching a pair of workmen dig a rectangular hole. At Rushing's feet a naked man lay, his right arm twisted under his body, one cheek pressed into the dirt. As Reen approached, he noticed the houndstooth pattern of burn marks, the ruined feet. And he recognized the bleached blue of the slain man's dumbfounded eyes.

Kapavik.

Rushing saw the Cousins. He tapped Marian's arm and nodded toward them.

Marian, seeing the direction of Reen's gaze, said, "We had to do it this way. There wasn't time for anything else."

So Marian had ordered the tortures. Did Le Doux and Kapavik scream? Did they beg for mercy? Marian always got what she wanted.

Reen peered into the open grave at his feet and saw what he first took to be the glint of dark water. *Only water,* he thought in relief. *Nothing to be afraid of. And in a minute all of this will be over.*

The workmen bent to lift the water, which turned out to be black plastic sheeting.

"Not yours," Marian told him, reading Reen's expression. "Ours. We're taking her home."

Rushing knelt and flipped back the plastic. Dirt tumbled down the gleaming sides. A gaseous stench escaped, spoiling the night air.

Natalie lay curled in her comfortless shroud, legs slightly bent, hands at her chest. The fingers were broken and bent backward. There were needle marks along her arms, some torn and jagged. The bullet that killed her had entered the back of her cranium and, leaving, took her forehead with it.

Reen looked down at Natalie's body, at which both worms and humans had plucked. Natalie of the bright clothes, all her color gone to a dull blue-gray. His throat closed. His voice emerged in a rasp. "Why?"

"Natalie died protecting you, Reen," Marian said. "Everything I've done was meant to protect you."

When he glanced up, she was giving him a speculative look.

"Jonis is over here, Reen," Marian said.

Jonis was wrapped in a soiled white sheet, and he lay, a cocoon without prospects, on the brown winter grass.

"I don't know if you should look," Rushing said gently.

Reen kept his eyes lowered until the sheet was peeled from the body.

Ants had visited Jonis. Disagreeable houseguests, they were crawling in and out of his punctured, wrinkled eyes.

"Where are his fingers?" Reen asked, his voice nearly failing him. "Where are his feet?"

Rushing went to the ambulance and returned with a small box.

A clumsy Pandora, he unfastened it, and from the opening came a thick puff of corruption.

"They buried the feet and fingers separately," Rushing said, closing the box. "Kapavik said they were planning to dismember the rest of him, to conceal what they had done. Jonis died before they pulled the third finger out of its socket."

Reen turned to Marian. "Where were you going to bury Jonis?"

"At the Virginia farm."

"Take him there. Take him there and bury him again."

Marian seemed surprised. "You don't want—"

"Take him!" Reen shouted. "Bury him, damn you! Don't you understand that the Community can't comprehend torture? That they believe the Cousins who were kidnapped died in peace, without a human raising a hand against them?"

She blanched. "We didn't have a thing to do with Jonis. We don't kill Cousins, Reen. That's not what we're after."

"You murdered Sidam, didn't you? You planted the bomb on the commuter ship. Tali was talking with Hopkins. Despite all we have learned from you, no Cousin could have murdered as coldly as that. And no other human could have got that close."

She drew back, as if fearing Reen would strike her. "I knew Tali and Hopkins were planning your kidnapping. I thought I could stop it."

He looked across the lawn to the two rectangular holes. The opening into Communal Mind was softer, its depths free from importunate insects and decay. "How did you get the explosives on board?" he asked. "Tell me on your own or I will bring the Helpers over and you won't have any choice but to tell me."

"I caught Sidam by the ship," Marian said, "and gave him a teddy bear for Angela. I told him you'd be going to West Virginia the next morning and that you'd give it to her then. There was an altitude-triggering device inside it. I never thought I'd kill Sidam, Reen. When Natalie called, I left for Langley. I thought it was Tali who died."

In a day and a night, Reen's entire life had soured. Marian turning against him. Jeff's laughter gushing onto a yellow carpet. Hopkins and Tali conferring in the basement of the White House, planning Reen's destruction. And at his feet the shell of Jonis in its filthy shroud.

Abruptly Reen turned and walked away.

"Reen," Marian called. "Where are you going? What are you going to do?"

Reen didn't answer. Hopkins was the problem. Hopkins, who had ripped out Jonis's fingers by the roots to learn Cousin secrets; Hopkins, who had murdered Jeff and had led Tali down the twisted path of treason. As Reen stalked past the other Cousins and the three Loving Helpers, they swiveled and followed him to the ship.

Oh, yes. Reen was going to see Hopkins.

24

LIKE COUSINS, HUMANS SENT OUT SIGnals when they slept, signals so resonant that if a Cousin listened carefully, he could hear the mutters of their slumber.

Below the darkened ship Reen could hear that murmuring. He felt a woman in a neighboring house toss in a restless dream; sensed beneath him Hopkins's mind drifting like a boat across a dark sea.

When they landed and walked to the door, Oomal slid an opener into the key slot. Reen could hear its metal fingers probing the lock's tumblers. Beside him, the Taskmaster was fumbling a trace into an outside plug where it would send a command through the network of electrical nerves in the house telling the security system to slumber, too.

There was a soft click. Oomal turned the knob and opened the door to black, warm silence.

The floor was marble, and the hall smelled not of death but of peach potpourri. In the living room to the right, the glow from the VCR's clock cast an eerie deep-ocean green on the carpet.

Reen turned left and found the stairs that led to where Hopkins was riding the slow breakers of his slumber. Behind him, quiet as thieves, soft as cats, the Loving Helpers followed.

Five rooms, all open, the cobalt of night gathered in the doorways. Downstairs the furnace came on with a low rumble and an exhalation of heated air. Somewhere in the darkness a mechanical clock ticked. Reen chose the second of the right-hand doors, the one from which Hopkins's sleep licked at the edges of his mind.

Hopkins lay, a graveyard hump, under moonlit covers. Reen, whose ancestors had crawled in twilight tunnels and had eyes that pierced all shadows, saw Hopkins's hand curled innocently under his jaw.

Two bruises on the jaw, Marian had told him, where strong unexpected fingers had clutched Jeff's face. Reen could almost hear the sudden, frightened squeak of the rocking chair, the clink of teeth against metal, the felling explosion.

The Loving Helpers, dainty and elfin, were drawn by body warmth, by curiosity, to Hopkins. One grasped the man's hand. In a milky spill of moonlight from the blinds Reen saw Hopkins's eyes fly open.

"Who am I?" Reen asked, stepping to the bed.

"Reen," Hopkins whispered, not needing to read the nameplate, for now Hopkins could see as a Cousin saw. He could look past the unremarkable face straight into Reen where the soul itself murmured identity.

"Get up," Reen said.

With a thin moan Hopkins sat up in bed, the Helpers clustered around, touching him like street children in some strange Third World country.

"You murdered Jeff," Reen told him. "You murdered Jonis."

Humans responded in different ways to a Helper's touch. Marian quietly, steadily wept. Hopkins was the speechless type, his terror so profound that it couldn't be given tongue. He shuddered. His face poured sweat. His eyes were tender, moist, globular, like peeled plums.

"Tell me," Reen said.

"Yes."

"Do you have a gun in the house?"

Hopkins's reply came in a reedy squeal, the sound of a saxophonist hitting a bad note. "Yes."

"Get it."

The man's mind fought to escape; his body ignored it. When his feet hit the floor, he looked down at them in surprise.

"Get it now," Reen told him.

With trembling hands Hopkins slid open the nightstand drawer. In it lay a nickel-plated pistol.

Hopkins looked up at Reen in mute, apprehensive hope, as though praying the exercise was over.

"Pick it up."

When the hand obeyed, Hopkins's jaw dropped in slapstick surprise.

Against a wall of the darkened room sat a rolltop desk. Reen walked over and pulled out the chair. "Sit here," he said. "Bring the gun."

Hopkins's mind was obviously screaming for him to stop. He walked stiff-legged. The Helpers led him to the chair, and Hopkins collapsed into it.

"Put the muzzle in your mouth," Reen said.

A twitch ran through the muscles in Hopkins's cheeks. His breathing was shallow and rapid. Reen heard a drip-drip on the carpet. The man was urinating. His maroon pajamas were soaked.

Hopkins's face twisted grotesquely. His jaw worked. He was struggling to talk. "Tali. Tali."

"I know all about Tali. Put the muzzle in your mouth."

"The others . . . not me. Marian Cole. Yes. Yes. Jonis. But didn't mean—"

"Do what I said."

Hopkins's mouth twitched closed. His eyes bulged as he watched his hand turn on the pivot of its wrist. His lips parted in a rictus of a smile. His teeth stayed clenched, the only mutiny he could muster.

"Pull the trigger," Reen said.

Hopkins moaned. On his teeth the muzzle was playing frantic castanets.

The Taskmaster leaped forward. "No!"

Reen looked into the white-rimmed blank pennies that were Hopkins's eyes.

"Pull the—"

An explosion. The head snapped backward. The back of it blossomed open like an autumn-blown rose, strewing red petals of skull to the floor.

Hopkins's right foot kicked the desk once, hard. His arm jerked out away from him, flinging the pistol in an arc to smash the dressing-table mirror. His body heaved, then flopped wearily back into the chair.

After the boom of the gun, the silence of the room was so complete that it seemed to Reen he had been struck deaf. A sliver of mirror fell from the frame and tinkled on the dresser.

A Loving Helper shrieked, rubbing its hands as though Hopkins's death had left gummy acid on its palms.

"How could you do this?" the Taskmaster cried. "How dare you do this thing?"

The Helpers were screaming, screaming until the house echoed with their high-pitched cries.

In the Green Room, Reen knew, Jeff was laughing again, laughing to beat the band.

"Get them under control, damn it," Oomal said.

The Taskmaster glared. "I can't. They absorbed the death agony. No one can control them now."

Thural retreated. Oomal did, too. The noise the Helpers were making was the noise of forged steel as it bends.

"Someone will hear," Oomal said, glancing nervously out a window.

"They'll make every Helper we have go mad." The Taskmaster slipped a rod from his belt and touched one and then another of them. The small Helpers crumpled to the ground soundlessly, like crusts of charcoal that, unnoticed, had burned to ash. Somewhere in the darkness of the house a clock chimed the hour.

"You killed them," the Taskmaster said as he contemplated the outcome of his sad, final chore.

At their feet the three Loving Helpers lay in a tumble, the obsessive light of Communal Mind extinguished in their eyes, their gray skin dim as smoke.

The furnace clicked off. The clock gave one last peal and then fell silent.

Reen thought he heard Hopkins's never-voiced pleas echo from room to empty room. And somewhere in the silent house he thought he heard a Helper scream, its cry like tearing metal.

25

REEN PICKED UP ONE OF THE CHILD-sized Loving Helpers and made his way down the steps, cradling his burden as snugly as he might have held Angela. Behind him he could hear Oomal, Thural, and the Taskmaster following, none of them speaking.

There was nothing to say. Reen walked across William Hopkins's dead lawn, the small head of the Helper nestled lifelessly against his shoulder.

They're not as intelligent as dogs, he had once admitted to Marian. But, oh, how much more loyal was this flesh of his flesh, Reen's skewed mirror. He pressed his cheek against the smooth cool cranium of the Helper, the bulbous case where no thought but duty had ever sparked.

Reen had never touched one, and now he marveled at the feel of that thick skin which was a copy of his own; he wondered at the solidity of its body and the twig-fragility of its limbs.

Halfway across the grass he stopped. Thural tried to take the body from him, but Reen pulled away. The others were now waiting with their own limp burdens at the ship's door.

"Come, Reen-ja. Come," Thural urged softly.

Reen twisted away. "No."

Reen wanted to weep for the Helper but couldn't. Cousins were made from emotionless clay. Only when they reached sapience did they discover there were things to weep for, but by then it was too late. They hadn't the genetic tools for mourning.

He heard Oomal's gentle voice, Brother to Brother. "Let me have the Helper, Reen-ja. It's time to go."

After a hesitation Reen put the corpse into his Brother's arms. The Helper's head lolled back, sharp chin pointed to the sky, eyes huge, opaque, and sightless. As Oomal turned, the Helper's arm swung like a heavy rope.

In the ship the others went to the lounge, but Reen sat alone in a small blue meditation room near the door. He fingered the lightning bolt at his chest, the symbol of his intelligence: a brilliant spark from earth to sky.

Fully ninety-three percent of his Brothers had been culled from the nest, raised separately from those who would have individual temperaments and individual names. Reen didn't know what his Helper Brothers looked like. He doubted he could pick them out from the others. Loving Helpers were interchangeable. They were the faceless night that surrounded the lightning.

Reen sat until Oomal came to tell him the ship had landed.

"Reen-ja, you're in no shape to go into the Cousin Place," he said after the door had closed behind him. "So let's talk for a minute. I have something I need to tell you."

Oomal sat beside his Brother, not slouching in the chair, as was his new style, but ramrod straight, his old.

"You're the First and I'm no Cousin Conscience, but I have to tell you that you fucked up."

Reen didn't bother to nod.

"Tali's going to crucify you with this. For a while tonight you had the upper hand. I mean, here Tali knows about Jonis, lies to the Community, and you kill your only goddamned witness."

"I have proof!" Reen said heatedly. "I have pictures: Tali bringing

Loving Helpers into the West Wing. I have names and dates. Everything, Oomal! Jeff had everything!"

"So you have pictures. So you have documentation. Photos don't tell the whole story. And the Community thinks all humans lie. We had to have Hopkins, Cousin Brother. They'd believe what Hopkins said if he was in the hands of the Loving Helpers. I thought you were just going to put a little scare into the man. Drag him back with us to the Cousin place, make him spill his guts. God, Reen, what a mistake."

"Do I disgust you?" Reen whispered.

Oomal stared at the wall. "You offend the hell out of me, First Brother. You and I and maybe Thural—we don't see the humans as strangers anymore. Christ. However much Hopkins conspired against you, how could you do it? How could you stand there and tell him to pull that trigger? Wasn't seeing Womack's body enough, and Kapavik's, and Jonis's? And you made me stand there and watch. It's something I'll never be able to forget. I don't know if I can forgive you for that."

"I'm sorry."

"Sorry doesn't cut it, First Brother. Nothing can make up for what you've done to me. And to yourself. Tali's been using Hopkins against you, and he probably thinks you've been using Marian Cole against him, like one of those old Third World wars by proxy the United States and the Soviet Union used to have. Now you murdered Hopkins. You upped the ante. Tali's not going to let you get away with it. So what did they do during the Cold War to keep it from heating up? They negotiated. You're going to have to negotiate with Tali, First Brother. As much as you hate it, you'll have to."

"Tali tried to kill me," Reen said.

"No, Reen. Tali didn't try to kill you. Cousins don't kill Cousins. He hired a human instead. Tali knows more about Communal law than you ever will. That's his job, and he's damned good at it. He knows that Cousins never dirty their hands, and they don't use Loving Helpers as weapons."

Reen looked away.

"Listen to me, Firstborn. Thural won't talk, but you can bet that the Taskmaster will. As far as he's concerned, you're *Tulmade,* you're egg-eater. He thinks you're crazy. That's all he talked about on the flight home. Now you're going to have to walk in there and give Tali something to make him happy. What does he want?"

"To breed the female."

Oomal was quiet. The lighting in the room was cool, blue, and lulling: nest color. Reen wanted to put his head down and go to sleep.

"That's stupid," Oomal said after a while. "You sure?"

"He can't accept what is happening to us."

"Yeah, well, Tali will quiet down once the first eggs are hatched and he has another thousand or so Loving Helpers to feed and house."

Reen turned to his Brother. "I can't allow the breeding of the female. Who would I choose? You? Thural? Any of the others? And as First, I would have to stand witness. I couldn't, Oomal. I couldn't watch that. I won't order a Cousin to die simply because our Brother can't accept reality."

Oomal spread his hands in defeat. "So what do you plan to do?"

"I will go in there," Reen said firmly, "and apologize for my actions."

"Oh, *that* should work. *That* should make everything all right."

"I'm not finished! Then I will tell the Community that Tali knew about Jonis. That he tried to have me murdered. I will ask Tali to step down as Conscience and put another in his place. You, perhaps, since you seem to like the job."

Oomal ignored the barb. "You're skirting the edge of disaster, Reen-ja. Brother bonding goes only so far. Tali may have your chains around him, but he chafes under their weight. If you don't play it very, very cautiously, you'll end up in rebuke, and Tali will be designated to make all your decisions for you."

Reen got to his feet. "The Community won't do that. At least not after a hearing. And I have you and Thural as witnesses to Hopkins's confession."

"Reen-ja, sit down. You can't—"

"Are you coming with me, Third Brother? Or are you afraid of Tali, too? When I call on you to speak up for me, will you lie?"

Oomal jumped to his feet, and Reen found himself slammed against the wall. He nearly fell. Oomal jerked him upright. "Listen, Cousin First Brother," he said in a low, deadly tone. "Get hold of yourself. You always had a bad temper, even when we were children, and time hasn't taught you shit. I'd jump off a cliff if you told me to, if you had a good reason, so don't take your rage at Tali out on me."

Reen felt as though he were under rebuke already, that every shred of authority had been taken from him. He was suddenly afraid of Oomal, afraid that his Brother would strike him as the Sleep Master had.

But Oomal let him go and stood back. Reen slid to the floor.

"Are you all right?" Oomal asked.

"No, I'm not. I'm sorry for everything. For trusting Marian Cole, for not suspecting Hopkins. I'm sorry for Jonis, for the Loving Helpers, for my anger."

"Quit saying you're sorry."

Reen looked up at his Brother. "What else can I do, Oomal?"

"Breed the female. Close your eyes and point. Choose somebody. Please point away from me."

Reen looked at the lozenges of blue light set along the tops of the walls. "Then I will have murdered five times tonight: Hopkins, the Helpers, and my own blood."

"Too bad that by law you can't choose Tali," Oomal mused. "That would be a sound executive decision. Come on. We'd better get inside and get it over with." He bent and helped his Brother to his feet.

It was late. The moon had set, leaving the sky adorned with a meager sprinkling of city stars. Oomal at his side, Reen walked into the chamber, stopping dead when he saw that a crowd of Cousins had gathered there.

Reen's arrival was met with silence. The Sleep Master, his face grim, was standing next to the Taskmaster. Thural was frozen, one hand still out to Tali in entreaty.

The Taskmaster broke the spell. "Egg-eater," he spat.

Reen searched the crowd, found nothing but hatred or caution. Prudently Oomal stepped away from Reen's side.

"I . . ." Reen began.

The Sleep Master brought him up short. "We cannot identify your voice. We do not recognize your face."

Reen saw Thural's hand fall uselessly, wearily, to his side, all appeals abandoned.

"You are in that place where the eye does not see."

26

REEN STAGGERED FROM THE COUSIN
Place, looked around a moment, realized there was nowhere to go,
and, dazed, sat on the steps.

A death sentence. The Community had given him a death sentence.

Along the dark horizon, the lights of Washington, D.C., painted
a glowing dome on the bottom of the night. The air was brittle with
frost. The moon, high and silent, was a lamp in the hands of Orion.
Reen looked up, searching for home; but the star was too far and too
faint to be seen.

Reen had misjudged how far and how fast Tali would go. *Now
what?* he asked himself. There was no use going back inside and
pleading. No one would listen.

Behind him, a quiet pop. The door opened, spilling light down
the stairs. "Reen?" a low voice called.

Oomal. Oomal had called his name. Reen got to his feet. His
Brother was looking at him, looking into his face as if nothing had
happened.

Reen wasn't sure about the etiquette involved, if he should respond to his Brother's call.

Like a luminous eye closing, the door pressed shut. "You okay?" Oomal asked.

"Should we be talking?" Reen whispered. "If they hear us talking . . ."

"Tali already tried to rebuke me because I said he was the egg-eater and not you. He's in there shouting orders, and about half the Community is acting as if he were the one thrown away. It's a mess, Reen."

With a moist, kissing sound, the door parted again. Thural stumbled out. His dark gaze slipped past Reen and fixed on Oomal. "Tali cannot lead and be Conscience as well," he said. "Oomal, you must be Conscience. Go back in there and tell him."

Oomal shrugged. "I am already Conscience, Cousin Thural. Tali has nothing to do with the destiny of birth order. He'll understand that when he gets over his snit."

"But you are under rebuke, Cousin. How can Tali put his Conscience under rebuke?"

"He can't. Tali knows Communal law. He's bluffing. Go on back, Thural, before Tali tries to put you under rebuke, too. I'll let him cool off and then remind him how the Community works."

"He cannot be the First!" Thural shouted. "He cannot simply throw away his Brother and then take over his place! This has never been done! Another First should rule."

"We don't have another First," Oomal reminded him gently.

Thural's cry shattered the night as Hopkins's gun had shattered the mirror. "What he does is human, Cousin Conscience! This is a human thing Tali does, to murder a Brother in order to rule!"

"Yes," Oomal said with a malicious chuckle. "I agree. Very human. You might go back in and point that out to the Community, too."

Reen thought for sure that Thural, so full of indignation, would turn on his heel and march back to confront Tali. Instead his Cousin looked out at the dark landing strip and was silent for a long breath-less moment. "What the Nameless did was evil, Cousin Conscience," he finally said, "but not evil enough for this. If the Cousin Who Has No Voice should ask for help, I might hear his request and sleep at his side."

Reen clapped his hand to his own cowardly mouth to keep from uttering an appeal. Enough murder had been done that night. A pair of Cousins didn't make a Community. If he accepted Thural's offer, they would spend the next three days in a sleepless wait for death.

"Never mind," Oomal told him. "The Nameless will be taken care of. I have some Gerber execs who like the Nameless a lot more than they like Tali. If he wants to come to Michigan, he has a sleeping place. Now go back in there before Tali starts plotting against you."

Reluctantly Thural went to the door and let it swallow him.

"I meant what I said." Oomal turned to Reen. "You come on up to Michigan. Tali can't do anything to me or my employees. Don't worry about us. We won't get thrown away just for hanging around with a Nameless Cousin."

A Nameless Cousin.

Reen took in a ragged breath that tasted of ice. There were difficult things he would have to remember: that he would never again be able to give an order; that he would make no more decisions other than his own.

Commuter ships and the smaller runners squatted on the tarmac like a gathering of toadstools. Soon he would leave in one and never be able to return.

There had been a time when the Cousins' obedience to him had been instinctive; when his Brothers, all but one, had loved him.

"I can't go just yet," Reen said.

"Don't be a jerk, Reen."

"If Tali does not have a consensus, he won't dare go against the humans. But he will go after Marian Cole. I must warn her," Reen said.

"Let her go. She hates us. Don't you see that yet? Someday, Reen, she's going to drink you dry."

As a child, when Reen had first felt the sightless nuzzle of his Brothers exploring him for allegiance, love had poured from him like milk. It wasn't just Marian who would drink him dry, it was the Community, it was the humans, it was Angela.

"I know," he said.

27

HE HAD ALWAYS COME TO HER LIKE A thief, sneaking into her house, rummaging through the closets of her mind. Down the hall, Howard wrestled with his nightmares, but Reen stood in the doorway watching Marian.

Her eyes opened. When she raised her head to look at him, he turned and went down the stairs to the kitchen. At his back a breathy whisper: "Reen?" He could hear her groping her drowsy way from the bottom of the steps to the hall.

"Here," he replied, pulling out a chair and seating himself in the breakfast nook.

She shuffled into the dark kitchen and fumbled for the light switch. The fluorescents came on with a chill dazzle, igniting color in the room: the turquoise countertops, the terra-cotta-tiled floor.

Marian had hastily tied a pink terry-cloth robe over her nightgown, and she was squinting in the glare. "You always come to me like a dream," she told him, rubbing her eyes with the tips of her fingers.

He sat, his hands linked on the tabletop. It was late, and the hours sagged around his shoulders. The colors in the room were painfully iridescent. Surreal.

"You want some coffee?"

Without waiting for an answer she went to the cabinets and pulled out an acid-green can of Folger's. A hiss of water from the tap. The clunk as the glass carafe was set on the Mr. Coffee hotplate.

"I murdered William Hopkins tonight," Reen said.

A crash. He turned and saw Marian staring down at a broken cup.

He reached for her, but she was too far away. In some ways she had always been. "There's no reason to be afraid."

"No, of course not." With a fussy gesture she pushed her hair back from her face. "How silly," she said, bending to pick up the pieces of shattered cup. "How clumsy."

On the counter the coffee maker spat. The aggressive scent of coffee pushed through the heavy air in the kitchen.

"Come here," he said. "Please."

She placed the shards of porcelain on the drainboard, then walked over, tucked her robe about her knees, and sat. "You look tired," she said.

She was the one who looked tired. Without makeup, her eyes seemed smaller, a more watery blue. Her cheeks were a wan, weary color. Tiny lines checkmarked the skin around her lips.

"Sit with me awhile," he said, his voice trembling a little. "I want to apologize."

She looked down at his hands and stroked the smooth gray surface of his fingers. "Don't feel guilty about Hopkins. He deserved it. The man was a shit."

"I know," he said softly. "I want to apologize for what I've done to you."

Her fingers halted in mid-caress. Her touch was warm but light as feathers.

"I've thought about what you told me, Marian. I've tried to understand what I did. I think that sometimes we fall in love with our opposites. Then we try to erase the differences. That's what I did to you."

"It was over a long time ago, Reen. It doesn't matter."

"Of course it matters," he snapped.

They looked at each other, and he saw that, despite everything, they were the same irascible Reen and the same vexing Marian that had existed from the beginning of the genetic experiments.

"When you married Howard, I should have left you alone, or at least not allowed you to remember. You and Howard could have bought that country house you always wanted. You could have had your dogs. Your horses. I kept you from that."

"Howard?" She was surprised. "You think I wanted Howard? You never told me I was putting on weight. You never noticed I was growing old. You never criticized the way I dressed or laughed at my opinions."

"There are things I am unable . . ."

"Don't!" she said sharply. "For God's sake, don't blame yourself. How do you think that makes me feel? I wanted things from you that I knew you couldn't give. You love as if everybody were important. As if everybody were the same. You know? Once I even slit my wrists so you would love me best."

He drew his hand away in shock. He always thought she slashed her wrists for Howard.

"If you didn't love Howard, you should have left him. You might have met someone else, someone who understood you . . ."

Her sour laugh stopped him.

"A *man* who understands me? Shit. Little boys grow up in some damned club called No Girls Allowed. And by the time they get to adolescence and start thinking about girls, they only want to know how to get into our pants. Later, when they're grown, they start trying to understand us, but by then it's too late."

Blinking hard, she said, "Women spend their whole lives wondering what we did wrong. Wondering why the ultimate insult for one eight-year-old boy to another is to call him a girl. Don't you dare apologize to me, Reen. You're no good at it. I've been apologizing my whole fucking life."

Bracing her hands on the table, Marian pushed herself to her feet. "Let's have some coffee."

Then she walked away. Reen heard the clinking sound of glass against china, the gurgle of coffee pouring. A moment later she was back, pushing a cup and saucer across the butcher-block table toward him.

He stared into the liquid, dark and brown as blood. "Oomal wanted to use Loving Helpers to find out why you were lying to me. I didn't let him."

There was a long silence. When he glanced up, he saw that she was watching him over the rim of her cup.

"I want to trust you," he said.

She put the cup down, turned it this way and that on the table, as if trying to find some perfect but elusive alignment.

"In a few days, I will die."

Her eyes rose.

"Tali is now First. Oomal is now Conscience. Oomal is strong enough to keep Tali from using the virus, or at least he will be if I stay away. But he either can't or won't stop Tali from coming after you. I want you to leave tonight. Pack a few things. Drive to some safe place. Surely you have one."

She gave a flat laugh. "Stop joking."

"I will die, Marian. There is no way to prevent it. The Sleep Master and Tali have ordered me from the Community because of what I did to Hopkins."

She grabbed at his arm, nearly spilling his coffee. "Don't leave me, damn it!"

Reen put his head in his hands. Lack of sleep was already getting to him. His arms shook; his head felt heavy.

Suddenly she was kneeling on the tiles, pushing herself into him, arms around his waist, head to his chest. He sat back in confused and awkward alarm.

Marian was so good at embraces. In all those years he had never really learned to hold her. He lowered his arms to her back.

Pressing his face into her hair, he smelled the apple scent of her shampoo.

When he lifted his head, he saw Howard standing in the shadowed doorway watching, just watching. Reen wondered how long the man had stood there and how much he had heard. For a moment they looked at each other, then Reen turned away and put his head again on Marian's silken, fragrant hair.

"We'll go away together," she said, "just the two of us. Let Oomal handle everything. I know how tired you've been lately, how the stress has gotten to you. Just walk away from it, can't you? Can't you do that for me?"

Reen looked up, but Howard was gone.

"I have to leave," he said.

She clung to him. Now it seemed that her hot, hungry arms were eating at him; that if he sat any longer, he would be consumed.

He shoved free. Her hands fell away. She sat back on her heels, her eyes shuttered with hurt. "I was never enough for you, was I?"

"Cousin is tied to Cousin, Marian. I can't help that."

"Since I was five years old you've been my whole goddamned world. You . . ."

He stood.

She stood, too. Her face was so twisted with anger that he thought she would strike him. "They always meant more to you than I did. Sometimes I hate you for that. Tali tells you to die, and you crawl off somewhere and stop living. Reen, you can learn to do without the other Cousins. I know you can."

"We are hive creatures, Marian!" he shouted in exasperation. "I have to have other Cousins around me to sleep! Listen to me. I want to know that you're safe. Pack some things. Leave the house."

She paled. "Wait. Stay here. Stay right here, just for a minute. I have something." She rushed into the next room.

Through the dark doorway, the slam of a drawer. A muttered "What are you doing up?"

"You're leaving, aren't you?" It was Howard in the shadows, his tone thick with hurt.

Marian's fierce whisper: "Where did you put it?"

"Just . . . don't do this. I know I can make things right. Just stay with me. Talk to me. Tell me what to do."

The bang of a cabinet. "Goddamn you. Where is it?"

A pause. A hollow reply. "In the blue vase."

Riffling sounds like paper. The clink of a diamond ring against porcelain. "Go to bed, Howard."

"Please. You—you'll be up in a few minutes, won't you? We'll talk. We'll—"

A hoarse "Go to bed."

A hesitation. Then Reen heard a heavy tread on the stairs. The squeak of a floorboard.

Marian rushed into the kitchen, her eyes wide. "Here! Take it! I killed for this!"

She shoved a cassette tape at him. He took it.

"You said you killed Hopkins, and it looks as if you didn't get anything out of it. If you're going to kill, Reen, at least do it right. This tape proves what Tali was up to. It proves everything." Her voice caught. "This will save you, won't it? They'll forgive you now, won't they?"

He turned and walked from the kitchen. Marian called his name. He closed the door on her voice, snapping it like a thread.

28

IT WAS NEAR DAWN WHEN REEN ARrived at the White House. Alone, he parked his small ship at the edge of the landing pad and trudged past the darkened colonnade to the stairs.

He was the only thing moving in the halls. A four-in-the-morning hush had fallen over the White House, time holding its breath for the sun.

When he got to the second-floor study, he noticed the light was still on. He lifted a heavy hand to switch it off. Shuffling into Womack's adjoining room, he arranged himself on the bed. The mattress was so soft and so open that he couldn't decide whether he was in danger of being swallowed or of falling. After a few minutes of tossing he got on the floor and positioned his body between the safety of the bed on one side and the rigid frame of the dresser on the other.

There was no way he could sleep. The corners of the room were too sharp and hard, its Georgian design too fussy. Predawn light, the wrong shade of blue, seeped around the heavy curtains. The room smelled not of peppery rest but of potpourri.

With a little moan, Reen pressed his head closer to the dresser, gathering what comfort he could from the hard surface.

The first day would be the worst. The first day his struggle to sleep would be frantic. After twenty hours or so, when his weary mind gave up the fight, the going would be easier. He would lie in dazed insanity until his heart gave out. Reen had never seen a Cousin die from *mitalet,* but he'd been warned enough by his elders.

Intelligence was too heavy a burden to carry alone.

Reen fought to drive out thought, but like a boorish dinner guest it refused to go. Lying there, he remembered the smooth tunnels of childhood. He pictured his Second Brother: the resolute victory in a face turned to cruel stone.

Memories assailed him. He pulled the pillow over his eyes, as though the press of the satin might keep out the visions.

But they paraded: Angela and Marian in the snow; Oomal, pity and revulsion in his gaze; Jeff Womack's head leaking pinkish gray brain; the fear in Hopkins's face.

Without the tether of the Community, his walleyed imagination bolted. Tali would find Marian and kill her. The Community would unleash the virus on the humans if the humans didn't revolt and kill the Cousins first. Thural, for his sympathy with Reen, would be chosen to die as consort.

Thural. Reen wished now that he had accepted his Cousin's offer. Two weren't enough to make a nest, but some of the edge might be blunted.

Thural. Reen tried to get up to go find him, but his body refused to move. Instead of rising, he flipped over on his side, his neck at an uncomfortable angle.

Reen heard a Cousin whimpering, then realized he was alone in the room and the whimpering came from him. Two more days.

The door hinges squeaked.

Reen lay in a tiny defenseless ball near the bed. Another squeak. Footsteps whispered across carpet.

"Reen?" Oomal called.

Reen rolled over. Oomal was standing at the corner of the bed, looking down.

Oomal should never have come. Reen's defenses were down,

and like Marian he would envelop the nearest victim in his own selfish need. He wanted to tell Oomal to run for his life, but he couldn't.

"I took a little nap when I got back to Michigan," Oomal said. "Then Sakan woke me up to say you hadn't arrived. I figured you'd do something stupid."

Another Cousin stepped around the side of the bed. "Hi, Reen," Sakan said. "You look like shit."

The two bent, grabbed Reen by his sleeve, and pulled him to his feet. Blearily he saw that four other Cousins were standing by the door, Louis Vuitton suitcases in hand.

"Oomal says we're camping out," Sakan said. "Like the time we went on the fishing trip."

Oomal made quick introductions. "You know Sakan. He's our director of marketing, the one who came up with the strained pea tartlets, remember?"

Sakan muttered, "Right. Bring that up again."

"Radalt," Oomal went on. "He's our controller. Kresom, vice president in charge of personnel. Zoor—the humans call him Zoomer—vice president of sales. And Wesut, production manager."

The Cousins gave Reen little waves of acknowledgment as they threw their suitcases on the bed.

"Zoomer," Oomal said. "Go find us some sheets."

Zoor nodded. "Where's the linen closet?"

Reen pointed to the hall, and Zoor left.

Oomal said, "Follow the logic, Reen. We evolved from tunneling creatures." He held up his opposable claws. "So we like semidarkness and confined spaces. Sleep's our way of getting back to the larval stage."

Radalt opened his suitcase and took out a blue light bulb.

"Communal Mind is part of it, but the ambiance has to be right, too," Oomal said.

Zoor came back in, holding up a sheet patterned with red and blue cartoon dinosaurs. "Hey, guys. Get a load of this."

Radalt stopped what he was doing. At the window, Kresom turned.

Looking down at the sheet, Zoor asked, "Our extinction or theirs?" Then he left on his quest again.

When the chuckles subsided, Oomal went on, "Anyway. The camping trip."

"Zoor kept asking why they didn't just cut out the middleman and eat the worms, remember?" Wesut said. "He popped a worm into his mouth, and Harvey Cohen from accounting fell over the side laughing and nearly drowned before we could get him back in the boat? Remember that? And then—"

"The humans kept telling us how much fun camping would be," Oomal said. "So, what the hell, we decided to try it. That night we pitched a tent and slept just fine."

Radalt switched on the lamp, flooding the room with blue. Kresom closed the heavy velvet draperies on the gray morning. Zoor came back with a sheet and tossed it to Sakan. "Colored sheets, but that's all I could find."

"If we wrap ourselves up tightly enough, we feel we're in the security of the nest," Oomal lectured as Sakan flapped out his sheet and rolled himself up in the material. His gyrations fetched him up against a nightstand with a thud.

"Comfortable, Sakan?" Radalt asked the pink cocoon.

A shiver went through Reen. He was looking at Sakan, he knew, but thought of Jonis, Jonis in his shroud.

Sakan's reply was muffled. "Just fine."

Zoor passed out sheets to the rest of them. Oomal helped Reen into his, showing him how to hold his arm down, demonstrating how to flip the end over his head.

"Sleep, Reen," Oomal said gently when his Brother was a tight cocoon in the corner.

Reen's sheet was a pale yellow, and once he was rolled up in it, the blue tinged the color light green. Arms pinioned at his sides, he caught the first whiff of spice. One of the Cousins had quietly and without the least difficulty fallen asleep. A moment later the room was heavy with the dumb inescapable weight of Communal Mind. Reen fretted for a moment against the confines of his shroud before he, too, dropped into the dim, thoughtless regions of slumber.

Reen, the Old Ones called.

Reen couldn't see them, but he could hear them. His mind was falling, falling.

Reen, they said, but he was plummeting too fast to answer, his guilt wrapping him as tightly as the sheet.

He couldn't reply. He shouldn't. All ties with the Community were gone except for Oomal's unbreachable pity.

Aerodynamics, Reen thought giddily. The word dropped from his mind and fell with him, a small, round, heavy thing. Down and down and down. He imagined he could feel the edges of the sheet flutter.

Reen. The voices of the Old Ones echoed like thunder from the mouth of a well. And Reen knew they couldn't understand why he refused to answer.

29

REEN WAS YANKED OUT OF HIS DOZE
by the clamor of angry voices. He was awake but couldn't move. He
couldn't see. He tussled frantically until he remembered that he was
wrapped in Jeff Womack's sheet.

"—back to Michigan!" Tali was shouting.

Oomal's reply was calm, but Reen could hear the anger in his
voice like the throbbing bass note in a musical chord. "Order the
other Cousins if you can, Tali. By law I don't have to listen to your
shit."

Reen flipped the sheet from his head and wriggled his way out
of the tangle. Tali and Oomal were standing in the doorway, the other
Gerber executives watching, their empty, makeshift cocoons littering
the floor.

Radalt smiled down at Reen. "Oh, hi. You awake? Want a bath?"
he asked pleasantly. "We filled the tub with tannic water and set a
fresh uniform out for you."

Tali's fury shifted from Oomal to Radalt. "You speak to the air!
There is no one there! No one!"

It looked as though Radalt was longing to make some snappy
rejoinder but couldn't quite work up the courage. Zoor bent and
started picking up sheets.

"This is the law," Tali said, speaking into the averted faces of the Michigan Cousins, who seemed to be engaged in trying to pretend that Tali was invisible instead of Reen. "It is cleanliness to throw the dead from the Community because if the dead stay, they breed disease. And this Nameless Cousin, like a dead thing, will breed a terrible illness, a sickness of the soul."

Burdened with his pile of sheets, Zoor made his hesitant way past Tali and out into the hall, searching, Reen supposed, for a maid, for deliverance, or at least for a washer and dryer.

"Go back to work, Cousin Brother," Oomal said, snagging Tali's sleeve. "There's nothing to interest you here."

Tali jerked away. "You speak to me of *work*?" he shrieked. "You who bring your workers here with nothing for them to do? Where are we without purpose, Brother? Illness and insanity are the fruits of idleness."

"You know, Tali," Oomal said with amused irony, "you're just like a damned elderly Cousin looking for spots of fungus in his claw and telling scary stories to the young. But I'm grown now, and those Communal myths don't frighten me anymore." Turning, he motioned the other Michigan Cousins out of the room. "Go on down to the office we set up in the East Wing, guys. It's okay. Let my Brother and me scream at each other in private."

When the Gerber execs had all filed out, with backward looks of concern, Tali muttered, "Envy-eyed liar. Spiteful stomach for eggs. You want my place. It eats at you that I am First now and you are Second. Do not think I am blind to this."

"Paranoia is a human malady, Cousin Brother," Oomal said gravely. "You should add it to your list of diseases. As Conscience I thought you might need to hear that."

Tali pivoted on his heel and marched out of the room.

When he had left, Oomal said irritably, "Get up, Reen. Get off the floor, damn it! Take a bath. I have work to do." Then he slammed out the door.

In the bathroom Reen stripped off his uniform and lowered

himself into the water. There he sat, heartsick, knowing that Oomal still loved him but would never forgive him.

When he had sloughed off the coating of sleep, he dressed in a fresh uniform, and after a moment's thought pinned his nametag to his tunic. Then he walked into the study, the one room in the White House where Jeff Womack had always said he felt comfortable.

Reen didn't feel comfortable there. He went past the strip of bare carpet padding and out into the cold wind on the Truman balcony. An itchy sort of need crawled his spine. If sleep was drink to Cousins, work was food. Reen was hungry for something to do. He walked back through the warmth of the oval study and down the grand staircase to the colonnade.

It was as though an invasion had begun in the executive offices. Cousins were everywhere, striding purposefully down the halls, stacks of paper in their hands. They passed Reen without a glance. An unfamiliar Cousin was perched behind Natalie's desk. And in the Oval Office, Reen saw with bitter shock, Tali stood conversing with the Sleep Master and Thural.

For a heartbeat the conversation paused. Of the three, only Thural's gaze flickered as Reen entered and sat on one of the loveseats.

"We will bring the law to bear on him," the Sleep Master was saying, eyeing Tali so hard that Reen imagined he was fighting not to let his eyes slip to Reen.

"Do not be stupid," Tali shot back. "If he has other Cousins here, his sleep may be uncomfortable but not impossible. They slept last night, apparently. Oomal has learned many things in Michigan, Cousin. And one of them is how to do without the Community."

"A dangerous precedent," the Sleep Master agreed. "For without the Community, what are Cousins? And how chaotic may such lives become?"

Tali looked down at the presidential seal woven into the thick wool carpet. "The humans infect us. I believe it is time to cleanse this place. I will tell the Guardians to prepare the viruses."

Reen jumped to his feet. Only Thural's calm voice stopped him from launching himself at his Brother. "You are not so much in the law as that, Cousin, to order such a thing. After all, you are no First. There are others, like me, who will refuse you."

"Back to the ship," Tali commanded.

"I think I will stay. You have a gift for avoiding witnesses, and you have too great a love of secrets. I wonder what you would talk about if I left the room. And I wonder where you went last night alone when the rest of the Cousins were settled into their niches."

Tali gasped. He whirled on Thural. "Back to the ship!"

Thural didn't move. It seemed to Reen that the Cousin was scarcely breathing.

"Didn't you hear me?" Tali screamed, the fury in his voice surprising even the Sleep Master, who stepped away from the pair.

"Kill me, then," Thural said quietly, "as you once led my Brother Jonis to slaughter. Kill me so that all the Community will know you are *tulmade,* and Oomal can take your place."

"Enough of this," the Sleep Master hissed from his refuge against the wall. "The sickness of disobedience has fevered us. You, Tali, must accept the charges of your Cousin, for he heard the wrong that the human Hopkins admitted to. And you, Thural, must forgive Tali."

Slowly, slowly, Thural turned to the Sleep Master. The light from the French doors glinted in his eyes, making them seem less flesh than obsidian. "Have someone with clean hands point the way, then. Give me a First I can follow, and I will study forgiveness. The mother that spewed forth these Brothers was cursed, and she laid the germs of her insanity in them. Two Brothers as murderers. Perhaps if we breed the female, we will find that our seed is not barren but warped, and we will father a generation of killers. Ask him yourself, Sleep Master. Ask why he left the Cousin Place last night alone with three Loving Helpers."

From Tali's throat came a snarl of rage. He seized a vase from an end table and, before the Sleep Master could stop him, hurled it at Thural's chest. The thin porcelain shattered with a bang. Amazement on his face, Thural staggered into a loveseat.

The Cousin in the secretary's office came rushing in to stare aghast at the shards of china that littered the floor.

"Are you all right?" the Sleep Master asked in a horrified voice.

Shakily, Thural grabbed the arm of the sofa and pulled himself upright. "Yes. I think so."

"It is best that you rest now," the Sleep Master suggested.

Thural gave a weak nod.

"When your rest is over, the world will look better."

Thural's expression suggested strongly that he doubted that. Tali's secretary backed cautiously from the room. After a pause to gather his composure, Thural left, too.

When they were gone, Tali said, "Thural goes too far."

"Silence," the Sleep Master said. "And watch yourself, Tali-ja. I back you because you know the law, but I begin to see that for you the law is a surface thing. Perhaps Thural is right. Perhaps there was something wrong with the eggs in your batch. I warn you now: Break the law again, and you will find yourself a ghost like your Brother."

Tali looked thoughtfully at the Sleep Master as the old Cousin stalked out. From the anteroom Reen heard the tap-tap of clumsy Cousin hands on a keyboard, the quiet murmur of voices.

"Have you ever stuck a stick into an ant bed, Cousin Brother?" Reen asked quietly.

Tali walked over to the French doors and pulled back the sheers.

"That is what you have done," Reen told his Brother's back.

Somewhere in a neighboring office a phone rang, and Reen heard the high, clear, enchanting sound of a human laugh.

"You are stirring the stick, Cousin Brother. Ants, when disturbed, will sting. I have a piece of advice for you: Learn to love chaos, for you will be surrounded by it now."

When Reen left a few minutes later, Tali was still staring wordlessly out at the Rose Garden.

30

REEN WANDERED THE WEST WING UN-
til he wearied of being ignored, then went down to the main building
for lunch.

The pantry was a cozy, utilitarian room with an old kitchen table
in the center and cabinets all around. As Reen walked in, he found
the butler and Jeremy Holt having brunch. The burly black chief of
the serving staff popped the last of his omelette into his mouth, swallowed, and asked Reen, "Lunch, sir?"

"Yes," Reen said, looking at the new President, who was toying
with his coffee cup.

"Where do you want me to serve you, sir?"

The President spoke. From the broad Bostonian *a*'s Reen could
hear that he was dealing with Kennedy and not the medium. "Serve
him in here, ah, Kevin, if you will. It's always good to have a little
company with lunch."

"Yes, sir. Yes, it sure is." The butler wiped his mouth with his
napkin and rose, taking his empty plate with him to the kitchen.

In the ensuing and prickly silence, Reen sat.

Kennedy said, "Your, ah, Brother seems to have moved into
the Oval Office. I take that as a sign you're out of favor. Am I
right?"

"As I recall, that was one of your most annoying habits—always being right."

"There were a few glaring exceptions." Kennedy sliced the remains of his Denver omelette into fussy strips. "Anyway, I notice your Brother has taken over with a dexterity that must have come from careful planning. Always be cautious of people who are prepared, Reen," Kennedy lectured, one eyebrow cocked. "Beware of Boy Scouts."

"I thought you'd never want to talk to me again," Reen said.

Somehow Jeremy's mousy features arranged themselves into Kennedy's brilliant smile. "Oh, I learned a few things on the other side."

"Like forgiveness?"

Kennedy threw his head back and laughed. "No, no. I mean, I found out who to blame."

Fascinated, Reen asked, "Who? My Brother?"

A tired shake of his head. "No. J. Edgar. He suckered you, Reen. Hoover told you I tried to have you assassinated, didn't he?"

"Yes, that's why—"

"Don't apologize," Kennedy said curtly. "When I was President, you didn't understand humans very well. Or politics. I'm not angry with you for murdering me. Hoover was a master manipulator. But I wish you hadn't murdered my brother."

Brothers again, Reen thought as he watched Kennedy refill his cup from the silver pot. In the world of Brothers it was perfectly understandable that Jack would forgive Reen for killing him yet still resent his murdering Robert. In the world of Brothers, Oomal would protect Reen because he hated Tali more.

"So you're saying you *didn't* plan to assassinate me," Reen said.

"I don't know why you were so gullible as to think I'd try."

Gullible. Odd, Reen thought, how he believed in his own keen insight, and others thought him naive. "You plotted against Castro. Hoover told us that, and he had proof. He said you wanted to control everything: Cuba and Russia and the Cousins. He told us you wanted to get rid of Khrushchev and me, too. You were dangerous. At least that's how Hoover explained it. Personally, I had no interest in killing your brother, but Hoover insisted on a trade."

It struck Reen that he knew where Tali had learned some of his trickery. Not from Hopkins. And not all from Hoover. Some of it came from Reen himself.

Kennedy seemed amused. "I told you Hoover played you for a sucker. Think about it. It made sense to assassinate Castro. Castro was a one-man band. Khrushchev, on the other hand, was an orchestra. Kill Khrushchev, and I'd have the whole politburo to deal with. And what sense would it have made to assassinate you? I'd stop the woodwinds, maybe, but the strings would only play louder. Action in politics has to make sense."

The butler came out of the kitchen with a plate of finger sandwiches and fresh fruit.

Reen speared a slice of melon, then put it down, uneaten.

"The Senate is up in arms," Kennedy said.

Reen gave him a questioning look.

"Womack had two more years to his term. That even makes the Democrats uncomfortable. In spite of my assurances, the Senate feels the country is adrift. Partially your fault, you know, for urging the passage of the unlimited term amendment. Fifty-one years of Womack. Fifty-one years. The people can't imagine another president. Ah, well. If you'll excuse me, I have a state funeral to arrange."

When Kennedy left, Reen took a couple of finger sandwiches and ate them as he made his way upstairs.

The maids had been in the oval study. The surface of Womack's scarred table was agleam with lemon oil. Fresh flowers had been set out: chrysanthemums and hothouse roses. Reen went into the next room.

The bed was rumpled, the floor cluttered. His uniform still lay on the bathroom floor. As he bent to pick it up, his claw clicked on something in the pocket.

Marian's tape.

He took the cassette out, went to the oval study again, and closed the door to the hall. In the cabinet of the bar he found a tape recorder, the one Womack had been using to dictate the eighteenth volume of his autobiography. Popping the cassette out with his claw, Reen replaced Jeff's tape with Marian's.

He turned on the recorder. From the speaker came the squeak of a chair, the empty hiss of white noise. Then, "Do you know why the President has called the press conference?"

The words were distorted, but Reen recognized the voice. It was Tali.

A tap-tap-tap. Someone rapping out a rhythm on wood. A pen against a desktop?

"No idea."

Superstitious horror made Reen nearly drop the recorder: Hopkins's voice was so clear. The man must have been sitting much closer to the mike. "The Speaker says there's gossip that Womack will spring some surprise on Congress tomorrow. Doesn't know what it is yet, but he says not to worry. Platt's dense but malleable. I've told him to take care of it. He will. We hit Womack, anyway. You bring the Helpers in and put them on Security Chief Landis. It can't be one of my men. I want Landis to pull the trigger, you understand?"

"We do not need the Loving Helpers. It is dangerous to bring them into the building. I am afraid one of the other Cousins might see. Besides, the suggestion has already been implanted, and the man is under my control. I will say the word, and he will do anything I ask."

"Bring the Helpers," Hopkins said.

A sigh.

"So. It's all decided. And the kidnapping's set up. A few minutes from now my men will snatch Reen, take him out to Camp David, and bury him with Jonis." A pause. Then Hopkins said slyly, "That's what you want, isn't it?"

Tali made a small throaty sound. "It is not what I wish. It is simply what must happen. Reen-ja is wrong about many things. And he lacks the morality to lead. But this decision about Womack is different. It is a human one. I have done as you requested. I have put Landis under control. I do not wish to know what you do with my Brother. And I do not wish to watch what happens to the President. These violent matters are disturbing to me. I will give the order, I promise you, but other than that . . ."

Hopkins's laugh was rich and careless and vibrant, nothing like the laugh of a dead man. "No. I want *you* to do it. I want you to bring the Helpers in, and I want you there when Landis blows Womack's brains out. Otherwise I'll see the Community gets all the evidence I have. They'd be shocked, don't you think, to learn how you traded Womack's assassination for the murder of your Brother?"

The angry squeal of a chair, a thump.

"Sit down. You're not going anywhere," Hopkins said calmly. "I have copies of that evidence salted all over Washington. And an interrogation session with the Helpers isn't going to help, so don't even think about it. Sit down. Sit down!"

The chair squeaked again. Tali's voice was plaintive, hurt. He hardly sounded like himself. "You told me J. Edgar Hoover was your hero. That's why I had Reen appoint you. That's why I trusted you enough not to use an implant. Hoover would never do such a thing to me."

"Tough shit." Then in a conversational tone Hopkins said, "Tomorrow."

"All right." Tali's voice seethed. It sounded like Tali again. "Tomorrow."

Reen started, hearing footsteps in the hall. Quickly he turned off the recorder and slipped it into his pocket. The footsteps continued down the hall to the elevator. Just the Secret Service. Or one of the staff.

Taking out the recorder, Reen held it in his hand. Marian was right. This was all the proof he needed. He would go to the Oval Office and confront Tali and the Sleep Master. The Sleep Master wouldn't listen to Reen, but he couldn't ignore the tape.

He hurried out of the oval study, ran down the steps and through the colonnade. He passed a Cousin typing in the reception area and threw open the Oval Office doors.

The room was empty.

Reen whirled to the Cousin secretary, set the recorder on his desk. "Listen. I know you are not allowed to hear me, but listen." Reen punched the REWIND button, fumbled for the PLAY. From the speaker the squeak of a chair, a thump, Hopkins saying, "Sit down. You're not going anywhere . . ." And Tali's injured response.

The Cousin never paused in his typing.

"Listen to it!" Reen shouted.

REWIND. PLAY. Tali: ". . . put Landis under control. I do not wish to know what you do . . ."

Picking up a pile of papers, the Cousin walked from the office. He never looked back.

Reen sat on the edge of the desk, looked at the recorder, tapped a defeated, listless finger on the buttons, REWIND, PLAY. ". . . snatch Reen, take him out to Camp David . . ."

STOP.

Sighing, he looked through the open doors and saw that in the Oval Office the portrait of Millard Fillmore was crooked.

A quick three-step throb of his heart. Stuffing the recorder into his pocket, he walked into the office, pulled a chair up next to the fireplace, and checked behind the painting.

The manila envelope was still there. Reen, in his haste, had left the portrait awry.

As he pried the envelope from its hiding place, a slip of paper dropped from the open end. He picked it up: that nine-digit number.

What could it be? It was about the right length for a bank account but one number too short for Social Security.

7039713991.

703. The first three digits leaped from the page, and the picture fell into place. There were no dashes to indicate area code and exchange, but it was obviously a phone number. A phone number in Fairfax County, Virginia.

Reen walked to the telephone and dialed. There was a pause as the circuits clicked through, then a shadowy, faraway ring.

For some nonsensical reason he thought of the Old Ones. Oomal had said Jeff was setting up an AT&T long-distance line with the Old Ones. For an instant Reen had the absurd thought that the Old Ones had rented a house in Fairfax County, and Jeff had found out about it.

Ring.

A nice house. The Old Ones would rent a nice house. A traditional Fairfax County place with red brick and white trim and a pretty garden.

Another ring.

They'd have flowers, a few trees, and maybe a springer spaniel. Heritage would demand it.

Click. The sound of the receiver being picked up. "National Wildlife Federation," a female voice chirped.

Reen hung up. The National Wildlife Federation?

He left the Oval Office and went to the East Wing to find Oomal.

31

Oomal was in an office barking into a phone. He looked and sounded more like a leader than Reen or Tali ever had.

"Goddamn it!" his Brother was shouting. "I don't give a flying fuck *how* the bugs got into the macaroni! We have a warehouse full of weevils, and we're not feeding them to one-year-olds! You come—no, no, *you* come and take that macaroni out of our warehouse. You—I'm not finished. No, Cousins don't have some magic wand that makes weevils—no. Hey, but I have a team of lawyers with twelve-inch dicks. What? Watch me. I said *watch me!*"

Oomal slammed the phone down so hard that it gave a broken-piano complaint. "What do you want?" he snapped at Reen, who was standing, a penitent, in front of his desk, Womack's envelope in one hand and the recorder in the other.

The phone rang again.

"*What?*" Oomal screamed into the receiver. Abruptly his face and his tone softened. "Yeah, Jerry. Sorry, I . . . Right, uh huh. Burn the production records. Trust me. Just trust me on this. . . . No, nothing's going on. Just tell the reporters you don't have any comment other than what I said at the press conference. What? No, no. Of course I wasn't making it up. The birthrate's just going into a little dip.

It's nothing to worry about. . . . Come on, Jer. Have I ever lied to you? No. . . . No need to apologize. Just— Yeah. I appreciate this."

He hung up, this time softly, and sat staring into space.

The official photo of Jeff Womack, taken during his first term, smiled down impishly from its perch on the wall. Hurriedly, Reen slipped the recorder back into his pocket, hoping Oomal hadn't seen. He had been wrong to play the tape for Tali's secretary. The truth was a responsibility he now wished he didn't have.

Tali's treachery was merely his way of following in his big Brother's steps. Reen and Hoover taught him how to use assassination and deceit.

Oomal wiped his hands down his cheeks. "Well. Have you seen the front page of the *Post*?" He shoved the paper across the desk.

Reen glanced at the top half of the front page. More about Womack's suicide. A piece on the birthrate. He flipped the paper over and looked below the fold.

INDICTMENT SOUGHT IN KENNEDY ASSASSINATION

WASHINGTON, D.C.—The Justice Department is looking into allegations that the White House chief of staff may be implicated in the November 22, 1963, death of President John Fitzgerald Kennedy.

"We have talked to the President, and he is disinclined to pursue the matter," Ted Rice, Justice Department Special Prosecutor, said in an interview with the *Post* today. "But this is not a civil case, and there is no statute of limitations on murder. The Justice Department feels that there is cause to bring charges of criminal conspiracy before a grand jury."

President Kennedy/Holt could not be reached for comment.

"Murder?" Reen said in a weak voice. "I'm going to be accused of murder?"

"Not that story. Forget about that story. I'm talking about the one that's not there. The Hopkins piece. He had a maid. Why didn't the maid report the body?"

Because that's where Tali went last night. He went to get Hopkins's evidence, didn't find it, and then hid Hopkins's body to buy himself more time.

Hopkins had been a good teacher.

Oomal sat back and linked his hands across his belly. "What's that you're carrying around?"

Reen stiffened, then realized his Brother wasn't asking about the recorder. "Oh. Jeff's envelope? I found the National Wildlife Federation's phone number in it."

Oomal sat forward. "Let me see," he said, taking the envelope from Reen. He thumbed through the pages, pausing momentarily to wince at the autopsy photo. Then: "This one? This 703 number?"

"Yes."

"I keep getting the feeling that the other shoe is about to drop. And I keep wondering why the humans who know about the sterilization haven't talked. Maybe this will give us a clue." Oomal pressed a button on his intercom. "Zoomer? Come see me." His face pensive, he asked Reen, "Where's Marian Cole gone off to, Brother?"

Reen stared at Oomal, Oomal the Conscience, Oomal who was burdened now with upholding the law. "I don't know."

"You have to know, Reen. I know you know."

Zoor's entrance saved Reen from answering.

"Zoomer," Oomal said, getting to his feet. "Round up two or three Helpers and meet us at the ship."

Reen's heart sank. He followed his Brother's quick stride from the East Wing and to one of the small Michigan commuter ships. "Why do you suspect Marian?" Reen asked.

"We did a fly-by of the entire border of China. There were no troops massed there. If there were no troops, Reen, and if Womack signed the tariff bill, what are those tanks doing still stationed in front of the White House?"

Reen looked at the fence. The soldiers were staring at them. The cannons of the tanks were pointed at the street, but they could just as easily be turned. They could . . .

"Just before Hopkins died," Oomal went on, "he was trying to tell us something. Something about Marian. And she got rid of her competition very conveniently, don't you think? We go to Camp David, and Kapavik's already dead. She tells you Hopkins is behind it all, and you kill Hopkins before he can tell his side."

Reen tore his anxious gaze from the tanks. "His side? We know Hopkins's side. He admitted it. You heard him. We all heard him."

The door of the ship spread open, and Oomal threw himself into the navigation seat, leaving Reen to crawl around him to the back. "I heard him admit to killing Womack and Jonis. That's all I heard. He never said he kidnapped the others. Besides, if Marian was so worried about what Hopkins was doing, why didn't she just come out and tell you earlier?"

"Maybe she was frightened," Reen said miserably as he watched Zoor herd three Loving Helpers out the door and across the lawn to the ship.

"That doesn't solve the problem of why the humans haven't talked. Or why the other Cousins were kidnapped. Come on, come on, Zoomer," Oomal said anxiously under his breath.

"Maybe Hopkins kidnapped the Cousins to put more pressure on Tali, Cousin Brother."

The Helpers began to file into the ship, taking their places behind Reen. When Zoor got into his seat, Oomal jerked the command ball upward, and the ship shot into the air.

"You don't believe that," Oomal replied.

No, Reen didn't believe that. But in the press of other dilemmas he had put the problem of the kidnappings out of his mind.

"It was a good thing that you saved Marian from Tali," Oomal went on. "If he killed her, we'd never learn the whole truth. But we'll have to talk to her sooner or later, and when that time comes, I want you to tell me where I can find her. And don't lie to me, okay? You know that frequency like a human baby knows its mother's breast. And when I ask for it, I want you to give me that frequency, understand?"

Reen watched the noon traffic on Route 50. The spidery winter trees of the Virginia countryside flashed by. He had always said he would kill Marian if she proved too dangerous, but he had lied to the Community. He had lied to himself. "I took the transmitter out of her two years ago."

"What?" Oomal tore his eyes from the controls to glare at Reen. "You did what?"

Zoor flung himself across Oomal and righted the ship before it could dive.

"There was no sense in keeping it in her. Angela was a viable embryo."

"Goddamned Marian was the CIA director! You made her CIA director, Cousin Brother! And you thought it would be a nice idea to let her walk around unsupervised?"

"Watch where you're flying, Oomal," Zoor said quietly. "Can you just watch where you're flying?"

Oomal took back the controls and looked out the window. "We passed it. We're halfway to fucking West Virginia. Shit on a stick." He jerked the ship around so fast that the angle overrode the baffles. Reen was flung into a wall with a thump.

They flew to the National Wildlife Federation in silence and didn't speak as the ship settled into the parking lot beside the red-brick building.

The Cousins left the Helpers on board and went up the long sweeping concrete ramp to the entrance. In the huge lobby two receptionists sat behind a doughnut-shaped desk where two young raccoons were playing.

"May I help you?" one of the women asked while a raccoon went through her Rolodex with its quick, inquisitive fingers.

Reen found himself staring at the bandit eyes, the furry banded tails. It looked as if the animals had been placed there as part of the Wildlife Federation decor.

"The director, please," Oomal told her in a no-nonsense tone.

Near the second receptionist, the second raccoon had managed to pull out a drawer and was trying to fit its body between the hanging files.

The first receptionist whispered into the phone, then turned brightly to Oomal. "He's on his way."

A thud from the drawer. The raccoon had apparently gained entrance. Neither receptionist paid any attention to the animals, as if the raccoons, like Reen himself, were sentenced to invisibility.

People sat on chairs lined up near the windows. A man who looked like a farmer waited next to a cardboard box that periodically made a mewling sound. A housewife sat holding a plaster cast of a hoof.

"Good afternoon!" a boisterous bass voice said. Making his way across the carpet, hand out, was a friendly looking bald man in a dark suit. "I'm Ralph Gunnerson. What can I do for you?"

Oomal stepped forward and shook the man's hand. "You can tell us why the National Wildlife Federation's number was found in papers that belonged to a murder victim."

Gunnerson's rosy skin went pale from cheek to scalp. "I think," he said, licking his lips nervously, "we'd better talk in private."

The Cousins followed the director through a room of secretaries. In the back of the building Gunnerson ushered them into a large paneled conference room and sank into a raspberry-colored velour chair. "First off," he said, "you have to guarantee all of us protection. All our wives, all our kids."

Reen kept silent. Across the table from him, Zoor sat mystified.

"Promise me," Gunnerson urged. "You have to promise."

Oomal nodded.

Gunnerson passed an unsteady hand over his forehead. "Look. We're dedicated to animals. Everyone here loves animals. It's a job requirement. I get choked up when I see a bald eagle. I've seen one of our staff bawl when someone brought in a wounded deer." He stopped, as though either afraid or ashamed to go on.

Oomal said gently, "Continue, Mr. Gunnerson."

"It was the men." The director picked at a nail.

"What men?" Reen asked.

"I don't know. I don't know who they were. They wanted animals. You see how people bring in wild animals. They bring them in all the time. I don't know why. It's not like we're a zoo. But we never turn an animal away. We've had coyotes, rattlesnakes, you name it. If they're hurt, we patch them up. If they're sick, we tend to them until they're well. Then we take them back to the wild and let them go."

The director picked at the nail until he brought up a bead of crimson blood.

"The men," Oomal prompted.

Gunnerson's head bobbed. "They wanted wild animals. I told them no. I started getting phone calls late at night. Threatening calls. They harassed my wife at work. At the store. It got so she was afraid to go out. They followed my children. . . ." His lower lip trembled. Tears gathered in his eyes. "They . . ." His voice lowered. "They raped one of our assistants."

"You don't know who they were?" Reen asked after a decorous pause.

"No. But they came every day to see if we had animals. If we had any, they'd take them. I had to give up the animals. You can see that, can't you? I was responsible for my staff. I couldn't let anybody else be hurt. Then one day, about three years ago, the men stopped coming. About four months after the men left, I found a bug in my office. It was poorly hidden, so I'm sure I was supposed to find it. A reminder not to talk. When AT&T installed our new phone system last year, they said there were indications that someone was tapping our lines. I don't know what the men did with the animals, but I imagine . . ." His voice trailed off, and he swallowed hard.

Oomal asked, "When did these men start taking your animals?"

"Five—no, six years ago. It started six years ago."

"Do you have any idea who they are?"

Gunnerson let his breath out in a sigh. His body sagged. "You might ask the SPCA. One of our receptionists came from there, and after the men stopped coming to us, she said the SPCA started having problems with them, too."

32

AT THE FAIRFAX COUNTY SPCA A well-dressed woman filled out forms at a counter while on the other side stood a lanky young man with a beard and ponytail. The building stank of disinfectant. A cacophony of muffled yips and meows came from behind double doors.

Run, Reen thought suddenly. *We should run as far and as fast as we can. Because what we find out here won't be about Tali and Hopkins at all but about something else. Something I don't want to know.*

The two people looked up as the Cousins entered.

"The director, please," Oomal said.

The young man behind the counter indolently scratched his cheek. "You don't want to adopt, do you? I mean, I don't know that we could clear that."

The woman wore an expensive fake fur, and she was eyeing Reen analytically and somewhat contemptuously, as if Reen were a mangy prospective pet.

"We want to speak with the director." Oomal snapped his finger on his claw. "Now."

Suddenly the double doors burst open, and a petite young woman in an apron came through, holding the collar of a golden retriever.

When the dog saw the Cousins, he staggered back a few feet in astonishment and then, perhaps considering some aspect of canine integrity, lunged forward. The dog had a bark that made the walls tremble.

The girl held on. "Down!" she shouted. The dog paid her no heed.

Reen, the closest to the dog, shrank from the yellow snapping teeth, the frantic scrabbling of claws on linoleum, and the harsh panting as the animal strained against its collar.

"Harry," the girl said in exasperation.

Harry opened a swing latch in the counter and sauntered out to the dog.

"Door to the right," he said over his shoulder.

Oomal and Zoor fled through the steel doorway, Reen not far behind.

On a dusty cabinet in the main office of the SPCA a phone was ringing. The two typists in the room paid no attention to it.

"The director?" Oomal asked.

A typist looked up from her ancient Selectric, a myopic editor's frown on her face. "Go on back," she said, jerking her head in that direction.

The Cousins made their way past a mountain of dog food that sandbagged one side of the room. To the left of the Purina was an unassuming door, the kind that might lead to a bathroom or mop closet. Behind it was a scarred metal desk and a pile of manila folders paperweighted by a slumbering calico cat. And behind the folders was an impressive battleship of a woman, who said, "What the hell do you want?" in a voice not unlike the retriever's.

Awakened, the cat gave the Cousins a sleepy double take, then leaped off the folders, scattering the top two inches of the stack onto the threadbare carpet. The cat vanished, a streak of white, black, and russet, into a dark back room.

That's how I should run, Reen thought. *I should run as though all the nightmares humans ever dreamed were at my heels.*

Oomal took the only available chair, a cheap steel and plastic thing. "Somebody's been threatening you. They've been taking animals."

The woman blinked. "Lots of animals. Hundreds of animals. You going to get the bastards?"

"Who are they?" Oomal asked.

"Russians," the woman said. She leaned back in her chair and laced her hands across a generous belly. "Germans. A few Latin Americans."

Reen asked, "How can you be so sure?"

She gave him a sour smile. "Got a master's in linguistics. They speak English well enough, but I can tag 'em. I can always tag 'em."

"They still come around?" Oomal asked.

"Not for a couple of days. So you know who they are?"

"Yes," he said quietly.

"They're doing experiments on the animals, aren't they?"

"I think so."

"Castration's too good," she said by way of suggestion.

The Cousins left. In the secretarial area the phone was still ringing, but the dog and the fake-furred woman had disappeared from the lobby. Under the stares of the girl and the ponytailed man, the Cousins exited and made their way to the ship.

"So you know who's been taking the animals?" Reen asked his Brother.

The ship's door spread open in welcome. Zoor took a wordless seat in the back. Reen sat next to Oomal.

"The CIA," Oomal said.

Apprehension crawled, dainty-footed and insectile, up Reen's spine. "How can you be sure?"

"Because," Oomal said as the ship lifted into clear, bright air, "when the consolidation hit, the CIA merged with the KGB, North Korean intelligence, and every thug in every crappy little police state south of the American border. I know who's been taking those animals because I know the FBI is xenophobic. The FBI has stayed as all-American as goddamned apple pie."

Reen remembered Hopkins's accusation of Marian at the last NSC meeting. *Start investigating at Langley.* Too bad that Reen had not believed him until it was too late.

Twenty-eight of the Community, both Loving Helpers and Cousins, had been kidnapped— and it all started the same time the confiscation of animals at the SPCA began.

33

CIA HEADQUARTERS, TUCKED BE-
tween parks on the west and the Potomac on the north, looked more
imposing from the ground than from the air. In fact, flying in low
from the northwest, Reen could hardly see the massive installation
until the ship was nearly on top of it.

As they approached, Zoor said, "There's nobody in the guard-
house."

"I know." Oomal's voice was tense.

Reen studied the rolling tree-studded lawn of the complex. No
one moved on the walkways. No one was outside to catch the last
gleam of the Indian summer sun.

And the parking lot was empty.

Oomal settled the ship on the lawn. "Get the Loving Helpers,
Zoomer."

The Cousins and Helpers climbed out and walked through the
porte cochere to the huge brick building. The lobby was brightly lit.
No guard sat at the station; no receptionist sat at the desk. The building was so silent that Reen could hear the whisper of air through
heating ducts and the far, faint hum of a PC.

The corridor was a deserted river of beige carpet banded by sun
slanting from western windows. Somewhere in the bowels of the

building a phone was ringing. Ringing. In the SPCA, the ringing had been part of the din. Here, it was a hammer tapping against brittle silence.

The three halted before a red EXIT sign. The phone rang again.

"Let's not get on the elevators. No telling what traps they've set up." Oomal opened the steel door, and they entered the stairwell.

As Reen mounted the first step, Oomal snagged his sleeve. Reen turned and saw a look of determined, fearful intensity, as though Oomal were an exorcist about to enter a haunted house. "Downstairs."

Oomal was right. Downstairs. When humans wanted to hide something, they went to basements. They went to ground.

No one spoke. The only sound in the stairwell was the slippery, soft steps of booted feet, the feathery echoes of breathing. At the bottom, in a pool of shadows, Zoor fumbled for the knob.

"Do you hear something?" Oomal asked, holding out his hand to stop them.

Reen froze. In the dim light he could see Zoor's eyes move back and forth as though searching by sight for the noise.

"No," Reen said at last. He grasped the knob and opened the door into fluorescent brilliance.

The fourth level of the basement was a rabbit warren of offices, all empty. A door to the right was open, and on its painted steel surface were the words CLEAN ROOM. Reen walked inside. The telexes were silent, their power lights off. On a small table sat a red phone, its receiver a foot or so away. A persistent waa-waa came from the speaker, the Chesapeake Bay Bell reminder that the phone was off the hook.

Reen heard Oomal's faint "Reen? Come here."

Someone had slipped a tumbler into a door marked RESTRICTED, and it was standing ajar. Past the security-card access was a long linoleum hall where Oomal stood. Reen made his way down the corridor to his Brother and looked at an office plaque. At first the name didn't register. Nothing registered. Not the implications of it, not his Brother standing next to him. Then Reen's head started to pound.

DR. HOWARD FRANKLIN, PROJECT SUPERVISOR

"He was working for the CIA, too," Oomal said. "Working for them the whole time, and she never told you. Now you know who was important to her and why, Cousin Brother. Now you see—"

A muffled cry.

"Zoor?" Oomal called.

"Here, Cousin! Here! It's . . ."

Oomal hurried toward Zoor's voice, Reen lagging behind. The corridor led to a huge room that held the earthy stench of a zoo. Under the stench was a cloying odor, sweet and at the same time metallic.

This room, like the SPCA, must once have rung with barks and plaintive questioning meows. Now it was silent. Dead animals lay in their screen cages, forlorn bits of bloodied fluff. A thick crimson sea, just beginning to congeal to black, ran down the sloping floor to a center drain. The Helpers, oblivious, stood in the pool of blood, amidst the carnage. Zoor, his face anguished, was trying to call them to higher, cleaner ground.

"Why kill the animals?" Zoor asked. "They've been shot, all of them. Why do this? It doesn't make sense!"

Oomal rushed back to Howard's office, Reen at his heels, pleading silently for them to leave now.

Oomal rounded the doorway at a dead run and began frantically flipping through papers. He jerked open a credenza drawer, sending it tumbling, spilling accordianed computer printouts and staplers and rolls of masking tape. The heavy drawer hit the floor with a crash.

"You had to take her into your confidence, didn't you? Goddamn it, Reen." Oomal booted Howard's computer.

The expression in his eyes was wild, savage, nearly human. "It crashed! See? They left in a hurry, but Howard had time to run a viral program to wipe the hard drive clean! They knew we'd come."

"Oomal?" Zoor called. "I found something."

In the empty hall, sticky red footprints tracked messily on the shiny linoleum, across a threshold, and over the beige carpet in the next room. It might have been a conference room anywhere but for the crimson prints on its carpet, and Zoor and the Helpers standing there. Twelve plush aqua chairs were placed equidistantly on either side of an oak table. Charts and graphs lined the walls, and in one corner stood a television hooked to a VCR.

Oomal halted at Reen's shoulder. He was breathing hard. "Onset of Death," he read from the top of the nearest graph. "Goddamn her."

He lunged to the television, turned it on, and hit the VCR's PLAY.

Snow. A long minute of snow. Then on the screen Hans Krupner was peering directly at them, his face distorted by the fish-eye lens. His eyes too round, too wide, and his balding head Cousin-bulbous.

His voice was distorted, too, garbled by terror and by the echoes in the bare room. "Marian? Marian? I know you are angry with me, yes?"

What sort of room was it? Tiny, windowless, more like a closet. The walls were seamless gray metal. At the bottom of the television screen was a series of red numbers: 00:00:00.

Like a digital clock set to time a race.

Krupner turned. Two paces, and he was at the back wall. "*Gott*," he whispered.

Two agitated steps. He was pleading into the camera again. "Please. What was so important about the fax, Marian? You are the one who told me to feed the German ministry information. You remember, yes? So they would not become suspicious I was a double agent? And I was fired! I could not help that I was fired! Sent back to Germany. And the ministry wanted something. A little something, Marian. It was just a small item I found. Something amusing. Nothing of importance. You were the one who said——"

A loud clang. At the left of the screen, a door opened. Two men with sticks herded a Loving Helper into the room.

"Zoor! Get the Helpers out of here!"

Oomal's curt order jerked Reen's attention from the TV.

"Take them down the hall. Quick!"

On the screen the abandoned Helper shrieked its loneliness. It charged the open door, the men. Its Brothers must have been just beyond, close enough to smell them. Nothing but longing could have made it that desperate.

A prod from a stick. A bacon-fat sizzle. A short-circuit *zzzt* as voltage hit flesh. The Helper squealed, staggered backward, turning in frantic circles to escape the pain.

Eyeing the Helper, the men backed out. The door closed with clanging finality. Krupner sat down in a corner, hugged his legs, and eyed the Helper, too.

Pain now forgotten, the Loving Helper stopped spinning. It faced the door expectantly, as if it were a compass needle and its unseen Brothers magnetic north.

00:00:01

The red numerals began clicking off tenths of seconds, time unrolling with dizzy speed.

00:02:39

Something was wrong with the Helper. It scratched urgently at its throat.

00:04:21

A spasm sent arms and legs flailing.

Krupner got to his feet, clamping hands over the bottom of his face. He was breathing in hard, jerky pants. Above the cage of his fingers, his eyes were demented, luminous, as if terror were burning him inside-out.

00:06:03

Blood leaked from the edges of the Helper's eyes. A mad chatter from the television speaker, the sound of the Helper's claws against the metal floor.

00:08:42

The Helper's mouth bubbled blood. The feet twitched, then were still.

00:10:31

And Krupner was alive. He was sitting in a corner, body tucked into a small ball.

Reen jumped at the abruptness of the white-noise hiss as the picture changed to snow.

With a blow of his fist Oomal turned off the television. "Goddamn her."

Reen caught his arm. "Let's go now, Oomal."

Oomal shook off the warning claw. Reen pursued him from the conference room, past a confused Zoor, past the animal cages. Oomal slipped on the bloody tiles and fell. He heaved himself upright, uniform wet, hands and cheeks a gelatinous crimson. One savage push on an adjoining olive-green door. It swung open.

And the Helpers with Zoor began to shriek.

"Come see, Cousin Brother," Oomal said. "Come see what Marian was up to."

An immaculate white room. White tile walls, white tile floor. At the center two steel tables. Krupner and the Helper lay on those cold hard beds, their skulls and their chests open.

For all its uncompromising neatness the room had a cluttered look, of things left in haste. A bone saw, still bloody, lay on a table next to Krupner. A scalpel sat forgotten atop the Helper's ruptured chest.

There was a humming in Reen's ears as he watched Oomal walk to a bank of steel cabinets. As he saw him slide open a drawer, saw him peer in.

It was a pleasant room, really. All steel-gray and white. The ordered squares of the tiles and the larger squares of the cabinets all fitted perfectly. Like fractals. Even the autopsy Ys and the clean-edged openings into the skulls had been done with a meticulous hand. Not at all like the ruin of Jeff Womack's head. Or Hopkins's.

Oomal drew back with a gasp, as though something in the drawer had bitten him. His bloody footprints disturbed the pattern of the floor. His bloody palm prints disturbed the pristine surface of the cabinets.

He began pulling out drawers, one after the other. "Damn her!" he shouted. "They're all in here! The room's full of dead Cousins and Helpers!"

The place was so quiet, so antiseptic that Oomal's loud carelessness annoyed Reen. He walked out, his boots making sucking noises in the animals' blood.

Oomal caught up with Reen in the hall near Howard's office.

"Where do you think you're going, Cousin Brother? Are you afraid to see what she's done?"

Reen looked away from the red on the linoleum. The wall was soothing and white, like blank beginnings. Like the potential of paper before it is written on. Like the untrampled snow of West Virginia.

A fierce tug on his arm. "Marian! Marian was the kidnapper!"

Reen's eyes shifted. Zoor was standing at the end of the corridor, the Loving Helpers around him.

"Oomal," Zoor said. "They're still nervous. Something down this way, I think. You'd better come see."

Oomal nearly pulled Reen off his feet. He dragged him, stumbling, behind.

Images in flashes. A door open to a littered office. A paper shredder adrift in a snowfall of confetti. A pressure door. A sign: WARNING—TOXIC GAS. A border of yellow and black stripes, pleasing, systematic stripes, but just the wrong colors.

And a smell, too. Stale sleep. Spice with a hint of decay.

Oomal spun Reen around to face a quiet blue room. Nest blue. In a padded corner two Loving Helpers and a Cousin lay tangled.

"That's how she kept them alive!"

Reen wanted to tell Oomal to shut up, that he would wake the sleepers. So serene, the Helpers and the Cousin, their arms around one another.

Zoor saying, "I left the Helpers by Howard's office. What was it? What made them nervous?"

The three lying so still. A broad dark stripe down the Cousin's head. A splash of brown on the floor, like a check mark or a bird in flight.

"Something must have happened," Oomal was saying. "The agents dropped everything and got out quick. They couldn't take the Helpers and the Cousin, so they shot them, like they shot the animals."

A smudge on a wall like a flower, petals opening. Reen pulled his sleeve from Oomal's grasp and walked toward the exit sign.

"Brother!"

Reen's pace quickened. He started to trot. Wrenching open the door, he hurried up the stairs. By the second floor he was taking the steps two at a time, and when he reached the lobby, he was running.

"Reen!"

Panting, taking air in huge gulping whoops as he ran clumsily past the reception area, toward the sunlight. His legs knew no rhythm, only haste and direction. He burst through the glass and steel entrance and ran across the cement of the porte cochere. Thrashed through a border of flowers. Shouts of concern behind him.

The ship, round and cool and silent, waited on a grassy hummock. He stumbled, tripped, sprawled facedown in the smell of loam, fallen leaves, and the quiet natural death of autumn.

Boots stopped near him. "Brother?" Oomal whispered.

Reen didn't answer. And Oomal waited as blue shadows barred the lawn, as daylight faded to gray, as the first stars began to peer from the violet sky.

Finally Oomal said, "You trusted her too much."

Reen somehow managed to get back on his feet. He dusted his hands. "Don't you think I know?" he said.

34

"WE HAVE TO FIND HER," OOMAL SAID as they walked to the ship. "And we'll use the Loving Helpers this time. It looks as though the CIA perfected that toxin they were working on but didn't have the time to put it into production. Still, we have to make sure."

Reen kept pace with him, his eyes on the grass at his feet. "There's a farm in Virginia," he said. "Fly up Chain Bridge Road to Wolf Trap. I think I might be able to find it again."

In the smoky dusk, lights were going on in houses, and each looked as warm and friendly as home. Marian could have been hiding in any one of them.

The ship flew on in the cold, dim evening.

"Now where?" Oomal asked when they reached Wolf Trap.

"North, I think."

They circled the area for a long time, over dozens of dilapidated barns, hundreds of solitary farmhouses, but nothing looked familiar. They went to Camp Peary, but the CIA farm was deserted.

Oomal gave up around midnight and flew back to the White House. When they landed, he motioned Zoor and the Loving Helpers out, to sit alone in the ship with Reen.

"From the notes I found," Oomal said into the dark silence between them, "the wild animals were a dead end. That's when they started experimenting directly on Cousins. I don't know how this toxin works, Reen, but you saw that it's effective and fast. Tali wants to find Marian, and he's bound to search Langley. When he discovers what the CIA was working on, the Community will panic. They'll order the viruses used."

Ahead, the portico lights bathed a solitary marine guard.

After a moment, Reen reached into his pocket and took out the tape recorder. When Oomal saw the recorder, he cocked his head in mute question.

"Oomal?" Reen asked. "How much is Tali's life worth? Ten humans? A thousand? Thirty billion?"

"I don't understand."

Reen hit the REWIND button, then PLAY. He heard Oomal's gasp at Tali's voice, Oomal's low moan when he realized what Hopkins was saying.

"God, Reen," Oomal said when the tape was finished. "Poor Tali. Murder. Blackmail. I thought *I'd* become too human. I thought you had. But Tali . . . Christ. None of us is really a Cousin anymore."

"You'll be First."

"Tomorrow." Oomal, in his anger, sounded so much like Tali that it startled Reen. "Tomorrow I'll go to Andrews and present this to the Sleep Master."

The White House lawn was dark, with only the fountain lit. Reen could imagine the Old Ones walking there, searching, trying to find where Reen and his Brothers had so carelessly misplaced the Cousin legacy.

"If you know where Marian is, Reen, tell me."

"If I knew, I would."

Oomal climbed out of the ship, Reen following. At the top of the grand staircase, Reen paused.

"Aren't you coming to sleep?" Oomal asked.

"In a moment."

"About what we saw at Langley . . .you're not going to do anything stupid?"

Reen gave his Brother a lopsided smile. "Haven't I always?"

Oomal gazed longingly down the hall toward the promise of sleep. "Look, what happened wasn't your fault. You may have trusted Marian too much, but Tali also trusted Hopkins. It's hard for us to understand human deception. I see it all the time, and even I don't understand it. Suppliers and their lies about the freshness of their produce. Salesmen making overblown claims. They look you right in the eye and lie. It's not—"

"Go ahead and sleep, Oomal. I'll be there in a minute."

Reen watched his Brother turn and make his reluctant way to Jeff Womack's old bedroom. When Oomal was safely inside, Reen went downstairs.

In the pantry one of the staff was sleeping in a chair, his head on the table. At the entrance to the colonnade a dull-eyed Secret Serviceman sat at his desk, watching a bank of monitors.

The White House was as dead as Langley had been.

Reen paused at the entrance to the Green Room. In that plush, silent chamber someone was sitting in a chair by the fireplace, his back to Reen.

Reen entered. It was Jeremy Holt, staring into the cold hearth. The medium looked up. "Oh, hello."

"Who are you tonight?" Reen asked. "Kennedy? Van Cliburn? Rachmaninoff?"

"No," Jeremy said with a shy shrug, as if ducking a blow. "It's just me this time."

"Then why are you sitting in here?" It wasn't a place for the medium. It was Jeff's room. Jeff's chair.

"I got lost," the man said miserably.

Reen sighed and sat down.

"It's a big place, isn't it? The White House, I mean." Jeremy's glasses magnified his pond-brown eyes. "When President Kennedy's here, he knows his way around, but he never bothers to tell me. Do you know where I'm supposed to sleep?"

"The Lincoln bedroom."

"Yes, I know that," he said, regarding a Remington oil without interest. "I know I'm supposed to sleep in the Lincoln bedroom. But I'm not in myself much anymore, and I forget where it is. I went to where I thought it was, but that was a big room with a piano in it."

"The East Room. You needed to go up a floor."

"Oh."

Jeremy was a small man, Reen realized with a stab of pity. A little soul who was easily misplaced. "I'm going upstairs. I'll show you where it is."

The man's face brightened. "Thanks. I'm very tired."

"Just don't come in this room again."

"Is it the laughter?" Jeremy asked.

Halfway to his feet, Reen froze.

"I hear laughter in here sometimes."

"Yes," Reen said. "It's because of the laughter."

They trudged up the steps in silence. At the door to the Lincoln bedroom, Reen said good night.

Jeff Womack's old bedroom smelled of sleep, and in the blue glow from the lamp Reen could see the pea-podded lumps of the Cousins. On the bed he found a sheet laid out for him, and he wrapped himself in it tightly. He fell asleep more easily than he thought possible.

He awoke before dawn and inched himself out of the sheet. Quietly, in order not to wake the others, he crept from the room and into the study next door.

The air was moist and cold on the Truman balcony. Across the Potomac the lights of Arlington shimmered. The sun, just below the eastern terminator, had turned the sky a bruised purple.

"Reen," a voice said.

He turned. The speaker was hidden in shadow, but he knew the voice.

"I was hoping you'd wake up," Marian said. "I kept thinking of you. Is that the way you used to wake me?"

Sunrise began to paint the tip of the Washington Monument lavender.

"I went to Langley," he said.

A yellow flame in a corner of the balcony. The gentle glow cupped Marian's cheek. She lit her cigarette and with a click extinguished the lighter.

That face. He had seen it softened in sleep, contorted with fear. He had seen it grow old. Forty-seven years, and he had never really known her.

"You planted the bomb at Dulles," he said.

She tilted her head and blew a thread of smoke at the ceiling. "Yes."

"You kidnapped Cousins and Helpers, and Howard experimented on them."

She pulled her leather jacket tighter against the moist dawn chill. "Yes."

Reen looked across the lawn. The tops of the tallest trees had netted the morning and were ablaze.

"You told me too much," she said quietly. "You handed me all that responsibility. What did you expect me to do? Did you think only Cousins loved their own? Did you think that just because we're not as good as you, you could destroy us and we wouldn't care?"

"No. No. I never thought that," he whispered.

"King Leopold in the Congo." Her voice was wry and amused. "That's how you acted. Sometimes you were such a condescending bastard, Reen. You had to love everybody, and I was only good at loving one thing." She looked out pensively at the tender apricot sunrise. "But it came down to genocide, didn't it? Secrets and genocide. If I wanted to live with myself, I had to stop you before the birthrate went any lower."

A promising ruddy sun peered over the horizon. "The birthrate doesn't matter, Marian. Your DNA is now infected with the same flaw as ours is. Except that we produce Loving Helpers. Sometime in the next generation you'll begin to produce nothing. Your DNA will not replicate anymore."

A throaty sound of surprise. She got up and walked to the edge of the balcony, resting her elbows on the railing. The Potomac below was a dusky pink ribbon in the dawn.

He thought she would weep. It shocked him when she chuckled. "God help me. I've been a spook too long. If I were normal, I wouldn't find this funny. But I've never been normal, have I?"

A flick of her adroit human fingers. The cigarette arced toward the lawn, a ruddy falling star.

"You outfoxed me. That sweet innocent little face. That pint-sized childlike honor. I thought humans were better at deception, Reen. We were so good at it, I felt sorry for you. Oh, Jesus." She laughed. "You learned a lot from Jeff Womack. Political half-truths. You even hid things you shouldn't have. I didn't know you couldn't sleep without others around. When you told me that, you scared me to death. I thought I could always protect you."

"If you hadn't put the Cousins in with the Helpers, you would have found out that we die if left alone."

She turned to face him. Behind her, down the gentle bowl of the sky, the violet brightened to a rim of gold.

"Here," she said, taking a plastic bag from the pocket of her jacket.

He took it. Small pink squares at the bottom, like confetti.

"It's an antidote. Enough for you and Oomal and the Cousins from Gerber. It works like adrenaline. Under stress, your body produces an endorphin that shuts down your system."

Confetti. Like something from a child's birthday party. And pink, the color of dawn.

Her voice was hurried. "When everything starts, put one in your mouth. It's adhesive. There will be a burning sensation. Your pulse will race—"

"When what starts?"

"Stay in the White House. You'll be safe here. The troops will guard you. Vilishnikov promised me that."

"Marian!" he shouted, alarmed. "What's going to happen?"

"Vilishnikov put all military troops on alert two days ago. At nine o'clock Eastern Standard Time they'll attack the Cousin installations. Your defense can scramble electronics, but I know from what you've told me that you're not prepared for a sudden overwhelming attack. I don't want you to set foot outside the White House, Reen. I don't want you to try to stop it."

The plastic bag fell from his fingers.

"Pick it up!" Marian ordered angrily. "Damn you! Pick that up! Go in there and give it to the rest of those Cousins! At nine o'clock put one in your mouth. Make sure the others do, too."

A quick triple pump from his heart. His head swam, and he sat down hard on a lounge chair. The delicate light of morning flooded the Mall and the leafless cherry trees.

He checked his watch. Six A.M. Oomal was wrapped in slumber in the room next door. At Andrews the Community was tucked into niches. In West Virginia the children were still riding their dreams.

"Will it work on the children?"

"What?"

"Will it work on Angela? Marian, did you ever once think about your daughter?"

He could see the answer in her face.

"Get out," he told her.

She hesitated. "Promise me you'll use the antidote."

"Damn you. Goddamn you." Oomal's words, but his own hushed voice. "A house in the country. Me all to yourself. Marian, must you always get everything you want?"

Turning his back on her, he watched morning fill the streets. No cars moved on Constitution Avenue. The windows of the nearby buildings were dark. Saturday, he remembered.

It was Saturday, and the morning was so quiet, he could hear her every soft footstep as she left.

35

"Give me your gun," Reen said.

The Secret Serviceman in the colonnade looked up in dazed and sleepy alarm. Reen recognized him: the same agent he had encountered on the stairway after Jeff Womack's assassination.

"Excuse me, sir?"

"I need a gun. Give me your gun."

Indecision. Then, "Sir, there *are* regulations. I can't give you mine, but . . ." The agent got up and walked with Reen to Landis's office. A jingling of keys as he opened a steel gun safe. "This is a nine-millimeter federal issue. Ever handle a gun before? No? Okay, this is the slide. Pull it back to chamber the first bullet. After that, well, it's an automatic, sir. It pretty much does the rest on its own. Here's the safety. Leave that on until you have to shoot. The magazine's loaded with Hydra-Shok hollowpoints. The gun's light. Should be light enough for you to use. But it's got plenty of stopping power."

Reen took the automatic. Heavy, not at all light. It looked very much like Hopkins's gun. His three-fingered hand and claw felt unwieldy on the grip.

The Secret Serviceman was young, earnest, and anxious. "About the assassination . . . are you worried we can't protect you? Or is there something going on the Service should know about? I admired President Womack very much, sir. And I know he was fond of you. Both President Womack and President Kennedy left very specific instructions as to your safety. An agent hasn't been assigned to you, but that can be remedied. I can call—"

"Don't bother. It's nothing. I'm fine."

Reen took the gun and left. On the landing of the staircase he remembered to pull the slide to chamber the bullet. Then, despite what the agent had said, he flicked off the safety.

He took an old gym bag out of the desk drawer in Jeff Womack's study. Stuffing the gun into the tote, he walked into the bedroom and looked at the slumbering Cousins.

They seemed so peaceful, so innocent that some compassionate thing in Reen wanted to go away and leave them there.

"Oomal," he called.

In the dim blue light, one of the cocoons stirred.

Louder: "Oomal!"

Radalt pulled the sheet down from his face. Next to Radalt, Oomal grunted and shrugged himself out of his bonds.

"Get up. All of you need to get up. Don't bother bathing."

"Are you okay, Cousin?" Zoor asked, crawling out from his sheet. "You sound—"

"In three hours the army will attack. We have to get the recombinants off Earth."

Oomal's fingers slowly unhinged, and his sheet fluttered to the floor. "Get the Gerber commuter," he told his staff. "Fly up to one of the main ships to get more runners. There are twenty-one recombinant centers. I want them all cleared in two hours and those children up in space where they'll be safe."

Sakan made a graceless, overwrought gesture. "But what about the payroll? What are the workers going to do if we're not there to sign the checks?"

"It's all right," Oomal said. "Everything will be all right. Go on."

With troubled backward looks the Gerber execs left the room.

"She was here, wasn't she? Marian was here," Oomal said when they were alone.

"I want to go to West Virginia."

"Yes, that's fine, Reen. But I have a responsibility. The Community—"

"Oomal, think! Humans and Cousins are becoming extinct. If there is to be any future, we *must* save the children."

The truth hit Oomal like a blow. He looked around the room, bewildered, then shook his head to clear it. "The Community ship's over by the West Wing. We'll take that."

He hurried from the room, Reen after him. At their passage the maids looked up from their cleaning; the Secret Service agent in the colonnade glanced up from his daily report. The ship was parked on the lawn, Thural standing by it. His sleep must have been thin for him to awaken so early.

Thural's gaze flicked to Reen and then settled on Oomal.

"Get on the ship's net. Alert the Community at Andrews. Tell them to send the word out," Oomal called. "The humans are planning an attack."

Thural tipped his head as though he thought Oomal was making a poor joke.

"Do it now, Thural," Oomal said as he bounded onto the ramp, Reen at his heels. "And take us to West Virginia."

Thural followed them. "But I am under rebuke, Cousin."

"Just *do* it!"

"They will not believe me."

Oomal turned, his face contorted. "Goddamn it to hell, just *do* it!"

Stunned, Thural walked down the short hall to the navigation room.

When the ship lifted, Reen said, "I want you to take the children to Mars station."

Oomal stared out the window.

"Did you hear me?"

"Yes."

"I want you to keep them away from the rest of the Community. Promise me that."

Reen saw the glimmering string of lights along the George Washington Parkway blink out. For a moment he feared that it had something to do with the coming attack, then realized that it was only the automatic timer kicking in.

Time had come for the Cousins. Past time. In his mind he saw lights going out all over the universe.

"When you're safe," Reen said, "I'll go back to help the Community."

After a silence Oomal asked, "What do you have in that bag?"

"A gun."

"For Christ's sake. A gun?" Oomal's voice wavered between amusement and grief.

Reen looked out the window at the gold dawn streaking the sky. "Oomal, I shouldn't have trusted Marian."

Oomal hooked the side of Reen's tunic and drew him near. "Listen to me." His Brother was so close that Reen could smell the spice of sleep on him. "I loved my human employees. And in a few hours the whole truth will be out. They'll be wondering why I lied to them. They'll wonder how I could have eaten dinner in their homes and gone to Little League baseball games, all the while doing my best to make their race extinct. You don't have a corner on the guilt market."

They stood like that, perilously close, closer than Communal Law allowed, and together they watched the ship leave the lights of Fairfax County behind.

Reen put his finger to the emblem on his Brother's chest, thrilling at the contact of childhood Mind.

Oomal didn't move but looked at Reen in query.

"Intelligence," Reen whispered.

"Yes?"

"Both of us. We should have been more intelligent than to love the thing we were destroying."

It had snowed in the West Virginia mountains, and the trees were thick with white.

"You know?" Oomal said wistfully. "In Michigan we used to go sledding with the human kids. I'll miss the snow."

The snow. The trees. Oomal's humor. Angela's beautiful hands.

Reen and Oomal made their way from the ship. At the door they met Thural.

"Did you call ahead to warn them?" Oomal asked.

"I warned them, but I do not know if they believed me."

Oomal nodded. "You've done all you can. Go round up the West Virginia Cousins and get them on the main transport."

The children's house smelled of blueberry muffins. In the dining room the recombinants were having breakfast. As Reen and Oomal entered, Angela jumped up from the table and ran over to hug Reen's waist. His hand dropped to cradle the warm bulge of her cranium, the wisps of blond hair.

Quen came around the table, his expression furious. "You bring him here?"

"Get the children together, Quen," Oomal said. "Get them on board the transport. We're going to Mars station."

"Mars station is deserted!"

"Now, Quen." Oomal's face was strangely impassive. Shock? Reen wondered. Or an effort not to alarm the children?

Mrs. Gonzales emerged from the kitchen, a spatula in her hand.

"The army plans to attack the Cousins," Reen told her. "Stay here if you like. It will be safe enough for a while. We must take the children."

After a long, steady look at Reen, the caregiver bent down to Angela. "Come on, sweetie, let's get your clothes. We're all going for a ride together."

She ushered the children from the table and into the dormitories.

Quickly, without looking back, Reen hurried outside. Thural was still standing by the commuter, pretending not to have noticed Reen's exit. Behind him the West Virginia Cousins were packing the transport to leave.

Stepping off the porch onto the snow, Reen went around to the side of the house, Jeff's gym bag bouncing at his side.

Tali had spies, Reen knew. Hopkins had been a teacher of deception, Tali a good student. The spy from West Virginia would have been told to keep an eye on Reen. Whoever the spy was, he would follow.

He heard the door of the house open. Heard footsteps crunch in the snow. He paused and looked over his shoulder. Quen was walking behind him, and Thural was a few paces back.

Seeing him stop, they stopped, too, and peered at the snowbound trees in a parody of innocence.

"Go back to the ship," Reen said.

Neither Cousin moved. Thural was engrossed in a tiny black-green pine, Quen in the eaves of the roof.

"Go back," Reen said. "Please." *Please, not Thural.*

Thural finally turned and made his way slowly to the other ship, his boots leaving blue-pooled indentations in the white.

Reen turned and kept walking, hearing the squeak of his own steps, of Quen's. Around a corner, in the center of a winter-blasted garden, he stopped and looked back. Quen was standing against the wall, beyond a row of spindly fig-tree corpses and the stick grave markers of withered tomato plants.

Reen unzipped the bag, took out the gun.

"Quen," he said.

The Cousin didn't look up.

It took both hands to lift the automatic. Reen sighted to the center of Quen's chest, just to the left of the lightning bolt.

"Quen," he said in low apology and pulled the trigger.

A sky-splitting crack. Reen's arms were jerked up over his head. Quen was flung backward. Blood sprayed the white wall, the snow.

On the ground Quen made a little sound, like someone surprised by bad news. He put his hand to his chest and then stared idiotically at the brown covering his palm.

Reen approached, and Quen finally looked up, looked right at him despite Communal law. His eyes were terrified.

It would take only a few minutes; Cousins never took long to die. But Reen couldn't walk away and leave him. He lifted the gun again. Quen raised his hand as though to ward off the bullet.

The explosion made Reen's ears ring. Quen's hand dropped. Without a single tremor, without another breath, he lay still.

Reen slipped the gun back into the bag. When he walked around to the front of the house, he saw Oomal and Thural by the door of the transport. The children were boarding.

There was horror in Oomal's face. "Reen? My God. I thought I heard—"

"No one will report back to Tali now. You're safe enough. I'll go to Anacostia and try to warn the Cousins."

Angela stood in the line of children at the ship, making a snowball. When she saw Reen, she stopped her play and ran over, flailing in the ankle-deep snow. He sank to one knee and gathered his daughter to him.

Too bad, oh, too bad. If only he had broad shoulders and a wide strong back, he wouldn't have failed her. He could have kept the world at bay.

"Go for a ride, Daddy," she said.

"Yes," he whispered into her hair.

The human need for embraces, it must have something to do with never wanting to let go. Angela against him, stomach to stomach, chest to chest, furnished him with a sort of magic. A daughter-shaped impression that, if his mind ever failed to remember, his body would never forget.

"Reen. It's getting late." Oomal took Angela by the shoulders and gently pulled her from her father.

Reen couldn't get up. The cold snow had soaked his uniform so that he couldn't feel his legs. Angela, standing next to Oomal, was looking at him as gravely as any Cousin. Her thumb was in her mouth. Then Oomal turned her around and walked her inside. Kneeling there, Reen watched his whole world rise, round and silver, into the robin's-egg-blue day.

36

THE HOUSE WAS EMPTY, BUT NOT IN the way Langley had been. It was as if the house had simply taken a breath and in a moment the children would return, carried on the warm, muffin-scented wind, to pick up the doll left on the chair, the mittens forgotten on the floor.

Reen slid his finger down one side of the long breakfast-strewn table and thought he could feel in the wood the vibration of high piping voices, of laughter, of small running feet.

The house remembered. It would remember for a long, long time.

Finally, hefting the tote, he walked out to the small runner they had left him. A glance at his watch. He was surprised to see it was only twenty minutes to eight, time enough to finish his duty.

All duties finished sometime, he thought as he lifted the ship into the clear morning air. All projects, all lives had an end. If he could, he would go to Mars when he was done. There he would spin out the remainder of his days, watching his daughter grow up and his own race die.

In a few centuries the Cousins would fade in the new race's memory like photographs in a family album. But the children wouldn't completely forget.

Here's my grandfather. He had a farm in Ohio.

Reen remembered looking at the family album Jeff had once placed in his lap.

And my grandfather on my father's side. Here. Here's a picture of him in Poland.

Perhaps Angela's children would inherit from the humans that specific love of family rather than the Cousins' generic love of race. If they did, Reen would grow old and sweet and distant, as Jeff's round-faced grandfather in Poland or the laughing Ohio farmer with his arm around his pudgy wife.

Below Reen, a few early risers in Falls Church were going outside to pick their papers from the lawn. Cars drove in a leisurely Saturday morning pace to the store or a weekend shift of work. It all looked very peaceful.

He took a moment to fly past the White House one more time, and even that huge building seemed sleepy. Angling southeast, he sailed over the poor neighborhoods of Washington and the boats bobbing on the sparkling Potomac. A few minutes later he lowered the ship on the flat center of hard white spume that was the Cousin complex in Anacostia.

The bag over his shoulder, he strode past the parked ships to the nearest door. A Cousin in the hall, apparently recognizing Reen, hurriedly turned his face away.

Reen said, "I know you're not supposed to hear me, but I came to bring you news, and you must listen. The humans will attack in an hour. Call everyone together and get them to safety."

The Cousin walked down the hall, and Reen couldn't be sure he was going to warn the others. He headed to one of the communication centers and on the way passed a Brother.

"Kredin?" he asked.

Kredin's eyes immediately sought sanctuary on the floor. Reen put out a claw to stop him, but Kredin changed course slightly to avoid the touch.

"The humans will attack in a little while," Reen said to the retreating back. "Get everyone together and into the ships." He watched his Brother disappear around a curve in the corridor. Kredin did not quicken his stride.

As Reen walked toward the communication modules, he lifted his arm to look at the Rolex and stopped mid-stride. The time.

Time had run out.

It was nine o'clock. When he had looked at the watch before, it was twenty to nine, not twenty to eight. He had never learned to read anything but a digital.

He ran headlong down the corridor. Ahead stood three Cousins in a gossipy knot.

"Get out!" Reen screamed as he raced toward them, the wet soles of his boots beating a frantic slap-slap on the soft shiny floor.

They turned in tandem, curiosity and disgust in their eyes. And in tandem they looked away.

Reen ran. His breath came in hard painful gulps. The gun bumped crazily at his side. At the first communications module, his feet nearly slid out from under him, and he grabbed a doorjamb to stay his fall.

In the room a Cousin sat before a screen, calmly talking to another Cousin in another communications room. He looked up, then jerked his head away.

"Who are you talking to?"

The Cousin didn't answer. He continued his calm conversation.

Reen pushed him out of the chair and shouted into the terminal. "Tell everyone! The humans are attacking!"

The distant Cousin on the screen stood and walked away. The Cousin on the floor got to his feet and brushed at his uniform.

"Go to the ships and lift off! Lift off!" Reen shrieked into the terminal. He punched the controls. "Get to the ships and lift off!"

The floor slipped a little beneath him. He staggered. The Cousin on the floor uttered an astonished cry, and the building moved again.

Reen pounded the controls so hard, his hand went numb. "Get to the ships!"

The walls and floor shook. With a wail of terror, the Cousin ran to the hall.

The next explosion was more than motion; it was sound, too. A bass rumble, and tenor Cousin shrieks. Somewhere in the complex a wall had been breached.

Reen ran into the hall, pulling the gun from the bag. Ahead of him Cousins were standing stock-still, watching smoke pour down the corridor.

"Run!" he shouted. But they didn't run. They couldn't. Cousins were genetically incapable of either fight or flight.

Suddenly soldiers, too, were running in the corridor. Reen watched as a man ran a tiny Cousin down and crushed his head against the wall.

Reen lifted the gun and fired. The man reeled back a couple of steps, then tried to rush Reen, but his legs weren't working well and he toppled.

The humans looked up from their murder like lions disturbed from a kill. Their arms were brown to the elbow with blood, and their eyes were wild with strange excitement.

They blocked the only exit Reen knew. He didn't know how to get out. Far to the back of the building he could hear the high, thin cries of the dying.

The closest soldier lifted his rifle and aimed it at Reen. Cousins didn't understand battle, they didn't understand killing, but what they knew was quickness. Precision. The automatic in Reen's hand barked once, and the man fell. The other soldiers retreated.

No one had told them a Cousin would fight back, Reen thought as he fled down a right-hand hall. Marian must have promised it would be easy.

A Cousin hunkered in a corner, babbling. Reen tried to grab him, but the Cousin pulled away.

"Come with me!" Reen urged.

The Cousin's small body shook. He had wrapped his arms around his knees, as if to make himself a smaller target. His mouth kept moving.

Reen left him.

The smoke was so thick that Reen wasn't sure in which direction he was going. Around a bend, the peppery sweet smell of blood hit him, and he saw that the corridor was littered with black-uniformed bodies. A section of the ceiling had fallen, exposing the building to a flood of sunlight. At his feet a severed Cousin head lay like a gray basketball.

Reen ran down another hall. Near the end were two doors. He blundered through the one on the right, into blue. The blue of nests. The blue of sleep. It was silent, everything in order. The meditation room was cool and serene in the manner of Cousins.

He lowered the gun and noticed that his arms were aching. The room greeted him with its distant welcome, as it might have greeted anyone. A smell in it of calm, and the light, heady spice of rest.

Looking down, he saw that his uniform and his boots were filthy. How tired he suddenly was. The gun dropped from his fingers and hit the floor with a clank.

He gasped, realizing he had very nearly dozed off. Not sleep. No, not at all. The little death.

Panicky, he bent and grabbed the gun. The little death tugging at him, he whirled to the door. It opened, and he was facing a human.

The man was in camouflage. His helmet was off, his uniform blouse askew. His eyes widened at Reen's unexpected appearance. His right hand came up, lifting a pistol.

There was no hatred in the man's face, only mild surprise, as though he had met someone he recognized at a party. *Oh, hello,* he might have said, *and how are you?* Instead, he fired.

Reen heard the boom, saw the flame from the muzzle, felt hot gunpowder stipple his cheek. Before the soldier could pull the trigger again, Reen fired. The man crumpled.

Reen squeezed himself through the left door the moment it started opening. Outside, the air was cold, the wind rank with oily smoke. Ahead of him the Cousin ships sat untenanted on their pads. He ran to the nearest and threw himself into the seat. As the ship lifted, he looked down.

All of Anacostia was burning, and the ruins of the Cousin center squatted in that inferno, one entire side of it open to the smoky sky.

Reen clipped the control ball southeast, and the ship hurled itself over Suitland Parkway toward Andrews. Tanks were moving on the Beltway, and fighter planes sailed the bright air.

As he passed over Andrews, what he saw made him weak. Loving Helpers were stacked at the fences, thousands and thousands of Loving Helpers, eight and ten deep.

At the Cousin Place he settled the ship onto the tarmac. Cousins were moving back and forth from the building to the largest ships, carrying boxes. Reen trotted past them to the door where Tali and the Sleep Master were standing.

"Forget the supplies and records," Reen told them. "Just get on the ship. Anacostia's on fire."

Tali looked away, but the Sleep Master didn't. He stared hard into Reen's eyes.

"The Helpers won't stop them!" Reen's voice rose in frustration. "Listen to me. They have guns! They have a new toxin. They— The Helpers won't get close enough to them to matter!"

The Sleep Master looked at Reen with contempt. "Leave. Go where you wish. You are not wanted here."

Perhaps because the Sleep Master had spoken, Tali at last found the courage to turn around. "It is your fault. All of it. Your fault. Go to your humans. See if they love you now."

Reen could hear the faraway rattle of machine-gun fire and the first reedy screams of the Helpers.

A bomber flew low, thunder in its wake. The ground shook. The Cousins carrying boxes ducked. And the entire western perimeter of Andrews went up in black smoke and red flame. It was as though the sky let go a cloudburst of fire.

From the throats of the few surviving Helpers came a shrill lamentation. Tali clapped his hands over his ears.

The Sleep Master's face changed. "Quick," he said to Tali. "Get the Cousins on board."

Tali hesitated. His hands dropped. "The Helpers . . ."

"Gone. All that are not gone are insane. Get the Cousins now."

Reen saw small bodies dancing in the hellish flames, saw demented Helpers, their mouths wide, running in panicked circles.

"Leave here," the Sleep Master told Reen.

"Yes," Reen said, nodding. "Yes."

He walked wearily to the nearest runner but halted when he saw the huge shape emerging from the building. Large as a room, slow and ponderous as a cloud. Sunlight turned the female's skin pearlescent.

Tali was barking orders, and the Cousins attending the female were trying to avoid her tail. She flowed over the tarmac, her body rippling.

Reen called to the Sleep Master, "This is wrong! The female never leaves the chamber! Let her die!"

The Sleep Master's eyes were as dark and expressionless as berries.

"You can't take a full-grown female on the ship! The attraction of the Communal Mind will be too strong! The Cousins can't fight it! She'll kill someone! You know that!"

The Sleep Master turned away.

The Cousins were trying to nudge the creature up the ramp, but she was balking. Terrified of approaching too close, they were prodding her with sticks, with raised voices.

She wasn't moving. And Reen knew that Tali wouldn't let the ships leave without her.

Without stopping to consider the enormity of it, Reen put his hand into the bag and brought out the gun. Tali saw him first. His mouth dropped. He held up his hand like a policeman ordering traffic to stop.

Around him Cousins were shouting, shouting at the stubborn female, shouting at Reen. Their voices were all but drowned out by the screeches of the Loving Helpers.

With shaking hands, Reen aimed. In front of him, Cousins scattered. Even Tali stepped away. The female inched around as though she was planning a return to the building.

Something hit Reen in the back. He staggered, fought to keep himself upright. But lethargy sucked him down. Over his shoulder he caught a glimpse of the Sleep Master's face.

The gun dropped from Reen's hand and clattered to the asphalt. He felt a claw rake his side only to be stopped by something hard in his pocket. Remotely he felt the Sleep Master's question the instant before they were both claimed by the murk of Communal Mind.

"The tape," he whispered.

37

BLUE. AN EERIE AND EMPTY NEST BLUE. A sensation of heaviness and a vague ache in his chest. Reen hung in sleep like a sodden log below a river's surface.

He drifted, wanted to sink further, but there was no drag of Communal Mind to pull him down. Unable to sink, he tried to rise but was swept by a current of exhaustion. In a timeless eddy he waited until, with a groan, he forced himself to sit up.

He was in a nest; the niches around him were vacant, haunted not by Communal Mind but by stale and long-abandoned spice. He swung his legs out and tried to stand, but his rubbery knees nearly gave out on him. Another smell overlaid the sleep: a fetid smell of human decay. He looked down at himself and saw that his uniform was stiff with dried blood.

Holding on to a wall for balance, he walked the empty tomb of the nest. Was this Andrews? And if so, where were the Cousins? Had they left him to face the humans alone?

He paused at the entrance to a hall. Ceiling lights sensed his presence and lit up in welcoming sequence. At the end of the hall was a door. He walked to it and found that it was locked. He rested there a while, leaning against the wall, letting his body, then his mind, gather the energy for the long trek to the baths.

The baths were neat and vacant. When he stripped off his uniform, he noticed the tape recorder was gone. Just below the center of his chest was a perfectly round bruise with an angry brown dot at its center. When he lowered himself into the water, he saw that his arms and legs were trembling, as if he had slept three hundred years and awakened palsied with age.

When he had finished bathing, he limped up the steps of the pool, found a uniform in a nearby closet, and put it on. Then he walked aimlessly through the strange silence of the abandoned nest, feeling a loneliness so keen that he wished he could end it by crawling into a niche and pulling oblivion in after him.

Where were they? Where were the Cousins? Why had they left him alone? He remembered the video of the Helper, how, without sight but with unerring precision, it had sensed the location of its Brothers.

Circling past the hall again, he stopped. The lights were blazing, and at the end near the door, Tali and the Sleep Master waited.

"The little death clings to you, Reen," the Sleep Master said. "You slept, and I thought you would die from it."

With that, he turned. The door opened for him, and he and Tali walked through.

Reen followed. The neighboring room was pale gray. Against a curved wall on the left was a row of chairs, where Tali seated himself. To the right, a single window looked out on a barren plain above which hung a slice of turquoise Earth.

Reen walked to the window and looked across the moon's dry sea. To either side of him the huge Cousin complex rose in stately billows that made Reen feel light-headed and small, like a bird lost among clouds.

His eyes rose to the white-whorled Earth. Over the eastern Pacific was a storm, dazzling as new-fallen snow. Reen wondered how they would live with the news, this fecund race gone barren. He wondered with what savage grief they would cling to the last of their children.

He took a breath. "How long have I been asleep?"

"Two weeks," the Sleep Master said. "I came every day to see if you were breathing. To touch you and feel your thoughts."

Reen pictured the old Cousin's hand on him, examining him for life as Reen had once examined Tali. He remembered feeling the darkness in his Brother and wondered if what the Sleep Master felt had been sadness. "There was a recorder in my pocket. It's not there now."

The Sleep Master said, "I have it."

"And?"

"I will keep it." The Sleep Master walked to Reen, stopped just at his shoulder, and looked out the window. "The Community is nearly gone."

Reen put a steadying hand to the wall. "How many were saved?"

"Forty-three."

Forty-three out of more than three thousand. The humans had nearly destroyed the Community.

"Never before have we waged war, Reen, and for good reason. The Cousins cannot sleep with visions of blood and death in their minds."

Of course the Cousins couldn't sleep. The butchery was over, but chaos possessed the collective Mind. As Reen himself had learned with the murders of Hopkins and Quen, killing was best done at a distance.

Kill but do not look, his ancestors might have said. *If you look, you will see brain on the floor. If you look, you will see your victim beg for mercy. If you dare look, you will see a beloved world die.*

History was supposed to be instructive, but Reen had ignored its lessons. He had wanted to know Angela's other parent, that hot-blooded human half, and had ended up with his Brothers' blood on his hands.

Three thousand Cousins. And how many humans? One last short generation, and he would kill them all.

He looked up. The Sleep Master was regarding him thoughtfully. "Tali cannot lead," he said.

Hope stirred in Reen's chest.

"So you must abdicate."

With a final exhausted twitch, hope died. "If you want me to leave . . ."

"There are those who would leave with you. Who are still loyal. It would deplete the Community even further. Tali needs you to acknowledge him as First, and that is what I am asking."

Reen shot an angry look at Tali. "He is no innocent. The tape . . ."

Tali jumped to his feet. "You are the one who brought this destruction on our heads, not me. You are the one who trusted humans too much, who—"

The Sleep Master whirled to Tali. "Silence!" he roared. "You will be silent! And take your seat! Remember, Tali-ja, that Reen is your Brother!"

Tali quickly sat.

"You can't do this," Reen argued. "Even under rebuke you can't let him be First. If you have heard what the tape says, then you know Tali has no heart for rule."

The Sleep Master took his eyes from Reen and let them rest on the star-strung space in the window. "I know he has no heart, and I know now where your heart belongs. But what matters is that the Community find its way out of turmoil. Tali was always the more ordered, the more disciplined Brother, so it is Tali we need. But Tali knows that should he seek revenge on the humans, I will use the tape against him." The old Cousin's expression softened. "Reen, I will hold your wishes dear, as though they were my own."

The Sleep Master was asking him to die. Reen opened his mouth, found himself saying, "How?"

Would they give him back the gun and leave him alone in the room, as courteous humans used to do with even more courteous traitors? Or would they open the door to the vacuum and expect him to walk outside?

"The sleep is thin, and only one thing can make it better. You have been tested and found viable. Go meditate your decision now, as custom dictates. Remember, not for Tali's goals but for simple, full sleep this is what we must do."

Simple, full sleep. Reen's exhaustion was back. His head was heavy, his arms and legs felt weighted, and he fought to swim against the current of the old Cousin's words. Somewhere in that cold numbing deluge was meaning, but Reen was too tired to find it.

"I have chosen you to be consort," the Sleep Master said.

38

REEN WANDERED THE ECHOING HALLS
that once had teemed with Cousins. He had brought extinction on
his Community too quickly, too soon. He thought he could avoid the
unavoidable with Angela. Fifty years of dreams.

He wanted to see her grow up. Wanted to know and love her
children. He should have gone with Oomal while he had the chance.
Even now he could escape to Mars, where Thural and Oomal and
Angela waited.

Guilt stopped him; remorse brought him back. Angela was only
his hope. Cousins, no matter how doomed, were his future.

When he returned to the room, he found three Cousins waiting.
Two were standing together at the window. The third rose at his
approach.

That Cousin. That unfamiliar Cousin.

"He has come a long way to see you," the Sleep Master said,
turning.

Beside the Sleep Master, Thural turned, too. One final betrayal:
Thural had left the children. Reen's pulse slowed as if it were coming
to a stop.

"Reen," Thural said, hands fluttering. "Oomal didn't go to Mars.
He went home."

Bewildered, Reen tipped his head to one side.

"Home," Thural explained. "He went through the Window to Setis. The home place."

Setis. The planet with a sky as blue as Earth's. Reen remembered the vast buildings riding the red oceans of its grass.

Oomal had taken Angela home.

The Sleep Master pointed nervously to the solemn wordless Cousin. "Mito-ja. Cousin First Brother of home place."

Beside the fretful Sleep Master and the embarrassed Thural, Mito stood as Reen himself must have once stood, as they all must have stood before being tainted by human impatience. With slow inevitability, Mito turned to regard Thural and the Sleep Master.

He did not order them away. He did not speak at all. But after a hesitant moment, the pair left.

The hush in Mito's eyes was spellbinding. *How beautiful he is,* Reen thought. And how alien. Reen had become accustomed to fleeting human expressions. Had become inured to faces in which fear, bemusement, and irritation chased and tumbled after each other like puppies.

Mito was an elegant still life.

"I come," Mito-ja finally said, "for Brother's love for Brother."

Reen felt the habit-formed human urge to ask Mito to sit down. He restrained himself and stood, feeling awkward.

"Oomal sends his message." Mito's words were eerily deliberate. If a mountain could speak, it would speak like this.

"The message is that he has done as he saw best, to seek my protection."

Reen looked at the floor and was silent so long that he thought Mito would leave. A human, an Earth Cousin, would have. But when Reen finally looked up, Mito was watching him, the universe in his eyes.

Reen shuddered. The Cousin First Brother of home was no ordinary Cousin sheltered from alien contact. No. Mito was a completely unfamiliar thing.

The First Brother of Setis was so still that for a moment Reen wondered if he was conversing with a ghost. Then Mito said, "Oomal wishes you to know that the children are welcome."

"Will they live with you?"

With stately grace Mito raised his hands. "We tunnel," he said.

"I don't understand."

"We tunnel. The aboveground no longer interests us."

We tunnel. Perhaps that was the solution every Cousin should have sought. Mito seemed larger, taller than other Cousins, and Reen wondered if it was poise alone that lent him height.

"Will Oomal live with you?" Would Oomal succumb to Mito's tranquility—that heady, abbreviated end to Cousin evolution?

Mito made a regal gesture with one arm, as though he were sweeping away thirty million years of history. "Oomal is *nadiye*. He is other." He gazed at Reen—sadly, it seemed, if the sea, the sky, could be thought sad. "You are, all of you, *nadiye*."

Without another word he left the room.

Reen watched the door close and fought the urge to run after. There was so much he longed to ask.

Did I fail, then? was the obvious question.

From that long black tunnel which led to extinction, Reen had plucked the closest and easiest answer. Mito had chosen the hard way: reaching farther than an arm's length.

Do I disappoint you?

The answer was plain. Mito had taken the Community in his keeping to where life was as ordered as crystalline structure. And in that unemotional order there was no place for disappointment. No room for heartache.

The door opened. The Sleep Master walked in and stood by the door as motionless as Mito, but stiffly. "I did not think to give you food. You might be hungry."

"No."

"So. Will you come?"

Before he lost his courage, Reen straightened his tunic. Taking a deep breath, he walked through the doorway.

He followed the Sleep Master down the hall to the right, down the next gray, sloping passageway. Down and down. In front of the female's chamber was a wall painted pale yellow in warning. There a knot of Cousins waited.

Reen came to a halt and stared at Tali, the Brother who had seemed most ordered until Mito came to show them the true pattern. If Reen had been wrong to cheat destiny for Cousin survival, Tali, so loyal to the old laws, had been wrong, too.

Reen's eyes must have contained something of his contempt because Tali quickly looked away.

"You do this willingly?" the Sleep Master asked.

Reen regarded the gathered Cousins one by one. No matter how much he loved Angela's new race, no matter how much he loved the humans, the Community always came first.

He caught Thural's eye. His aide would not have been able to live comfortably among the too-human Michigan Cousins, but he was too corrupted by alien contact for Mito to take in. Thural, in sympathy, Reen supposed, was trembling.

Reen walked on. As he neared the yellow wall, it opened. Inside was another wall, the next-to-last barrier, paler than the first.

DANGER, DANGER, the color said.

When Reen's people first left their nests in the earth and sought food and room above, the gleam of the yellow sun meant death. From its radiance fanged predators swooped. After thirty million years all that remained of those deadly hunters was the color from which they had come. Everything ended. Everything.

Turning aside to the antechamber, Reen pulled off his uniform and, for the second time that day, slipped into the bath. The ocher water was acidic and soothing. He washed until he was free of all human smells.

Nude, dripping, he walked up the steps to the second yellow wall and saw the Sleep Master standing there. They didn't speak. Dipping his head slightly, the old Cousin gathered Reen's uniform from the table where he had left it. Then he retreated to safety, where he would stand at the window and watch Reen die.

Reen stood, water droplets from his body making dark pimples on the floor. Suddenly he realized that he had gone through the ritual without having answered the Sleep Master's question.

He wanted to blunder back through the safe wall and shout "Yes! Yes!" to the Cousins waiting there.

But willingly? Die willingly? All the other decisions he had made had hurt those around him. And how could he watch as the rest of Earth Community declined?

We tunnel, Mito had said. All intelligent creatures tunneled. The burrowing itself should have been enough. It was for Mito. But Reen, digging for truth, had unearthed spurious and faulty answers.

His body had always been the ordered part of him, had always done the correct thing. Now, like a law-abiding good citizen, it moved him toward the second door. Beyond that would be the third door. The last. Between the two he would pause for a while, and gather his courage.

The door opened to cloudy light, and as he stepped through, it shut fast. The air was heavy with spice and with the narcotic torpor of Communal Mind. He halted in confusion. Instead of the final yellow wall there was a vast dim chamber where a huge shape moved.

High-voltage terror. Reen's heart raced into a frantic beat. He had made a terrible mistake. In those few paces from the second door he had somehow got lost and missed the meditation room.

Mito's stoicism now failed him, as did the Cousin instinct to stand and die. Reen whirled to the door and was dumbfounded that it didn't open.

He pounded his fists against the yellow wall even as he realized that it wasn't meant to open. No consort was that willing, not at the end. And that was the reason behind the final trick for the condemned: that missing meditation room.

A Cousin was watching him from the chamber's small window. Not the Sleep Master.

"Tali!"

Reen ran to the window and slapped his hands to either side of his Brother's face. His claws screeched against the glass.

"Tali, please!"

In his Brother's eyes was an expression so unexpected that Reen barely recognized him; for shame came naturally to Cousins, but repentance had to be taught. Tali lifted his fists to the glass as though he wanted to batter down the wall between them.

Too late. There was a slap on Reen's leg. His skin flamed from ankle to hip as the thick burr of the female's stingers pulled away. He howled and leaped to the side. His leg crumpled. He hit the wall with a thump and lay there, dazed.

"Tali?" he whispered. "I changed my mind, Tali."

A curious nudge at his hip brought him instantly alert. It was the female. Reen limped to the far side of the chamber. She was watching him, her eyes bright, not with intelligence but with something like cunning.

The huge body shifted.

The burning sensation was gone. Now tendrils of ice sprouted from his knee. He took another step, realized too late that his leg was numb, and toppled, his fingers splayed on the soft floor.

Something touched his arm.

"Tali!" he shouted and snapped his head around.

Pigeons on the south lawn. Pigeons, the feathers at their necks gleaming rainbow shades of emerald and lavender-pink.

"Pigeons," Marian said. "I like pigeons. They graze just like cattle, don't they?"

Reen looked at the fat compact bodies dotting the grass.

"A whole herd of pigeons." Marian laughed. "Must be forty head of pigeons."

And, just then, one took to the air. Reen's eyes followed it. Against his face it seemed he could feel the dry flutter of its wings.

Marian put her hand on his shoulder, and love rose in him like baking bread, a love so different, so alien, that it took his breath away.

He grasped her hand and held it, as though afraid that she, too, would take flight. He held her so hard that his claw must have dug into her flesh. He held her. He held Marian. And she didn't pull away.

The pigeons were gone, and the opalescent skin of the female was right against Reen's face. He tried to rise and failed. The vaginal tube detached from the base of the female's tail and wavered, as if trying to catch his scent.

Run, he told himself, just as he had shouted to the doomed Anacostia Cousins. Run.

He tried to pick himself up but fell, burdened by drowsy spice, by the stupor of Communal Mind. Numb, he tried to think. Something was happening. Something . . . Then he remembered he was dying.

Reen watched the tube approach. It was fluted, the outside pearl, the inside a rich golden brown.

The air was thick with the waxy smell of crayons. Kevin, large gray head down, was coloring a kitten. Beside Reen, Angela was working to fill in the stark, simple lines of a horse. Her small hands held the crayon in a stranglehold, and she sighed in disappointment when the brown strayed outside the lines.

Don't try so hard, he wanted to tell her, but then Angela had something of the Cousin drive for perfection. Warning would do no good.

She colored, she colored, her expression as intent as that of an engineer working on the blueprint of a bridge, or of a physicist laboring over an equation.

"I love you," he told her, swelling with so much affection that it seemed his chest might rupture.

She stopped coloring to look up. Kevin looked up, too. And at the end of the table Mrs. Gonzales paused in tutoring a clumsy Michelle to look at Reen in wonder.

"I love you," he told his daughter.

Angela went back to her coloring book. "I love you, too," she said.

An ache. Disoriented, Reen looked down at his chest. The female had already pushed his plates apart and had burrowed inside. He gasped as he felt the first sucking theft of sperm.

Run, he told himself. But he couldn't.

Desire blossomed from her touch, desire as quick and disabling as the ice of her drugs. He groaned and shoved the tough muscle of her deeper. His greedy hands reached out to the iridescent flesh, his claws digging, pulling her closer.

His body shuddered as lust gave way to satiation. His insides loosened. There was a gout of pain as his lungs tore free.

Oomal was handing him a box all wrapped in colored paper while humans gathered around the birth, their eyes as wide as Cousins' and black and deep as night.

"Open it, First Brother," Oomal said with shy, fierce pride. "Open it for Angela."

Reen ripped the paper. It bled and shrieked. And from Reen's hands blue worlds spilled out like doves.

When the planets had spun away, Oomal spread his arms. Reen had forgotten how warm, how soft his Brother's body could be.

Love, that never-ending thing. If only Marian had seen their daughter grow from a single cell, maybe then she would roll her name around in her mouth like candy.

Angela, small as a mustard seed, tiny as faith.

Angela, large as an arm's span.

In a wash of pewter light from the window Jeff Womack sat rocking, a gun stoppering his mouth. His silent eyes met Reen's, and there was something like ecstasy in them.

Oh, how strange, Reen thought. The Old Ones loomed in the chamber like mountains, while in front of him, under a female, a Cousin lay motionless and nearly consumed.

I must be dreaming.

Reen was a tiny creature, growing smaller, a being on the intoxicating edge of disappearance. He clutched at the rim of oblivion until he realized that there was nothing to hold on to, and no reason to be afraid of the fall.

Yes, the Old Ones breathed. *You are.*